THE ENGLISH KING

THE EARLS OF MERCIA
BOOK TEN

MJ PORTER

MJ PUBLISHING

Cover design by MJ Porter
Cover image by 165741493 © Tomert Dreamstime.com
ISBN: 9781914332128 (ebook)
ISBN: 9781914332081 (paperback)
ISBN: 9781914332760 (hardback/large print)

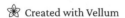 Created with Vellum

1

JUNE AD1042, LONDON, LEOFRIC

THE SWELL OF AMBITION THREATENED TO OVERWHELM HIM, YET HE STAYED firm, refusing to engage with the chattering of those who should have known better.

It still felt like a dream, or rather a nightmare. He might have known that Harthacnut would ail one day, but that day had come far too soon. Now, the great men and women convened to discuss who would be their next king. And they weren't short of potential claimants.

Harthacnut had extracted an oath from him, or rather a twin oath; the first that he would ensure Edward was elected king, the second that Lord Godwine wouldn't be allowed to resume his previous position of power and influence.

Leofric hoped the first would be easy to achieve, but he had no idea about the second.

He'd spoken to few people since Harthacnut's death. Archbishop Eadsige had sought him out, and so too had Osgot Clapa and Tovi. The first hadn't surprised him, and to be honest, neither had the other two, even though Tovi should have been enjoying his marriage bed. As all men in their situation would be, they were keen to ensure that no one blamed them for the king's unexpected and shocking death.

Leofric was aware it was rumoured that Osgot Clapa must have poisoned the king, and if not Osgot Clapa, then Tovi. He, of them all, knew with certainty that it wasn't the truth. But, many of Harthacnut's personal Danish servants had left, scurrying away before the death of Harthacnut, keen to avoid the finger of suspicion falling on them.

Harthacnut's body servants knew the facts of the king's health, but even Lord Otto had gone, clearly expecting nothing but recriminations despite the fact that he had been Harthacnut's man and might have expected to gain from his will.

If the matter came to a head, Leofric imagined being forced to vouch for Osgot Clapa and Tovi. With the support of Beorn Estridsson, Harthacnut's cousin, he believed he could clear the men's names if it became necessary. But he hoped it didn't.

It wouldn't do anyone any favours if the truth about Harthacnut became common knowledge. Then, it would appear that the English had willingly accepted an enfeebled king to rule them. That would only encourage other's covetous eyes from Denmark, Norway, and perhaps worse, from the kingdom of the Scots and Gruffydd Ap Llewelyn.

Now Leofric waited for the convocation of the witan in London so that Edward could officially be nominated and accepted as England's king. Then, they'd all be able to focus on the next most important matter, the need to bury Harthacnut with all the honours due to a king of England—even England's kings who had been unloved.

Harthacnut's body had been prepared and was ready to be conveyed to Winchester, once the court was free to move with it. Leofric shook his head, almost unable to process the truth; a boy he'd thought of as a son was dead long before his time. Never again would he clash with Harthacnut. Never again would he wonder where the endearing child he'd known long ago had gone.

'I take it Edward has your vote?' Earl Siward spoke from behind, his voice low so no one could overhear their conversation.

'Of course, he's the rightful king,' Leofric retorted, facing the other man. He noted Siward's fierce gaze and how his eyes roved over what was happening behind him rather than meeting Leofric's glare.

'Not King Magnus of Norway then, or even Lord Svein Estridsson, or the sons of King Edmund.'

Leofric narrowed his eyes at the other earl. The other man's despicable actions in the north had strained their friendship, perhaps beyond repair. Yet Siward had sought him out. Maybe, in choosing who would be the next king, they could act with one voice and find the means for reconciliation.

'I believe England has had enough rulers from overseas trying to run more than one country at once. England doesn't exist to fund the wars of absent kings. England isn't merely the treasure trove to be plundered by others.' Leofric was surprised to find his words laced with heat.

'But Edward is from Normandy. Who knows him here, in England, outside the witan?' Siward shrugged as he spoke. Leofric was unsure if it was a genuine question or a statement of fact.

'More know him than the other candidates. He might be somewhat of a stranger, but he's King Æthelred's acknowledged son. His right can't be denied; I don't believe it ever has. Correct me if I'm wrong?'

'There would be those keen to have another.' Leofric tensed at Siward's words, considering what the other earl was trying to tell him.

'And are you amongst those numbers?' He wouldn't be surprised to find that Siward would sooner have had anyone but an English king to rule over him. After all, he was Danish by birth. He owed his elevation and wealth to the Danish kings. That meant he might well prefer Lord Svein's claims to those of Edward, even if Svein was far away in Denmark, and Edward was here, in London, right now.

But Siward looked offended by the question.

'I serve the royal line, and my previous king, God Rest His Soul, has acclaimed Edward as his successor. It's my duty to fulfil that wish. You, of all people, should appreciate my loyalty to King Harthacnut.'

'Then, who do you speak about?' But really, Siward didn't need to say, not when Lord Godwine chose that exact moment to enter the rapidly filling room. His two oldest sons trailed behind him, or rather, Harold did. Sweyn walked with more arrogance than his father if that was possible. Despite the swell of heat that shimmered in the air as though made solid, his cloak was fixed around his shoulders so that he could proclaim the great wealth of the silver and gold thread, the exotic fur around his collar. It must have cost a fortune, no doubt, the proceeds from his mother's involvement in Dublin's lucrative slave trade.

'There are some who are even more desperate than I to have a Danish king rule them.' Siward's words were dark with humour as he, too spied Godwine and his sons.

Leofric pursed his lips, considering the enlarged figure of Lord Godwine, his black hair and beard riddled with grey now, the upturn of his lips visible even amongst the expanse of his expanded cheeks.

'I didn't think that Beorn Estridsson had any love for his uncle by marriage.' Leofric had never quite managed to decipher Beorn's intention in coming to England with his cousin, Harthacnut. Had it been to escape his brother, Lord Svein? Or more to do with a genuine affection for Harthacnut? Even now, Leofric didn't know. There was a curse in being the second brother, one that Leofric longed to endure, even now.

'It's not Beorn that I speak about,' but Leofric was already shaking his head. He knew the mind of Lady Estrid Sweinsdottir, sister to Cnut, aunt to Harthacnut and mother to Beorn and Svein. Her gaze had always firmly been on Denmark, not England. When she'd lived in England, at the beginning of her marriage to Ulfr she'd wanted nothing more than to return to Denmark. She'd been there ever since.

'I think Lord Godwine may be the one wishing, not Lord Svein.'

'Truly?' It seemed Earl Siward was genuinely surprised by the vehemence in Leofric's voice.

'You must know, you once served the family in Denmark.' Siward cast his two hands to either side of his body, a shrug of his shoulders, showing he couldn't say.

'But what of King Edmund's sons? They surely have precedence over Edward.'

'No one knows where they are,' Leofric confirmed. 'Whether they do or not, the English need a king, and they need one now. Look what happened to Harthacnut when he was absent from England on his father's death? Even Lord Godwine and Lady Emma couldn't hold England for him, despite their years of experience and Harald's perceived lack of it.'

Leofric waited for Earl Siward to rightly state that it was because of Leofric's support of Harald. Siward's failure to mention it perhaps spoke of a desire to allow the past to remain the past, a sentiment he no doubt wished Leofric to extend to him.

'So, you intend to name Edward your king just to prevent a war?'

'I intend to name Edward because that's what my king bid me do on his deathbed.'

Now it was Siward's turn to thin his lips. He was a tall man and distinctive because of that. He was somewhat younger than Leofric, although he had a son of a similar age to Ælfgar. His son had been born from a previous union before he'd married the daughter of the man he'd been instrumental in murdering on the orders of King Harthacnut. Siward was ambitious. Leofric knew that. He was ambitious enough to kill and endure problems in his domestic arrangements, provided it helped him gain power and influence.

'You, Earl Leofric, have always given binding oaths too freely, just as I hear your father once did. Don't you think it's about time you began to follow your own wishes?' And with that, Siward left his side, and Leofric watched him greet Lord Godwine with a mirthless smile.

He couldn't believe the audacity of Siward, but then, it was often the way with these Danish upstarts. If anyone could be accused of giving oaths too freely, it was the Danes. But, the difference between him and them was that he kept his. He always had. The Danes gave oaths more liberally than they groomed their hair or cleared their ears. Neither were they likely to feel any great compulsion to keep to them. Not if it became inconvenient.

And then the room hushed, and Leofric expected it to be for the appearance of Lord Edward, but it wasn't. He watched, almost wishing he could look away, as Lady Emma made her arrival.

He gasped to see her looking so frail. She wore a light wimple to cover her greying hair. Yet, she should have donned a veil as well. Her eyes were haunted, with all trace of fierceness melted away in the face of her grief. He swallowed heavily, remembering her sorrow for her dying son. She'd barely known Harthacnut, not the man he'd become, anyway, and now she was forced to mourn him rather than watch him successfully rule his father's rapidly disintegrating northern empire.

Once more, Leofric pitied her. No matter all the problems she'd caused his family throughout her nearly forty years in England, he wouldn't wish such torments on anyone. He still mourned his two brothers, killed decades apart, and he knew his father had never recovered from the death of Northman. No father should lose a child before their time, and the same went for a mother.

Lady Emma's dress was the darkest blue, the fall of it concealing her rounder figure, the plainness of the dress brooches and fabric, making him startle. She couldn't have made a more shocking entrance with her austere and grieving figure if she'd festooned herself with every gem in England she'd ever owned, gifted to her twice over by both Æthelred and Cnut.

Her eyes were clouded, her lips compressed tightly, and despite it all, he hazarded that he could see the traces of tears where they'd worn a furrow into her pale cheeks.

'My Lady,' he bowed low to her, somehow knowing she'd seek him out in that great room, choosing his familiar face above those of the ambitious ones. The whispering and plotting of everyone else dimmed a little but resumed quickly enough when they realised it was just Lady Emma entering the room and not Lord Edward.

'My Lord,' her voice was soft but cracked, the words an effort, her breath hitching even to say just that.

'There's no need for you to be here,' he offered, knowing there would be a quick denial even as he said it.

'No need, I know, but I must support my oldest son, even as I grieve for my youngest.'

Leofric nodded sombrely. She spoke the truth. Edward would benefit from her endorsement, but Leofric wasn't convinced he'd want it.

Lady Emma stood beside him, silence falling between them as they watched the crowd before them as it ebbed and flowed, men and women going from group to group, few standing alone, no one standing aloof, as they did. Leofric would have sooner Lady Emma had chosen to side with anyone but himself but equally realised that no one else would offer the quiet support he would.

He thought wryly of Earl Siward's taunting words about oaths. His father had forged this long-standing understanding with Lady Emma. His sister had, for some time, been one of her ladies in waiting, and yet they'd not always maintained such a friendship. There had been occasions when Lady Emma had abandoned the House of Leofwine. But equally, there had been some instances when Lady Emma must have thought herself forsaken by them.

The common problem had often been Lord Godwine, or Cnut, and his two families, with the divided loyalties his domestic arrangements imposed on his supporters.

But, both of them had been involved in the court and its politics for too long to hold lasting grudges, or so he hoped. Not that he thought Lord Edward would see it the same way.

Leofric felt as though a wall had formed around them, everyone else noting them but staying far away. He didn't want to feel so isolated, yet, from whom was he really isolated? Lord Godwine wasn't his ally; Earl Siward had disappointed him. It was no different than at any time in the last few years. Thuri was dead. Hrani's death was anticipated any day now.

Yet, Leofric carried a burden that none of the others did—his oath to Harthacnut.

'My son will be here shortly,' Lady Emma offered, her voice fracturing again. It was as though she'd not spoken for days.

'Were you with Lord Edward?' he asked, thinking it innocuous enough, but her piercing gaze dissuaded him of that notion.

'My son was speaking with his nephew and Lord Beorn.' The news was no surprise for him. Edward had been cool towards Lady Emma as Harthacnut lay dying. Leofric didn't believe that the ruptured relationship would be easily healed.

Leofric focused on the room within which they stood. He'd been here often enough when Harald was king. He'd made London his capital when he'd ruled north of the Thames boundary, not Winchester from where the kings of England had historically reigned.

The smell of the river lingered in the humid air, mixing with that of the many candles, and in the height of summer, it was impossible to escape where they were. Perhaps it would have been better to have met onboard a ship. At least then, the wind might have blown the unpleasant aromas of the turgid river away from them.

Somewhere, Ælfgar mingled amongst those assembled. He had more freedom than Leofric did. He could be seen conversing with others without the immediate rumours that occasioned Leofric's interest in any of the other earls, thegns and kings thegns.

Ælfgar was also a known associate of Lord Harold, Lord Godwine's second-oldest son. Perhaps. He'd return with news of

Lord Godwine's intentions. Not, Leofric thought, that it took a great deal of skill to decipher the man's desires. He'd do whatever was necessary to reclaim the position and influence he'd lost because of Harthacnut's restrictions.

With that thought, the audience again fell to silence, and this time, Leofric noted the light hair of Lord Edward making its way to the front of the hall. Bishop Ælfweard followed Lord Edward. In turn, he was followed by a bevy of clerics and other high-ranking holy men who'd been summoned to London from the surrounding area and those who'd happened to be within London anyway. While Archbishop Eadsige was absent from the group, Ælfwine of Winchester, Wulfsige of Lichfield, and Eadnoth of Dorchester surrounded the king, their approval of his election evident in their very presence.

Resolutely, Edward settled himself in the chair waiting for him on the dais, Bishop Ælfweard beside him. Lord Beorn and Ralph had taken seats in the front row, facing the soon-to-be-king. They were not far from where Leofric and Lady Emma now sat, Leofric having guided her there as soon as he'd realised the king had arrived. The other bishops, abbots, and abbesses settled on the opposite side, in the chairs waiting for them.

It was a striking position for the king to have chosen. Leofric considered whether such careful placement marked him as strong or weak. Was sitting alone a strength or weakness?

Beside Lord Edward, although partially out of sight on the raised dais, due to the shadows caused by the sunshine and the candlelight, Leofric caught sight of Harthacnut's huscarls. They still fulfilled their role as protectors of the king by guarding the dead king's designated heir. Evidently, they'd decided to support Edward, and they held fast, wearing their byrnies, with menace written into every line of their muscular bodies. Karl and Urk threatened just with their presence. Leofric didn't doubt that Thored was at the main door doing the same with the remainder of the huscarls.

Leofric wouldn't want to face one of them, let alone the three of them. He had no illusion that if called upon, the rest of the huscarls were prepared to act. If this didn't go as Lord Edward imagined, there might be violence.

'My lords and ladies,' everyone had shuffled to a seat as Bishop Ælfweard called for silence. He stood before them all, just to the side of Lord Edward. He'd discarded the ceremonial robes he'd worn inside the church, but his holy vocation was evident from the priceless holy cross that hung from his neck, sparkling amongst the folds of his tunic. He was tall, a booming voice ensuring his congregation heard and heeded his words.

They'd come from St Peter's church, where a mass had been raised for Harthacnut, although the king wouldn't be buried there. His burial place was to be beside his father and not where his despised half-brother had once been laid to rest in eternal slumber. For all that, the mood was far from sombre.

Leofric caught sight of men who'd been loyal to Harthacnut and now looked eagerly to see who their new king would be. Ælfstan, Lyfing, Odda, Dodda had much to lose if they fell foul of the new appointment and much to gain if they retained his loyalty.

'We must decide who'll lead England from this day,' Bishop Ælfweard began. Leofric was startled that he did not mention sorrow for Harthacnut's death, but perhaps, the Mass had been enough in his eyes. This meeting could hardly have been for any reason other than because of Harthacnut's death.

'I believe we all know the pedigree of Lord Edward, brother of King Harthacnut. I believe we all understand it was our previous king's wish that his brother should rule in his place. Now, before you all, I ask if any deny this?'

The bishop's eyes seemed to scour everyone in the audience. Leofric admired the stance he'd taken. Rather than laying out those who could rule instead of Edward, he presented Edward as the only possibility. Edward was Harthacnut's appointee and his brother. It was up to the other lords and bishops in attendance to name their alternative if, indeed, there was one.

Yet, while no one named the other potential candidates, Lord Godwine stood, bowing as low to the bishop as his enlarged waistline allowed, which wasn't far.

'Your eminence,' he began, voice oozing with confidence. 'I believe everyone knows that Lord Edward should be king, now, but there must be some conditions imposed upon him before the vote makes that a reality.'

Leofric felt his back straighten at the words. What game was Lord Godwine playing? About what conditions did he speak? Certainly, Leofric hadn't been consulted on the matter, and he should have been, as one of England's earls. Was Lord Godwine already making a play for more influence than he could currently claim? Harthacnut was barely cold and not yet in his grave, and already Lord Godwine was angling for an advantage.

Bishop Ælfweard fixed an arched eyebrow on the earl, perhaps dismayed to have someone speak against Lord Edward. Maybe just curious as to what would be said.

'What would these restrictions be?' the bishop asked eventually, the silence grown almost uncomfortable.

Leofric glanced at Lord Godwine, noting the slightly smug expression on his face but equally the sheen of sweat that touched his forehead below his retreating hair. His beard was speckled with grey, and Leofric took some thrill in knowing his oldest adversary was ageing and looked far from well with it. He ignored the fact that it meant the same for him.

'There must be an expectation, after the upheaval of the last seven years, that the new king will be compelled to rule using the laws laid down by King Cnut, under whom England flourished.'

Leofric huffed softly at the words. It sounded innocuous enough, and yet it wasn't difficult to understand the real intent behind them. Lord Godwine might say it was Cnut's laws he asked for, but really, it was a return to the way King Cnut had ruled and, more importantly, with whom he'd ruled.

Leofric was curious to see if Lord Edward understood the true meaning of the request. Lady Emma shifted beside him, her hands tightly clenched, one inside the other, and he couldn't help but think Lord Godwine was purposefully upsetting her. The mention of her son, the reference to her husband, and even the allusion to the years King Harald had ruled and forced Lady Emma to be banished from England. She'd only returned with King Harthacnut and his fleet of eighty-five ships barely two years before.

Equally, Leofric considered whether Lord Edward was aware of the last person to have such a charge levied against them, his father. Before he'd been reinstated as England's king, Æthelred had sworn to rule more justly. For Leofric, the coincidence couldn't be ignored. Lord Godwine would know that.

Yet, from the sea of nodding heads, Lord Godwine appeared to speak for more than only himself and his self-interest. Even Tovi and Osgot Clapa agreed with Lord Godwine, which surprised Leofric. But then, they were good English-Danes. They probably had no love for an English king who might not uphold the changes made in England since the death of Edward's older half-brother, King Edmund, twenty-six years before.

Equally, some looked offended, and Leofric noted how Wulfnoth, Kinewerd, Toking and Ulfcytel's faces filled with fury at the implied criticism of Harald and Harthacnut's reigns.

Bishop Ælfweard paused, turning to appraise Lord Edward. His face was blank, showing no hint of whether or not he appreciated such words. Leofric was curious as to how he'd respond. Lord Edward had no love for King Cnut. How could he? Cnut had banished Edward from England when he'd conquered the kingdom, fearing that one of King Æthelred's surviving sons would become the focus of a rebellion. It didn't matter that one son, Eadwig, had tried to incite such a rebellion. It didn't mean that Cnut had been right to banish Edward, Alfred and Godgifu.

While King Cnut might not have pursued Lord Edward to Normandy, seeking his death, he'd certainly offered no chance of

Edward ever having any of his inheritance, even that which had been left to him by his half-brothers.

Now Lord Edward stood, his hands folded demurely in front of him. Leofric noted then how Edward had adopted the opposite of his mother's approach. He was dressed as though he were a king already. Not that he was ostentatious, yet the value of the cloth that formed his tunic, the supple leather that made his black knee-high boots, and the few jewels that glimmered on his fingers and forearms couldn't be denied. Few could claim such wealth with only a day's notice, and that's all it had been since Harthacnut's death.

'England has endured a period of relative calm for over two decades, putting aside the issues surrounding the beginning of King Harthacnut's reign. It's not my intention to do anything that will jeopardise that.'

Lord Edward didn't directly address Lord Godwine with his steady voice, but rather, everyone within the hall. His eyes swept evenly from side to side, never settling on any one person, and at the same time, including everyone in his response.

Leofric approved. Edward didn't promise to do as Lord Godwine demanded, but neither were his words an admission that he'd bring about sweeping changes. In contradiction to Godwine, Lord Edward's words promised less than they said. Leofric felt his regard for the new king rising.

'England is a much-changed country from when I left it, not for the better or worse. It's merely different, and yet, also the same. Our Danish kings and our Danish countrymen are just as much English now as those who count themselves as English and have done since Athelstan first claimed the whole of England as his to rule.'

Lord Edward sat, his words at an end, but Lord Godwine still hovered, looking discomforted. Would he press the king for greater assurances? Did he genuinely believe King Harthacnut's restrictions against him could be lifted to ensure Lord Edward was declared king? It certainly seemed that way.

A heavy silence fell, eyes raking from Lord Edward to Lord

Godwine and then back again, some coming to rest on Bishop Ælfweard. He was the only man who could resolve the stalemate. Not that he seemed willing to do so.

'Perhaps, then, we need to consider those who also have a claim to England's crown?' A rumble of discontent greeted the archly given words Lord Godwine spat into the silence. He might crave the resumption of King Cnut's rule, but no one else wanted a return to the uncertainty that had befallen the kingdom after Cnut's death.

Cnut's sons had bickered and almost plunged England back into the type of war unseen since the beginning of Cnut's reign. If not for Harald's untimely death, there could have been bloodshed over who was the legal heir. His lacklustre responses had seen Lord Godwine fall from favour under both King Harald and Harthacnut. Leofric didn't welcome a resumption of Godwine's lost power.

'My Lord Godwine,' Tovi spoke, yet Bishop Ælfweard held up a hand for peace, beckoning to one of the clerics, who hastened to bring a parchment to him. He scanned it and then looked up.

'My understanding is that two sons survived King Edmund. It's also my belief that the boys didn't outlast their childhood. Is that correct?' Bishop Ælfweard's forehead furrowed as he spoke, peering at his clerics again for confirmation.

One stood and bent low to both Lord Edward and the bishop. When he spoke, his words were assured. This was a man who knew the answer to the question.

'We believe that the children survived. Their names are or were Edward and Edmund. However, no one knows where they are, and there hasn't been time to pursue or make enquiries.' There was no apology for that fact.

Leofric looked down at his hands. He didn't want anyone to look at him and guess the secret that he knew. Many years ago, Lady Estrid had told him what had happened to King Edmund's sons. But, just because Lady Estrid had known about the boys then, it was no guarantee that either still lived.

The news stirred Lord Edward, who spoke directly to the cleric, not the bishop.

'If I have nephews other than the children of Lady Godgifu, I should like to know of them. Perhaps this is something that can be pursued once I'm the king.' The final words, Edward directed to the witan at large.

Before anyone could respond, Lord Godwine promptly stood and spoke again. Leofric wasn't even convinced he'd been sitting, but rather squatting, waiting for the chance to interrupt the proceedings again.

'If we're to mention nephews, then shouldn't we consider those of King Cnut? Beorn Estridsson has made England his home, and Svein, the older brother, is in Denmark.'

Leofric couldn't stop himself from seeking out Beorn on the front row. His back was rigid, his head peering only forwards so that all Leofric could see were the curls of his blond hair at the nape of his neck. Perhaps he'd known to expect Godwine's words. Maybe, that was what Lord Edward had been speaking to him about before they'd entered the hall.

Condemnation thrummed through the air. Beorn and Svein were Godwine's nephews, even if Beorn all but ignored his uncle. Leofric believed the relationship wasn't a cordial one. It was Beorn's half-brother, Osbjorn, who was most closely allied with the House of Godwine. But then, Lady Gytha had raised him as one of her children after the execution of Ulfr when Lady Estrid had refused to acknowledge the boy.

Still, no one wanted Lord Godwine to have a nephew ruling England. It would be inevitable that his influence would be restored, just because of such proximity, even if Beorn or Svein refused to reward their uncle with greater wealth than he already owned. There would still be those who believed the path to the king's ear lay through the influence of the House of Godwine. Godwine wouldn't disabuse anyone of that notion.

Bishop Ælfweard raised his hand to hush the muttering unease.

'Lord Beorn has no interest in ruling England. Lord Svein will hope to claim the kingdom of Denmark when he hears of Harthacnut's passing. I believe that it's time England had a king of its own and not one with split priorities. And again, Lord Svein is unknown within England. It's Lord Beorn who's made his home here, but he's the younger brother.'

Lord Godwine finally sat unhappily, but Leofric caught sight of furious whispers between him and his oldest son, Sweyn. He wished he were close enough to hear the words, especially when Lady Emma seemed to note the same interaction and the words, 'never' issued from her rigid mouth.

What was all that about?

But Leofric didn't have time to muse on the matter, for the bishop brought the meeting to order.

'It seems we have the following options. Lord Edward, as the brother of King Harthacnut, will rule England. Or one of two men who will need to be found could rule. The second option will leave England without a king for the foreseeable future. A situation to be avoided, if possible. I would have your votes,' the bishop asked, and Leofric approved his stance. The matter needed to be settled quickly. And then the coronation could be arranged, and then a marriage for their new king so that England might have its own heirs.

'Those who wish to see Lord Edward as England's king, please stand and be counted.'

The clerics had moved from their places at the front of the hall and now stationed themselves in areas to get a full accounting of the dissenters, but really, there was no need for such an action.

Everyone stood, some reluctantly, amongst them Lord Godwine, but practicality prevailed. No one coveted a stranger as their new king. No one desired to wait for their new king to be found if indeed, he still lived.

'Then I declare Lord Edward, brother of Harthacnut, as England's new king. Long live the king,' and a muffled cheer greeted the bishop's words. Leofric wanted to join in the acclaim, but he didn't. Lady

Emma's shaking body spoke only of her misery, and instead, he bent low and spoke to her where she remained sitting.

'Come, My Lady, I think that's enough for one day.' Leofric expected to find her almost cheerful, but her face was white, her eyes haunted. He recalled that a man had died to bring Lord Edward to the throne. In fact, many men had died. Time would tell whether Edward was the true heir to the English crown or if he was merely the lesser of two evils.

Without allowing her to argue, he escorted Lady Emma from the chamber and out into the brightness of a hot day, a warm wind bringing the smell of fish to his nostrils as he grimaced and fought back a wave of nausea.

'My thanks,' Lady Emma offered a hand under her nose to ward off the aroma. 'I'll retire to my rooms,' she stated, one of her women rushing to her side, a courteous arm giving her some much-needed support. Leofric nodded at the woman. He knew her well. She would ensure Lady Emma had the required care.

Leofric bowed again, desirous of returning inside the hall as no one else had yet left. He didn't want his new king to miss him. These were important days. The future would be decided by a man he was already oath-sworn to but who owed Leofric nothing. He would need to step carefully, not allow Lord Godwine the opportunity to advance to his detriment.

Watching King Edward as he mingled through the assembled men and women of the witan, Leofric was struck by just how prophetic Lord Godwine's demand for a return to the past might have been. Everything was new and changed, and despite assurances to the contrary, it was possible that England could be returned to the status quo in place at King Æthelred's death. And that meant there could be a resumption of hostilities from the northern kingdoms that had categorised so much of Æthelred's reign.

Had they just decided on an English king when at least two men, King Magnus of Norway and perhaps Lord Svein Estridsson, might believe England should be theirs to rule? Bishop Ælfweard had made no mention of King Magnus as a potential candidate. It was possibly an oversight on his part because although King Harthacnut had made it clear that Lord Edward was to rule in England after him, there was another, older agreement between Harthacnut and King Magnus concerning Denmark.

As part of that agreement, they'd both named the other their heir in the event of their death. While most might think it only applied to Denmark and Norway's kingdoms, Leofric wasn't quite so sure that King Magnus would interpret it that way. Magnus was young and filled with ambition. He had the support of the ruling family of the land of the Svear as his most fervent supporters. It was a heady combination.

Leofric swallowed heavily.

He'd wanted Edward to become England's king, but had he been right? Only time would tell.

Leofric shook aside his unease, found a smile for his tight face, and went to mingle with the members of the witan. As he did so, he noted those who were pleased with the decision and those who'd merely accepted Lord Edward as the lesser of two unpalatable evils.

Amongst that number, he counted Lord Godwine, and he went out of his way to avoid him. It would be impossible to listen to his complaints, and they would be many and numerous. Instead, Leofric positioned himself close to Tovi and Osgot Clapa, only moving aside when Bishop Ælfweard beckoned him close.

The bishop looked serene at having performed his task well and yet showed some unease as he leaned toward Leofric and babbled, his words muffled by his hand.

'The king says he'll wait for his coronation.'

'Really?' This was news to Leofric, and he turned confused eyes towards the bishop. He'd only been gone from the room for a matter of moments. How could such a decision have already been made? Ælfweard nodded sagely, his eyes fixed on some point behind Leofric.

'Yes, he wishes it to be held on Easter Sunday, in Winchester, and not a day before or a day after.'

'Over half a year away?' Leofric scrunched his face at the words. The news was unsettling. Could it be that Lord Edward was reconsidering his desire to be king? Was he waiting to see if his nephews were found, or was it something deeper, more profound, that guided his decision?

'Well, that's for the king to order. It little matters. He's king. It's been decreed by the witan.'

'Perhaps,' Bishop Ælfweard commented, yet his voice was filled with foreboding, and Leofric swallowed down his unease. Already, King Edward defied Leofric's expectations. It wasn't what he'd hoped would happen in the first few moments after Edward had been declared king, far from it.

2

AD1042, WINCHESTER, LEOFRIC

LEOFRIC FELT NO COMPULSION TO DO MORE THAN HOVER ON THE EDGES OF the conversation. The swell of bitterness, resentment and ambition emanating from all those in attendance was just too much.

They were here to bury their young king in the Old Minster, yet few seemed to be mourning.

Whatever the trials and tribulations he'd endured with King Harthacnut, it didn't mean that his life should be forgotten, dismissed as no longer relevant, just because he was dead. Suddenly there was so much more to consider.

Leofric knew he was grumpy. There was no need for his wife to tell him as much, and in fact, he owed Lady Godgifu his respect for refusing to gloat over this turn of events. She'd had no love for Harthacnut. In all honesty, few had ever come to understand their Danish king. Leofric counted himself amongst that number. All the same, some modicum of respect was required, and he'd provide it even if more ambitious men and women wouldn't do the same.

He allowed his eyes to seek out Lord Godwine in the hall. If ever there was a more fitting example of a man who believed he'd escaped his family's inevitable downfall, it was him. It was his ambition, and that of his sons, and daughter, that hung over the gathering, thicker than fog. Leofric could feel it infiltrating all the spaces between allies and enemies; its insidious ways threatened to reignite long-running feuds and minor understandings. It twisted his gut to see it.

And not only because of his oath to Harthacnut. Also, because of what Lord Godwine's triumph would mean for him, his son, and his small grandchildren.

Leofric felt the heat of another's interest and turned, unsurprised to find the new king appraising him from where he stood with Ralph, his nephew, and Beorn, his sort-of cousin. Beorn was the son of his mother's second husband's sister.

He wasn't alone in failing to appreciate this assembly. Edward also looked distinctly uncomfortable, his gaze repeatedly straying towards where Lord Godwine and his wife, Lady Gytha, held sway over a fluctuating selection of thegns, king thegns, abbots and bishops. These people all realised that significant change was about to happen. Or at least, they suspected it was and were eager to be seen to be there from the beginning.

Lord Godwine was expansive, as he arrested everyone's attention, as though he were the king and not Edward. Leofric took the time to note the man. He was ageing. It couldn't be denied. He no longer had the vigour of a young man, which was never more obvious than when his sons were amassed at his side. But in losing his youth, Godwine had become keen to fill the void. It looked to Leofric that the man was overindulging in everything. His belly was swollen, and yet Godwine, or more probably his wife, had decided it was merely an extra canvas upon which to advertise their wealth.

Leofric felt his lips thin in displeasure. It wasn't his way to do the same. His wife might scold him for it, but he was content to wear the emblems of his noble house, the double-headed eagle, without the need for silks only available from distant lands and costing more than a fine horse.

'A pig in shit,' Leofric startled at the words and tried not to smile. His son had long understood Lord Godwine's ambitions.

'A happy pig in shit.'

'Just getting ready for the knife from the butcher.' Leofric felt his good spirits dissipate at the wistfulness in his son's voice.

'Lord Godwine is the sort to outlive his years. Such naked ambition seems to equate to a long life.'

'Perhaps. But enough of him. Tell me how fares our new king?'

Ælfgar had returned to his home in Oxford, and his young children, in the interval between Harthacnut's death and his funeral. Leofric had remained with Edward, travelling from London to Winchester, following the slow funeral procession, watching the people's faces as they pretended to grieve even as they were thrilled to know they were no longer under the repression of a Danish king.

'Content, for now, well, with all apart from his mother and Lord Godwine.'

'There's no rapprochement?'

'No, and not likely to be. The king has nothing in common with his mother. They're worse than strangers, the awkwardness of being family making everything that much harder.'

'And, how are you?' Leofric admired his son for not dwelling on the king's and his mother's relationship. He could think about little else.

'I'm here, and remain at the king's side, and will do all I can to assist him during this strange time.'

'Well, that sounds like an enjoyable pass time for the earl of Mercia.' The words were edged with dark humour.

Leofric sighed, but not with aggravation. His son was right to tease him, but what choice did he have? The more he aged, the more he understood his father's strange decision-making. Too many people pulled him in myriad ways. It was impossible to please everyone and, more importantly, to maintain the high standards he'd set himself.

He didn't wish to be like Ealdorman Eadric Streona, a man who'd been so ambitious he'd had no problems playing two sides against one another, with fatal consequences for almost everyone involved.

'First, I wish to mourn Harthacnut. He was too young to die. Like his father and his brothers. It's a tragedy.'

Ælfgar stilled at the words. He and Harthacnut had been the same age. While Ælfgar had a wife and children and yet walked amongst the living, Harthacnut had left no child behind him, had taken no wife, and was marbled in death. He might have been the king of Denmark and England, but Leofric knew he'd soon be forgotten. Just like Harald, his half-brother had been, and it was only two years since his death.

'Yes, come, we'll mourn at his tomb. There are few enough of the others doing as much.'

Leofric felt no need to reply. It was obvious enough from the number of men and women drinking the new king's wine and ale, laughter rippling through the air.

'We'll go to the Old Minster.' With the decision made, Leofric turned aside, and Ælfgar followed him into the day's heat. Leofric tugged at his tunic, ensuring it hung straight, and strode away from the king's hall. It wasn't a long walk, and he was struck by how much of a 'normal' day this was for Winchester's inhabitants. They might have lined the streets earlier that day, heads bowed, but they were now only concerned with their own affairs. Harthacnut had already been forgotten.

It was within the Old Minster that Cnut had been interred. And beside him, his son now lay. Leofric paused to consider that as he lithely crested the steps that led inside. It hadn't been the same for King Harald. No. Harthacnut had disturbed the body from its resting place in St Peter's in London and cast it into the Thames to punish his detested brother. Leofric and Ælfgar had been forced to recover the body and have it secretly buried elsewhere. It seemed that Harthacnut had regretted his hasty actions, but was the time now right for Harald to be moved? Should they meddle with his eternal slumbers again, or was it acceptable to leave him where he was?

Leofric considered asking Lady Ælfgifu, Harald's mother, but no one was supposed to know she yet lived. No. For now, Harald could stay where he was, buried in semi-secrecy in London. After all, his older brother was interred in Denmark. It wasn't as if the family was together or ever likely to be.

Leofric found himself looking upwards, considering the vastness of the Old Minster. It dominated Winchester and was a true statement of intent, equalled only by the New Minster next door. Yet, the Old Minster had been built by the Wessex royal family and not begun by King Cnut. There was an irony in the building that now stood a silent guard over King Cnut and his youngest son, one so deeply embedded in England's history that it had survived the Danish royal family's usurpation of England's crown.

Quickly, they passed from the heat of the day to the interior's cool. A hand on his arm caused Leofric to pause his steps. Before he could ask Ælfgar what ailed him, his eyes settled on Lady Emma, head bowed and on her knees before the vast altar. Leofric's steps slowed, only for him to speed them once more. Lady Emma might well mourn her youngest son alone, but it wasn't right, far from it. Harthacnut and Lady Emma might have known each other little and have cared even less for one another, but Leofric was saddened that she must sorrow for another of her children.

Ælfgar followed in his wake. Leofric was pleased to have his steadfast presence as he took to his knees, bowed his head, and cleared his head of everything except his genuine grief for Cnut and Harthacnut. Lady Emma's prayers didn't cease, and Leofric imagined she didn't even realise she'd been alone but was now joined by another two mourners.

Below his knees, he felt the coolness of the stone, welcome on such a warm day, and he considered the men who no longer inhabited the marbled bodies buried beneath the altar.

Neither Cnut nor Harthacnut had been easy on the House of Leofwine and its members. Yet Leofric had admired them in their own ways. They could both have been better men, but the past was the past. Nothing could be rewritten, despite Lady Emma's intentions with her great literary creation. The events and facts spoke for themselves, and Leofric refused to taint his memories further with a continuation of the complaints that were now irrelevant. He'd made his peace with what had happened. Others wouldn't, but they didn't concern him.

The monks prayers whispered through the vast edifice, and Leofric allowed himself to be carried along by those words, comforted by the familiar sound. They were a tribute to the past, a promise for the future, and a reminder that nothing ever truly changed. Time was immaterial.

3
AD1042, ÆLFGAR

'LADY EMMA,' HIS FATHER WAS COURTEOUS AS HE ASSISTED THE GRIEVING woman to her feet, an arm ensuring she remained upright. Ælfgar had no idea how long she'd been praying for before their arrival. Certainly, his knees thrummed with the uncomfortable position he'd been forced to adopt while he prayed beside her.

For just that moment, Ælfgar allowed his thoughts to cloud with unease. Lady Emma was a poisoned chalice, and all knew it. Her youngest son was dead, and now her oldest would be king in his place. It was all the wrong way around – all mixed up due to her two marriages to England's successive kings. Yet Ælfgar could find no element of pity for her. He knew his father admired and sorrowed for her, but he simply couldn't.

It was impossible not to hold her accountable for Lord Alfred's death, her second-born son with King Æthelred. She must have known what was likely to happen when she enticed Lords Alfred and Edward to England when Harald was proclaimed king. Had one family ever detested one another so much? He couldn't imagine it. Such ambition. Such rampant desire to rule. He didn't understand it and hoped he never would.

'My Lord Leofric,' Lady Emma's voice was rusty from lack of use, although he detected a hint of warmth and surprise.

She was richly adorned in a summer cloak, the fabric light enough to stop her from perspiring but flowing enough to ensure everyone could see the wealth of fine threads and material that constituted the cloak. The brooch holding it closed glimmered with the rich yellow of a diamond. Lady Emma wore her wealth well, but Ælfgar couldn't help but see beyond such frippery.

Lady Emma was getting old. She might have been ageing well, but the ravages of time were clear to see. She'd have no more children, not now, and of the five she'd birthed between her two husbands, three of them were dead. Ælfgar could admit that he didn't relish in her losses. How could he? He was a father. He wouldn't want to witness the deaths of any of his small children. It would break his wife. It would do the same to him.

'It's good of you to pray so earnestly for Harthacnut.' Lady Emma's fierce blue eyes sought out Ælfgar's, and he met them evenly with a dip of his chin.

'He was too young,' Leofric demurred, and yet those words covered a multitude of sins. Harthacnut was too young, too proud, and too much had been placed on his shoulders. Cnut should have treated all of his three sons favourably. It would have made the last seven years much easier for everyone if he'd split his northern empire and shared it equally between his sons. England had suffered during that time, and so had Ælfgar's family.

'He was,' and silence filled the vast space as they all turned to leave the Old Minster. Three women flanked Lady Emma, as did two of the huscarls, the men who'd once guarded Harthacnut. They gathered around her as she neared the back of the church. Ælfgar nodded as he met their eyes.

These men weren't here to protect Lady Emma. They acted on the new king's instructions. It was a clear sign that Edward believed Lady Emma capable of causing problems, even in the royal church of the Old Minster; even as empty as it was, and even while she sorrowed for her youngest son.

The knowledge made Ælfgar uneasy. Should his father truly be seen in such a public way with the new king's mother? Not, Ælfgar accepted, that his father would readily consent to a command that ran counter to his intentions. Leofric respected Lady Emma, even if he was wary of her motivations.

Lady Emma said nothing else, not until their small party had moved outside, through the wide door, and then taken the few steps down to ground level once more.

'Lord Leofric. My son needs your support.' Lady Emma spoke softly as though she imparted a great secret, her women and the huscarls standing a respectable distance away to not overhear her words.

'I'm always loyal to England's king,' Leofric offered, inclining his head. Ælfgar detected myriad emotions in his father's voice. He'd served many kings in his lifetime, all with the integrity his grandfather had used. It was wrong of Lady Emma to make the demand as though it contradicted his father's objective.

'I understand that,' Lady Emma agreed quickly, but she wanted to say more.

'You once accused me of colluding with Earl Godwine when Harald was king.' Ælfgar felt his stance straighten at her words. He knew exactly to what she alluded.

'I assure you that whatever agreement once lay between Earl Godwine and myself, it is long over with and finished. My loyalty is to Edward now and always will be.'

Ælfgar noted the flash of defiance that flickered in Lady Emma's eyes. He considered whether she expected his father to argue with her.

'My Lady. Lord Godwine has long served the royal family of England. I'm sure he'll continue to do so alongside his sons.' This time, Ælfgar quickly detected the fury on Lady Emma's face. These were not the words she wanted to hear, and in all honesty, neither did Ælfgar. Godwine's sons were not all the same as his father, but they were ambitious, and aspiration and a new king were not a good combination.

'As will you, your son, and grandchildren,' Lady Emma dredged her court façade to her face, and Ælfgar was struck by just how regal she was. She wore her years of service to England's kings easily, and yet he was sure it must be a trial to her. Maybe she should merely step aside and allow Edward to rule with his earls and the support of the bishops and archbishops. Perhaps it was time she retired to a nunnery.

'Ah, Priest Stigand,' a genuine smile touched Lady Emma's face as her eyes alighted on the man hovering before them. He was one of Harthacnut's household priests, yet even Ælfgar had heard of the man's pretensions. He quickly retracted his previous thoughts. Lady Emma was not done with her meddling and desire to rule as she'd done under Æthelred and Cnut. There were still accomplices willing to assist her.

The other man, tall and rigid, bowed stiffly to the king's mother, but there was genuine regard there.

'Excuse us,' Lady Emma inclined her head to his father, and the pair walked away into Winchester itself. Perhaps they went to her private dwelling far along the main street, eschewing the feast that Edward had ordered to be raised in memory of Harthacnut. Ælfgar expelled a breath he'd not realised he'd been holding.

'And just when I thought she might have decided to lay aside her interfering ways.'

Leofric surprised Ælfgar by laughing at his words, the sound brittle and too loud.

'She'll never be done, no matter what Edward might hope and believe. She might have been gone from England when King Harald ruled, but it was only for a handful of years. She still has her allies, and few can help but be swept up in the deception of power and prestige she presents to the world.'

'But it's a mirage?'

'It can be little else. And I imagine that Edward will move quickly to dissuade her of the ideas she currently has. He's determined to make his mark as England's king.'

'So, he'll attempt to set his mother aside. But what of Earl Godwine and his sons?'

'Ah,' and now Leofric's eyes clouded. 'I believe that it might not be possible to do the same with them. Unfortunately.'

Ælfgar wasn't sure how to respond to the resignation in his father's voice.

'But Harthacnut made you promise.'

'He did, yes. Like his father, he was the sort to force an impossible oath on a man. We will do what we can, but Lord Godwine is reinvigorated following Harthacnut's death. I doubt that Edward will have the same ability to overawe the man and his rampant ambitions that Harthacnut possessed.'

Ælfgar felt his mouth drop open in surprise.

'Never fear, son, I've not given up, but I'm conscious that some mountains can never be climbed, and the Godwinesson family may be one of those obstructions. Luckily, you have three sons and a daughter to aid you in ruling when they're older. We must hold on to what we have for now. Do what we can for now. At some point, Edward will find his stones. At least, I hope he will.'

Ælfgar's stomach felt leaden, and yet he nodded all the same.

'We know how to survive,' he tried to jest, and his father smiled in appreciation at the words.

'And so does our new king. Lord Godwine? Well, until he butted up against Harthacnut, he'd never had any experience of it. I imagine he'll quickly forget what it was like to be submissive. That'll be his downfall, mark my words.'

ÆLFGAR SAT JUST BEHIND HIS FATHER, WHO WAS WEDGED BETWEEN THE NOT-inconsiderable bulk of Earl Godwine, and the more svelte Earl Siward as the witan convened. News had reached them only that day of Earl Hrani's death, not unexpected, but just another problem for the new king to counter.

Ælfgar felt the pressure of Earl Godwine's four sons to his side, while Siward had his son, Osbjorn, with him. Anyone looking at the array of men would quickly assume who held the most sway with the king. But Ælfgar hoped that Edward would be a firmer ruler than his father seemed to think possible.

Not that the room was particularly filled with Edward's allies either. Ælfgar considered when more of the king's allies would arrive. Undoubtedly, Edward had associates in Normandy upon whom he could call. However, Ælfgar wasn't too sure. His father hadn't shared many details of Edward's domestic arrangements when he'd been sent to encourage Edward to return to England on Harthacnut's orders. The fact that only Ralph had come to England with Edward was perhaps telling.

Once more, the discussion was centred around the past. Earl Godwine determined to press Edward into asserting which laws now applied to England.

'I'll need to study the laws of Cnut, ensure that they were well-formed. I wouldn't wish to enact something I fundamentally disagree with.'

'I'm sure, my lord king, that you wouldn't wish to rescind any of your father's laws.' Earl Godwine's voice was slick and condescending.

Edward's cool gaze settled on Earl Godwine, no flicker of annoyance in the look.

'A wise man agrees to nothing without knowledge of it. I'll study the laws carefully. England needs her laws, which must apply to all men and women, regardless of rank and position.'

Earl Godwine bowed his head in acceptance and made to take his seat once more, but Ælfgar could detect the tension in the other man. It seemed he hoped that Edward would be easier to manipulate to his advantage.

'Tell me, have the ship army been paid recently? I know that

Harthacnut sent much of his Danish fleet back to Denmark two years ago. I assume the English fleet remains fully provisioned.' Edward's change of tact surprised Ælfgar, even as he appreciated it as a firm dismissal of Godwine's chosen topic.

'Yes, my lord Kking, they do. They're stationed in London and some of the other ports, most notably Sandwich. It's customary for one nobleman to have command over them.' It was Earl Siward who spoke now, standing before the newly-elected king. It was the day after Harthacnut's funeral, and Edward was keen to take control of his new kingdom.

'For the time being, Earl Siward, you'll ensure the shipmen have all they need. External enemies may threaten England. It would be a poor king who neglected such a valuable resource.'

Ælfgar was about to ask why his father hadn't spoken in response to the king's question when he realised. Earl Siward's focus was exclusively north of the River Humber. By allowing the man to answer, Leofric had ensured that, for the time being at least, Siward was interested in what happened in the south, as well as the north.

Ælfgar found himself looking to see who else attended the witan. He'd not been paying enough attention yesterday. He was unsurprised to find men who'd been staunchly loyal to Harthacnut in the crowd; Ordgar, Osgot Clapa, Brihtric, Odda, Ælfstan and Ælfgar. Edward gave the impression that he was keen to hold onto the prevailing status quo. Ælfgar approved of the tactic. Better to attempt to win over these influential men than begin by upsetting them and potentially inciting an uprising against him.

'I'll release my coinage as soon as the dies can be made. When it's ready for distribution, I wish to encourage moneyers to move to the ports and centres of trade.'

'My lord king,' again, Earl Godwine was on his feet, although he bowed his head to show some subservience. 'Such matters are surely beneath the attention of the king.' He infused his voice with scorn.

'Nothing should be beneath the attention of England's king, not when it affects my subject's wealth and access to resources.'

Now, Leofric did stand, bowing his head.

'My lord king, I know of a handful of moneyers who could be enticed to London from within my earldom. I'll ensure they know there are lucrative incentives for them to relocate. Perhaps they could purchase their dies at a discount or some such.'

Edward beamed with delight at Leofric's words.

'That would please the king.'

Leofric retook his seat, and yet Earl Godwine still stood. Ælfgar felt the man looked foolish, and indeed, Sweyn, his oldest son, murmured vehemently from behind him. If Godwine heard, he made a good show of ignoring it while Harold shushed his brother.

Ælfgar looked between the two men. It was impossible to glance at Sweyn and Harold and not be reminded of Earl Godwine and vice versa.

'Something else, Earl Godwine?' Edward's voice was pleasant enough.

'My lord king, I believe the witan should be concerned with the matter of your coronation.'

Edward smiled, although the movement didn't reach his emotionless eyes.

'I thank you for your interest, but I assure you, plans are already progressing for my coronation. The country swelters under a heat haze, and I know there are worries about the harvest and how the land will feed everyone. Such expenses as a coronation can be put off until all have safely survived the coming winter.'

Edward spoke so eloquently it would have been churlish for Earl Godwine to complain, and yet for a long moment, it seemed that he would do so. Sweyn grumbled at his father once more, and this time, Godwine returned to his seat with many eyes on him.

Edward spared him a final, lingering glance. Ælfgar knew a moment of regret that Harthacnut hadn't banished Earl Godwine when he'd had the opportunity.

THE ANGLO-SAXON CHRONICLE ENTRY FOR AD1042

(E – Peterborough Version) This year died King Harthacnut at Lambeth, on the 6th before the Ides of June: and he was king over all England two years wanting ten days; and he is buried in the Old-Minster at Winchester with king Canute (Cnut) his father. And his mother, for his soul, gave to the Newminster the head of St. Valentine the martyr. And before he was buried, all people chose Edward for king at London: may he hold it the while that God shall grant it to him! And all that year was a very heavy time, in many things and divers, as well in respect to ill seasons as to the fruits of the earth. And so much cattle perished in the year as no man before remembered, as well through various diseases as through tempests. And in this same time died Elsinus abbot of Peterborough; and then Amwius the monk was chosen abbot, because he was a very good man, and of great simplicity.

(C – Abingdon Version) and (D – Worcester Version) This year died King Harthacnut as he stood at his drink, and he suddenly fell to the earth with a terrible convulsion: and then they who were there nigh took hold of him; and he after that spoke not one word: and he died on the 6th before the Ides of June. And all people then acknowledged Edward for king, as was his true natural right.

4

EASTER, AD1043, WINCHESTER, LEOFRIC

THE OLD MINSTER WAS ADORNED WITH FINERY, AS IT SHOULD BE FOR THE coronation of a king. Leofric inhaled the scent of new growth and fixed a smile on his face. After a trying winter, the welcome brightness of Easter Sunday meant that few candles had to be lit inside the cavernous building. And just as when Harthacnut and Harald had been made king, he had a role to play in Edward's coronation service.

It was to be presided over by Archbishop Eadsige. Leofric considered how many men had enjoyed the honour of bestowing the ceremonial crown on three such royal heads, as the archbishop had crowned Harald and Harthacnut as well.

Edward had chosen to wear his wealth in an understated way that both spoke of his taciturn nature and new position. He wore the darkest purple, a regal colour if ever there was one. His hair shone as though a halo of gold and Leofric would have placed his age as at least a decade younger than he truly was.

Once more, he walked in the new king's procession to the front of the Old Minster. Like the archbishop, he'd been involved in more coronations than one man should in a lifetime, but this was taking place at the Old Minster. Harthacnut had been crowned in Kingston.

As Archbishop Eadsige began the extended service to make Edward a consecrated king, Leofric stood beside Edward with Godwine and Siward joining him. There were fewer earls than when Harthacnut had undergone the ceremony. Leofric didn't believe that would last long. Edward would have men he wished to reward for their loyalty, and the vacant earldom of Hrani was waiting to be filled.

Head bowed, eyes lowered, Leofric listened to the service conducted in Latin by the archbishop. He only raised his head when the new king was touched with the holy oil and anointed before God and his fellow men and women.

As a golden crown was placed on Edward's bowed head, Leofric watched with interest, noting that it wasn't the same one Harthacnut chose. Edward had ordered a new crown to be constructed using the extended delay between being declared king and the coronation. Leofric thought the crown more ceremonial than Harthacnut's had been.

Made with metal and silver and adorned with rich gemstones, the decoration was intricate. Somehow, and Leofric had no idea how, the goldsmith had managed to fashion the crown so that it glowed with the light of early summer. It seemed to warm with the promise of new growth and resurgence, even as it proclaimed its wearer as even holier than any who'd gone before.

As when Harthacnut had been crowned, it fell to Leofric to present Edward with his golden sceptre. It was dotted with rubies along its length and around the golden sphere, the item heavy and unruly in his hands.

Leofric bowed low before Edward before handing the precious item into his waiting grasp as he stood before the assembly. The two held one another's eyes for just too long, weighing one another. Leofric couldn't help considering what Edward saw when he looked at him.

It had been Earl Hrani who'd offered Harthacnut the silvery orb, but he was dead, and so the task fell to another, not yet one of the king's earls, but perhaps he would be soon. Leofric watched his son carefully, ensuring he made no mistake while playing his role in the service. Leofric was surprised when the king requested that Ælfgar do more than just watch the service. He'd expected Edward to ask Ralph or Beorn, but no, the king had decided to honour the House of Leofwine.

Leofric suppressed a smirk as his son stepped away from the king, the tension in his shoulders lessening with relief, a shimmer of sweat sliding beneath the collar of his tunic.

As with Harthacnut, Lord Godwine then presented the new king with the elaborately decorated rod, and Earl Siward had the honour of offering the ceremonial sword.

But, there was one final item for the king, which fell to Sweyn, Godwine's son. So, after all, the king had decided to honour two of his noble families, leaving aside only Earl Siward. Although Siward had left his son to rule in the north in his place, so perhaps it wasn't quite the slight that could be implied.

To Sweyn fell the task of presenting Edward with a ring to be worn on his right hand. This, similar to the crown, was a newly made item. Edward had proven squeamish and hadn't wanted to wear Harthacnut's recently discarded possessions. The ring's rich gold carried the same warm hue as the crown, but the flickering gems attached to it were far from ostentatious. Leofric found that Edward was a king who was well aware of who he was but felt no need to be gaudy.

So adorned, Edward was escorted to the throne by the archbishop and attendant bishops, his crown and ring still in place, but the other items placed to one side to make it easier for him to move.

Only then did the archbishop display the new king to the audience. They waited eagerly to catch sight of Edward, perhaps with the hope that he looked more kingly now consecrated. Maybe to remember this moment because who knew when they'd ever get the chance to see a king in the making again? Certainly, it was hoped that Edward would survive longer than Harthacnut, even if he were much older.

There was a thunderous reception at seeing Edward in all his regalia, led by the huscarls, their deep voices booming from the rear of the Old Minster. But the cheer died away too quickly, and even Archbishop Eadsige suddenly looked uneasy, his eyes peering forward as though he could force the audience to a more tremendous effort. Edward didn't seem to notice, but this was his first coronation. He wouldn't know it was any different to Harthacnut's ceremony.

Leofric moved quickly. On his throne, the king waited to take the oaths from his earls, bishops, and king's thegns. Leofric was determined to be the first of them all, even without the awkward silence clanging louder than the tolling church bell. Ælfgar knew of his intentions, and he was ready to interfere if it was needed. But Godwine and Siward seemed reluctant to be the first to pledge themselves, their movements tardy for men who knew what was expected of them.

Leofric knelt before the king, head bowed, the words of the oath tripping from his tongue.

'By the Lord, and these holy relics, I pledge to be loyal and true to Edward, and love all that he loves, and hate all that he hates, in accordance with God's rights and my noble obligations; and never, willingly and intentionally, in word or deed, do anything that is hateful to him; on condition that he keep me as was our agreement when I subjected myself to him and took his service.'

He tried not to consider how often he'd spoken these words to men who'd died before their time. Or even of the men who'd spoken it to him and were no longer by his side or had proven false to the oath.

Edward acknowledged his words with the smallest upturn of his lips, his eyes blazing with righteousness, before turning his expression to stone again. Earl Siward replaced Leofric. Siward bowed smartly and took to his knee, the movement fluid, the words flowing smoothly and loud enough for everyone to hear in the first rows of the congregation.

Godwine came last of all. Not for him the smoothness of bowing and taking the knee, not when his baulk was so vast. Leofric winced to hear the fabric straining at the shoulder and waist. While Lord Godwine spoke clearly, when he was finally settled, enunciating the words of the oath to ensure all understood he gave it freely, Leofric was far from convinced.

Yes, Godwine might rest his hand on the reliquary containing the bones of St Swithun as he made his pledge, just as Leofric and Siward had done, but only haughty disdain could be detected in Godwine's demeanour. Leofric was sure the king was aware of it as well, although his expression and stance didn't falter as Godwine hurried through the words.

Leofric listened intently to the familiar words. He knew men could be devious with even this outward show of respect and honour. Would Godwine risk it? It seemed he might. Yet, Edward acknowledged the oath as fully given, indicating that Godwine should rise, which he did, but only with the assistance of both hands on his knees, his breath rasping loudly.

Leofric stood to the side of the mass, waiting for his next task as Godwine moved away from the king. He'd caught sight of Lady Emma, observing this act of loyalty being sworn to her son. Her expression had been calm and accepting. Perhaps she'd finally come to terms with Harthacnut's death, although Leofric was unsure. It had been over nine months, but that wasn't long enough to mourn a child, and Lady Emma hadn't often been seen in company with her son, who still lived.

Did she somehow blame Edward for what had befallen Harthacnut? It was impossible and yet possible, all at the same time. Grief made people act irrationally, and think strange thoughts; he was no stranger to that.

Lady Emma needed to give her oath to the new king, and Leofric's task was to assist her at the correct time. She might have expected to do so before the earls, as a member of his household, as his mother, but Edward was making her wait.

Only now, when the bishops had made their obeisance, did the king indicate he was ready for his mother.

'My lady,' Leofric stood before her, extending his hand to assist her. The touch on his arm was no more than a feather, but he noted the fast pulse on her neck. He couldn't think that she was nervous, but perhaps she was. Leofric remained unsure how the king and his mother regarded one another. They weren't enemies, but neither were they allies.

'My thanks, Earl Leofric,' her words were firm as he released her hand to enable her to curtsey before the king.

She executed the movement perfectly, but Leofric considered what it cost her as she then kneeled and recited the words of the oath to her son. She spoke quietly, her voice designed not to reach the audience behind her. Her ploy didn't please the king as a swift glint of frustration touched his intelligent eyes. It forced Leofric to stand ever taller, aloof from Lady Emma, yet he knew that the king believed him to be closely allied with her.

For all the king's months in England, the nuances of some of his nobility were still a mystery to him. Leofric was convinced Edward was realising that not everything was as it seemed. How could it be with men and women who'd held their positions for so long? The mistakes of youth couldn't be undone, but they could be glossed over and perhaps, forgiven if the other party was so inclined.

Once more, he offered his arm to Lady Emma, courteous to the last. Together they walked to the front row, where the other earls and their families waited to either give their oaths or witness others doing so. Only now did Lady Emma's grip intensity, so much so that it felt like he was being pinched.

'My thanks, Earl Leofric. You've been a good friend to me. I hope it can continue.' So spoken, Lady Emma released her hold and settled back in the chair, eyes facing forwards, seemingly intent on observing her son as he took the oaths of every member of the witan within the Old Minister.

'Shall we?' he directed the words towards his wife and son. Lady Godgifu nodded, her expression pensive, while Ælfgar shot to his feet, Elgiva at his side. Once more, his nephews joined him, alongside his sister and niece. His brother had remained within Mercia. He would give his oath to Edward in the coming months.

As he chaperoned them to the king, Leofric allowed a glimmer of pride to touch his steps. His family might not hold high office throughout England, but they were without equal in Mercia, and he could only hope that the king would allow that to continue.

5

ÆLFGAR

'MY LORD HUSBAND,' ELGIVA'S VOICE ROUSED HIM FROM A GENTLE DOZE before the hearth, and he startled, looking around as though expecting the house to be on fire.

'What?' His voice was thick with sleep. She laughed, shaking her head as she watched him.

'You asked me to wake you, if you remember.'

He didn't, and then realisation dawned.

'Already?' he complained, but evidently, it was. 'Right. Wish me luck,' and he bent to kiss her cheek before pulling his tunic down from where it had hitched around his midriff. He hopped into his boots, smoothed his hair and walked towards the door as though he'd been awake all day and not just been roused.

Two of his servants worked quietly at their sewing, a sense of serenity filling the main hall of his home in Oxford.

'Don't forget Ælfwine,' her soft voice followed him to the door, causing him to turn, confusion furrowing his forehead.

Elgiva laughed again, her eyes bright with amusement. She nodded towards where his cousin still snored, head resting on his folded arms, before the hearth.

'Bloody hell. Come on, you damn fool,' Ælfgar took no delight in waking his cousin with a rough shake on his shoulder. Well, maybe he took a little when a groan and then confused eyes glanced his way.

'What?' Elgiva's chuckle at the identical response reached him, but he growled rather than laugh.

'Already?' Ælfwine came alert far more quickly than Ælfgar had, reaching for a beaker to swill water into his parched mouth and then moving to smooth his rumpled hair and tunic. Only then did he jump to his feet, disturbing the two hounds sleeping beneath the table. Two loud yawns filled the air, tails wagging against the wooden floorboards.

'Is Lord Leofric sure we need to do this?' Ælfwine demanded, not for the first time since they'd been assigned their task.

'He was adamant, I'm afraid,' Ælfgar retorted, even though he was as reluctant as Ælfwine.

'What does he think they're up to?'

'I rather think that's what we're supposed to find out, don't you?'

Ælfwine suppressed a yawn. 'Well, he must have some idea.'

'He does, but he's not shared that with me. He wants me to find out what's going on since Earl Hrani's death.'

'Poor sod,' and Ælfgar knew his cousin spoke of the old earl as they exited the building, moving into the yard where their horses waited. The servants had been more prepared than they had.

They'd all respected Earl Hrani, even if they'd not always agreed with him. Hrani had roused himself to come to their aid after the altercation with Gruffydd Ap Llewelyn.

'Yes, and now poor us, dealing with the aftermath.' Ælfgar's words were muffled as he mounted, but Ælfwine heard them all the same.

'Who will the king name as Hrani's replacement? Does your father think it'll be you?' While the idea wasn't new to Ælfgar, he still shook his head at his cousin's question.

'I can't imagine that Edward will want anyone too young in such a position unless he does decide to reward his nephew, but I can't see it. The Welsh borders aren't the place for a youth who's never been to war.' His voice was laced with the remembered horror of his uncle's murder.

'So what does Lady Gunnhild mean to do?'

'Well, the sooner we get there, the sooner we'll find out.'

While Ælfwine chuckled at Ælfgar's rueful tone, they both made their way to the gate that allowed access onto the roadway that ran from Oxford towards the west.

'Come on, let's not keep her waiting.' Without waiting, Ælfwine encouraged his mount to a gentle trot and then a gallop. Ælfgar hastened to follow him, his mind awash with the possibilities his cousin had brought to the fore, something he was trying not to think about in the mistaken hope that it might actually happen.

His father had told him not to expect the vacant earldom, a steely look in his eyes, and hunger on his face. He might be telling his son not to anticipate such advancement, and yet it was clear that Leofric hoped it would happen, all the same.

What, Ælfgar considered, would he do if he was named as earl of Hereford? He certainly had the requisite skills to rule alone, but it would be the first time he'd done so without the oversight of his father. All the years of practising would suddenly be put into effect, and he couldn't deny that it terrified him just as much as it thrilled.

He thought of the honour for his family if both he and his father were named earls. It would make it clear to others that the king highly regarded the House of Leofwine. There was only one slight problem with the image of the future that he imagined – he really wasn't sure what the king thought of his father and him. Ælfgar would have liked to be able to say, categorically, that his father was more greatly esteemed than Earl Godwine, but it was impossible.

Ælfgar was well aware of the words Harthacnut had spoken to his father as he lay dying, and yet, Edward hadn't seemed to appreciate the caution. After all the years of war and family dispute between Cnut and Æthelred's sons, was it too much to ask for some accord at long last?

And that, Ælfgar discovered as he entered the home of Lady Gunnhild later that day, was exactly about what she wished to speak to him and the other local nobility. Earl Hakon might have been dead for over a decade, but Gunnhild had held on to some of his properties in his old earldom centred around Worcester.

Ælfgar bowed low to her when he bid her good day, but Lady Gunnhild, in all of her finery, arms jingly with arm rings that he assumed must have belonged to her husbands, barely seemed to notice him and his cousin as she spoke in front of the select group of people she'd assembled in the hall. Ælfgar recognised her two sons, Hemming and Thurkill, both little more than children, yet swaggering as though they commanded a shield wall, and had the king's treasury to finance their wishes. He found a smile playing around his lips, and dipped his head low so that she wouldn't see it and neither would they.

Ælfgar took careful note of who else she'd invited to this strange meeting, unsurprised to find the vast majority had been adherents of Lady Ælfgifu, Cnut's first wife, holding land around Northampton. There was still much confusion about where she'd disappeared to, and Ælfgar felt no need to share the information he knew. She was safe. Her grandson was safe. And they were both hidden away where no one would ever think to look for them. That was all that mattered, not the hole that her disappearance had caused amongst the local nobility.

Equally, the fact that he could see Osgot Clapa didn't surprise him. Osgot Clapa's reputation had been tarnished by Harthacnut's death during his daughter's wedding celebrations to Tovi. It wasn't helped that King Edward, although owing his elevation to that death, was still markedly cool towards Osgot Clapa. Between one breath and the next, which had never come, Osgot Clapa and his family had fallen from the pinnacle of being the king's privileged ally to scrabbling around for favours.

Some of the local sheriffs and reeves were in attendance, who Lady Gunnhild believed would be swayed by her ideas. Ælfgar listened carefully to her words, even as he realised why his father wouldn't have been unable to attend the meeting.

Lady Gunnhild had determined her own means of keeping control of the Mercian lands she held in Jarl Hakon's name and those of Earl Hrani's. For some reason, she'd decided they should be hers as well. Not that the pair of them had been married or particularly close, but all the same, she was staking her claim to Hereford and wanted to ensure she had the support to do so.

'Earl Leofric,' and his interest pricked at hearing his father's name spoken by the woman, 'is my ally, and of course, he has the ear of the king. I believe it's only a matter of time before he speaks to the king regarding my suggestion. It's only as it should be that my sons are allowed to rule in place of Earl Hrani. They have Danish blood, as Hrani did, and the Danes who've settled this part of Mercia will welcome such staunch patrons.'

At her words, both lads somehow managed to puff themselves up even further than they already had.

'Bloody hell,' Ælfwine spoke out of the corner of his mouth, his voice filled with amusement at the sight. 'What does she think she's birthed? They look like they'd fall over if you blew on them wrong.'

Ælfwine was right, but what concerned Ælfgar was Lady Gunnhild's assertion that it was all done bar the king's agreement. That was far from the case. King Edward had made no move to replace the dead earl, and it wasn't expected that he would anytime soon, either. The king held a grand prize in his hands, and he wasn't about to bring the matter to a close, not yet.

And even if the king wanted to name a new earl, Ælfgar was not convinced that he'd listen to Earl Leofric's thoughts on the matter. And where did that leave his family's ambitions if his father supported an alternative to his son?

'And only Danes can keep the pestilent Welsh at bay.' Ælfgar reached out to caution his cousin with a hand on his arm at those words. They were lies. The Mercians had done more than enough to prevent the Welsh from attacking. But Lady Gunnhild was correct in that the Welsh were persistent bastards. He'd happily see them all dead, but slaughtering so many would never bring back his beloved uncle.

'Why should we want one of your sons as our earl? There are others, older men, who would be better fitted for an earl's position, men with battle glory and the ear of the king. I doubt the king even knows who your sons are, and would he truly wish to elevate a Dane to such a position? Their father, Thorkell, the Tall's son, was hardly the epitome of loyal to the kings he served.'

Swift fury covered Lady Gunnhild's face at the words spoken by Gloucester's sheriff, a man Ælfgar knew well and respected. There was a welling of support for his argument from the others in the hall.

'Earl Thorkell was loyal to King Edward's father. He helped him escape to Normandy when King Swein invaded. I'm sure the king will fondly remember my husband.' The resounding silence in the room at those words spoke to the contrary. Earl Thorkell had been a slippery individual. His son had never attained the same notoriety, yet he'd still been judged by his father's actions.

'Tell me, Lord Ælfgar. What does your father think of my suggestion?'

Ælfgar cursed his father then. It would have been invaluable to have some idea of what Lady Gunnhild was going to say so that he could have formulated an adequate response. He paused, trying to think of what to say.

'Earl Leofric is much taken up with the transition of power. I confess, I'm not privy to his thoughts about Earl Hrani's earldom.'

This, he quickly realised, wasn't the answer Lady Gunnhild was seeking. Even Ælfwine huffed with annoyance as he fumbled his way through the sentence.

'You said you had the earl's support,' an angry voice called from behind Ælfgar.

'I do have the earl's support, but it seems he's not told his son of that. No doubt,' and Ælfgar could almost hear Lady Gunnhild reasoning her way out of the conundrum, 'the earl has sent Ælfgar here to be convinced by listening to our arguments.'

'Then,' the same voice offered, 'I suggest you make them.' Ælfgar tried to determine who'd spoken but couldn't tell in the press of bodies. Rather than looking at the detractor, Lady Gunnhild had her eyes firmly on Ælfgar. The gaze almost made him squirm until he remembered that he was the son of an earl. He was a lord and sheriff in his own right. Lady Gunnhild wouldn't cow him.

'As you know,' and she finally turned away from him, her lips tight with concentration. 'This area of Mercia has been ruled by the Danes ever since King Cnut won the kingdom of England. The Danes have kept the border with the Welsh secure.'

Ælfgar almost choked at the repeated assertion. Gunnhild met his eyes, daring him to argue, but he snapped his mouth shut, refusing to be riled by her. What was his father doing in sending him here? Surely, he couldn't believe that Lady Gunnhild's intentions were good.

'It's the Danes who've given time, money and thought as to how the people can grow in wealth, who've argued against the imposition of unfavourable terms by the king on the people of Mercia.'

Ælfgar clenched his hands into fists. Lady Gunnhild spoke as though his father had played no part in this, and she certainly seemed determined not to accord him any responsibility. He couldn't believe that Gunnhild had made this particular argument when his father was present. Surely, she wouldn't be so arrogant?

'We've encouraged more and more of our countrymen and women to settle in Mercia. Without one of their own to speak for them, we could harken back to the St Brice's Day massacre, when men and women viciously hacked the Danes to death, some in their beds. I'll not allow a repeat of such. King Edward must be brought to reason.'

Now that Lady Gunnhild had stopped her derisive comments about his father, it seemed that she spoke some sense. Indeed, heads were nodding in agreement. Ælfgar realised this was something he'd not considered with the death of Harthacnut.

'The lands of the Danelaw have their rights written in the law, but the Danes of western Mercia aren't accorded the same, and of course, King Edward is a virtual stranger to his homeland. How would he even know to look for a problem? He might not even realise that he erred if taking directions from his other English earls.'

Ælfgar shook his head at the words. Lady Gunnhild, and indeed, everyone in that room, should be more than aware that his father counted the people of Mercia as Mercians, no matter from where they'd heralded. It had always been the same. It was an underhand tactic. The fact that it seemed to be working spoke of deep mistrust, both for his father and towards the new, English-born king.

No doubt, that was why his father had sent him here. Those in attendance were prepared to say things and react in ways; they wouldn't have done if Leofric had been amongst them.

'This is wrong,' Ælfwine whispered into his ear, and Ælfgar nodded. He could feel the current swirling through the audience. It spoke of too much and too little, and with Gruffydd Ap Llewelyn so powerful on the borders, it could portend disaster for the new king.

Ælfgar was beyond surprised that Lady Gunnhild could offer the caution that the other earls were English. Earl Siward was a Dane, Earl Godwine, married to a Danish woman. Both of them were most assuredly Danish.

But, he supposed, in the quest for power, Gunnhild was prepared to offer any excuse. If anything and Ælfgar knew he was right to think as such, it was the Mercians themselves who suffered the most. At the top of the hierarchy, his grandfather and father had endured when the three Danish men, Hrani, Eilifr and Hakon, had been given their earldoms. And they were just the most prominent victims. Ordinary men and women had lost out when land was gifted to Danes accompanying the new earls.

Lady Gunnhild appeared desperate to cement the status quo on the Welsh border. She didn't want a resurgence of the English

Mercians. There had been a brief revival for them under King Harald, thanks to his mother, who'd been so influential in Northampton. But that had not lasted into Harthacnut's reign, not just because Lady Ælfgifu had been forced to flee for her life.

'And the answer to this is to make one of your sons the earl in place of Hrani?' The voice was quizzical, and Ælfgar thought it belonged to Osgot Clapa.

'Yes,' Gunnhild's response was staunch.

'Would it not be better to have a man who was closer to the king or a tried and tested stateman? Your sons are children. Not men. They've never fought the Welsh. They've never argued the case of another before the king.' Both boys startled at the criticism, young faces flushing red with anger.

'My sons are well trained. All they need is the opportunity to become a man, just like their father.'

This response caused a soft murmur throughout the room. All knew of Lord Harald's death. He'd been murdered on a trip to Denmark only last year, leaving his wife a widow for the second time and his sons fatherless.

Once more, Ælfgar considered what had happened to Gunnhild's husband. Had Harald Thorkellson truly been unfortunate to be in the wrong place at the wrong time, or had he been gathering an army to rise against Edward, hoping to offer the kingdom of England to King Magnus? It was impossible to tell. Even his father couldn't say with any surety, and that wasn't like him. But, the rumours persisted all the same.

Ælfgar knew his father had allies he was ignorant about and that, no doubt, some of them were in Denmark. For now, he was content not to know too much. After all, it made sense. Earls Siward and Godwine had their networks of family ties. It would have been remiss if Leofric had neglected to develop some for himself.

'So, Lord Ælfgar,' and he was recalled to where he was by Lady Gunnhild's stringent tone. 'Have I said enough to convince you?'

He inclined his head at her words, the irony not lost on him that she advocated Danes to rule Danes, even though he was perhaps the most Mercian man in the room.

'I can see why my father asked me to attend your meeting. The proposal is an intriguing one.' He didn't wish to say more, and it seemed that his response was, again, less than welcome.

'Tell me, Lord Ælfgar; you can't possibly hope that the king will reward you with the title and responsibility?'

For all he tried to betray no emotion, he must have given something away because a cackle of laughter greeted his silence, Lady Gunnhild's mouth a wicked slash on her haughty face.

'It seems you and your father have ambitions far beyond your abilities. There isn't a single man in this room who would accept you as their earl.' Only it seemed that Lady Gunnhild was just as deluded as Ælfgar, for a man in the audience stood and looked his way.

Ælfgar sighed with relief. He should have trusted his father wouldn't send him and his cousin to such a meeting alone.

His uncle, Olaf, inclined his head toward Lady Gunnhild, a flash of white teeth showing as he turned to smile at Ælfgar, his presence already dissipating the thick tension that had formed.

'I must beg to differ with you there, my good woman. I think many here would support the rightful dynasty's return to rule from Deerhurst. And others would want to allow the king to decide for himself.'

Ælfgar wasn't sure what would happen next. Only another previously unseen figure stood and addressed the audience.

'I suggest we all decide what we want. Lord Ælfgar isn't the only young lord champing at the bit to be given his own earldom. I'd sooner the person chosen was one of our own, not one of Earl Godwine's litter.'

These words, spoken by a voice that Ælfgar recognised, jolted him. Would the king truly reward the man so instrumental in the death of his brother, Lord Alfred? It turned Ælfgar's stomach, even as he appreciated there was some sense in the idea.

'Then, I recommend we all support my sons, the sons of Lord

Harald Thorkellson. It will be better for all concerned if our new earl is removed from the influence of two of the earls that England already boasts. Better to have someone independent.'

'How can they be independent when you stand behind them?' Lady Gunnhild's face soured at the words flung at her by someone on the front row that Ælfgar couldn't see.

'Better someone untried and easier to manipulate, aye?' Another taunted.

'We should let the king decide,' someone else reiterated. The entire room felt as though it was close to erupting, but Lady Gunnhild did nothing. Ælfgar had the distinct impression that some audience members might have been placed there on purpose, to bring up such points when it seemed that consensus was far from being reached.

'We need to think of ourselves. We've had four bastard kings in almost as many years. They've all caused ructions. Earl Hrani was at least a constant.' That too was a good point.

Olaf made his way to Ælfgar's side, his expression neutral, even as he appraised his nephew.

'A hornet's nest,' he complained in a low voice. 'Your father's right to be worried. More rumours are flying through the earldom than when Edward was named king. They don't much mind who's in charge and who demands the taxes. What concerns them is who'll arbitrate in the courts, who'll keep the border secure, and of course, and to be expected, who they'll be able to bribe with the smallest amount of coin to maintain the present circumstances.'

'It seems to me that they all want something different,' Ælfwine offered.

'Yes, they do, but overall, they want what they have to continue as it has done for many years. Earl Hrani had been the earl for nearly two decades. Many people can begin to think that everything is set in stone after a long time. The threat of change only appeals to those who see it as an opportunity.'

Ælfgar eyed his uncle with interest. Olaf was often found at his father's side and was a formidable man. He might have lost the slab of muscle that made him an impressive warrior, but he looked no less lethal for that. He always looked ready to strike with his quick eyes and posture if he needed to do so.

'Why did my father send me here?'

'I think you probably know the answer to that,' Olaf raised one eyebrow. 'But, we've seen enough. Better to leave them to argue. I can't see Lady Gunnhild uniting the Danish, or the English, behind Hemming or Thurkill. But equally, I can't predict what the king will do.'

While the roar of conversation bellowed behind them, Ælfgar followed Ælfwine and Olaf outside, where fresh air was a welcome change after the stale smell of spilt ale and too many people in too small a space.

But here, Ælfgar spied something that made his heart sink. He'd recognise that horse with that stance anywhere. It seemed Earl Godwine had sent his son to this meeting as well, and no doubt, he'd take the news back to the king. Damn, Earl Godwine. He'd do anything to earn back the regard of the king, and for once, he might even be able to put such a spin on his tale that it might just work.

6

LEOFRIC

'I HAVE SOME ANNOUNCEMENTS TO MAKE,' THE KING'S WORDS WERE GREETED
with a sudden silence in the witan. Was this, then, for what they'd all
been waiting? Was he about to announce the man who was to
become earl?

Leofric eyed King Edward with mild interest. He didn't share the
relationship with the king he might have hoped for when
Harthacnut died. They were both too suspicious of the other's
motives. Not, Leofric appreciated, that Edward had done anything to
earn the unease. But neither had he done anything to dispel it.
Leofric had served too many difficult men not to understand the
difference.

It would have been easy for Edward to show his appreciation of
Leofric's oath and unswerving loyalty. But no, he'd chosen not to do
so, and now Leofric sensed that he was about to have his doubts and
questions proved correct.

Edward was unchanged from the man he'd first met on that
fateful day in Bolougne, but who he was and what he represented
couldn't be more different. He was no longer the forgotten son of a
little-lamented king. Now he was the king, and no one, to date, had

made any genuine attempts to unseat him. Yes, the rumours from Norway continued to swirl. Still, until King Magnus was seen on the horizon, Leofric wasn't concerned with his ship army.

King Magnus was being kept busy in his efforts to hold Denmark by Svein Estridsson. Leofric hoped that continued for many years to come.

'The first is an appointment. I'm pleased to confirm that of the royal priest, Stigand, to East Anglia's bishopric. I believe, as do the bishops and archbishops that such an elevation will benefit the spiritual health of the men and women of East Anglia.'

The news was no surprise to Leofric. He grasped that Lady Emma had been keen to have her ally confirmed in the vacant bishopric. Yet, the fact that the king had acquiesced spoke of insecurity. Even as king, he still needed to ingratiate himself with those who knew England much better than he did. Not for the first time, Leofric considered why the king hadn't summoned more of his followers from Normandy.

To date, he relied on his nephew, Ralph, who had no position other than as his mother's proxy for her English possessions and a burgeoning friendship with Beorn Estridsson.

Bishop Stigand stood at the king's words, a pleased expression on his long face, which just stopped short of looking self-satisfied. Lady Emma had chosen to distance herself from the meeting of the witan, and yet her closeness to Stigand was far from a secret. It was as though she attended, even though not physically. Perhaps, this is how it would be from now on.

Leofric appreciated that Edward might have made such a move to appease his mother. Perhaps. Or maybe, Stigand had merely been the next royal priest to deserve such a promotion. He might never know the truth of that.

'And now, for the need for a new earl. I've taken a great deal of time to consider the best solution to the loss of Earl Hrani from Hereford. I may not have had cause to know him well, but I'm aware that he toiled for the good of the kings he did serve, all three of them.

There's a lingering loyalty to Earl Hrani in Hereford and the surrounding areas from the Mercians and the Danes who make their homes there. All the same, the problems of the border dictate that a strong man must serve the king, a man likely to garner the respect of others, and one with the name of his family to support him as he does so.'

Leofric found himself sitting up at the words. Could the king be about to nominate his son as the new earl? He'd not honestly expected the king to take his son seriously, and yet, Ælfgar had proved himself to be a loyal man. And he had a good friendship with the king's nephew, Ralph. Might Ralph have prompted such a move by the king?

Leofric attempted to show no emotion on his face. He'd been disappointed before. Yet, he couldn't help but hope that the king would finally show his favour toward the House of Leofwine by making the nomination. Yes, it would be for the other earls and the king's thegns and bishops to give their agreement to, but it was unlikely that anyone would wish to disappoint their king by refusing the appointment.

He daren't cast a look at his son. He couldn't risk the slightest indication that he expected his son to be put forward. Leofric hardly breathed.

'And therefore, I nominate Lord Sweyn Godwinesson to the position of Earl of Hereford.' Leofric's heart began to beat too loudly in his ears at the words. He had to concentrate on just breathing, and on not offering an exclamation of surprise and disgust. Lord Sweyn, Godwine's son? What could the king even be thinking in setting that man over the border region of Hereford? The Godwine family held sway in Wessex and Kent, not on the border. It was destined to fail. How couldn't it?

But worse? Why was Edward rewarding the family of Lord Godwine? Leofric had expected much, much more from him.

Only slowly did he become aware of the babble of conversation within the king's hall. He wasn't the only one surprised by the king's decision. He tried to catch the eye of the king, but Edward was studiously avoiding him at the front of the hall, keen only to preside over the chaos his announcement had caused.

Leofric couldn't bring himself to seek out Lord Godwine's eyes but instead turned, eager to offer his support to Ælfgar. While he shouldn't have expected the king to raise his son to an earldom, it still seemed natural. The House of Leofwine had worked for over fifty years to protect Mercia. They'd co-operated with the Danish jarls that Cnut had installed as earls. They'd fought and died to protect the borders. But it seemed none of that was relevant to Edward

Ælfgar, sat a few rows behind Leofric, had adopted a stoic expression, even as Sweyn beamed with delight at the king's announcement. Sweyn stood to bow to his king and then face the rest of the attendees. Ælfgar wouldn't meet his father's eyes, but in that quick look, Leofric noticed Harold's confusion. Not jealousy, confusion, and that perplexed Leofric, until he remembered Ælfgar's defiant assertion that the two brothers weren't close.

'I'll second the vote.' Of course, Lord Godwine lumbered to his feet to give his agreement to the king's nomination. In his delight, Godwine looked as ambitious as ever. Leofric knew then that the years under Harald and Harthacnut's kingship would be quickly forgotten. The Earl of Wessex was back in the ascendant, and still, it made no sense to Leofric.

'Then we'll call a vote,' the king announced, his voice betraying no hint of either excitement or indifference to the news. Leofric considered that the king had been forced to make a choice. Had Lord Godwine found some political leverage to use against him? Or was it merely how Edward proved that he couldn't be considered beholden to Leofric because of Harthacnut's oath? He wished he knew.

The appointment was quickly confirmed without even the threat of dissent. Unwillingly, and yet wary of the arguments he'd only just voiced to himself about why Ælfgar would be an acceptable choice to the earldom, Leofric gave his vote to the proposal. It was evident that he'd been one of only a few not to know the king's mind before the announcement.

'Then, Sweyn, you're invited to join your fellow earls,' Edward's voice still betrayed no hint of his real emotions. While choruses of congratulations rang out for the new earl, Leofric scrutinised the king. Edward must have known that he sought him out but stayed resolutely focused on others.

'Well, that's a statement,' Earl Siward leaned across the space between them to offer the words to Leofric. 'Everything that Harthacnut did to counter the ambition of Godwine is ashes now.' Siward's voice dripped with suppressed fury. Only then did Leofric recall that Siward had a son who could have been offered the earldom, had the king so minded, and that Siward had murdered a man on Harthacnut's orders.

'It would have been better to have given the position to his nephew.'

'But Ralph lacks any military experience.'

'As does Sweyn,' Leofric retorted, but their conversation abruptly stopped because Sweyn stood before them. The youth tried to look arrogant, but his unbridled ambition ran across his unlined face. At that moment, Leofric appreciated that Sweyn would hold his position for decades and not just years. This appointment was for the rest of the man's life. Who knew what trouble Earl Sweyn would cause in that time. Leofric was only too aware that Sweyn could be only the first of the king's appointments. Edward had made it clear he didn't believe the country could be effectively managed with only three, or now four, earls.

'Did you know?' Ælfgar's face flamed as he demanded an answer, pacing before his father much later.

'No, but it seems I was the only one.'

'What game does the king play?'

'A dangerous one.'

'I don't understand it,' Ælfgar raged. Leofric was pleased they were within their personal lodgings, away from the eyes of the court and the courtiers.

'I don't either.'

'And I'll tell you this; Lady Gunnhild is going to be furious.'

'She is, yes, but whether she can do anything about it, I don't know.'

'Do you believe that's what's happened here? Has the king heard of her fantastical idea and determined to punish the House of Leofwine? After all, I know that lord, or rather, Earl Sweyn, was in attendance when Lady Gunnhild spewed forth the idea that her son should be named as earl.'

Leofric exhaled noisily. He sat before the hearth, the warm flames doing nothing to dispel the ice that ran through his body when he considered the future.

'I've no idea. I suppose it's worthy of consideration. But, I'd have expected the king to speak to me about it if there was a problem. He's been silent about the whole thing, even when I warned him of the problems building in Hereford and the surrounding area with the long delay in naming a new earl.'

'So, Lady Gunnhild has deprived me of an earldom?'

But Leofric was shaking his head.

'It's been decades and not years since there were a father and son whom both served as earl. Yes, the son might inherit the father's title after death, but even that hasn't been guaranteed. You need only look at Ealdorman Æthelweard. His son eventually became ealdorman, but it took over a decade after his death.'

'Then, why would the king do it now? Many others could serve him, men we know he trusts, such as Osgot Clapa, Lyfing or Odda. Or even Beorn. You can't get much more Danish than Beorn Estridsson.'

'I know all this,' Leofric stated, not to stop his son's complaints but because he wanted to move beyond the argument and try to determine a path for the future.

'The king hasn't taken me into his confidence about these choices. I knew nothing of Stigand's elevation to the bishopric or Sweyn's earldom. Somehow, I've lost his trust and support.'

'If you ever had it,' the words made Leofric wince, yet he couldn't deny them. Foolishly, he'd thought himself safe when Harthacnut died so young. He thought Edward would reward him for his loyalty. But no.

'He's no different to his father,' Leofric couldn't deny that those words hurt to hear, and yet they seemed to be accurate, all the same.

'The king means to dilute the influence of everyone other than the House of Godwine. Despite everything, he rewards the one man he should detest, the man he should have executed for the murder of his brother, Lord Alfred. But no, our illustrious king instead makes his son an earl!' Ælfgar slammed the cup he'd been gripping so tightly Leofric had worried he'd crack it onto the tabletop at the end of his tirade. It landed with a dull thud.

Ælfgar had drunk almost nothing, and now much lay gleaming in the candlelight. Ælfgar wasn't angry because he'd consumed too much wine or ale. No, Ælfgar was angry because he could determine the king's intentions towards the House of Leofwine.

'It seems that way. I won't deny it.' Olaf also sat brooding beside the hearth. He'd said little to nothing since the king's revelations. At least, he'd escaped the feast the king had held in honour of his new earl and bishop. Leofric and Ælfgar had been forced to endure the knowing smirks of all around them, even as they'd tried to carry on everyday conversations. Tedious discussions about trade and alliances and the recent news received from Denmark about Magnus' successes.

It had been agony. Leofric was incredulous that they'd both managed to get through the evening without making a scene. The same couldn't be said for the new earl, who'd raised his goblet to so many toasts, he'd eventually slumped to the wooden floorboards, vomit staining his deep maroon tunic.

Lord Godwine had merely called jovially for two of his other sons, Harold and Tostig, to take their brother away to his bed, no hint of embarrassment on his face. If Leofric had detected a note of unease on the king's face at the development, he put it down to wishful thinking. The king had been deeply engrossed in a conversation with the elderly Archbishop Eadsige, Ralph and Beorn.

'The king risks rebellion with his actions. Harthacnut threatened to tax the Mercians to their death, and now Edward inflicts an upstart over them, a man with more ambition than sense. I can't see this ending well, not at all.' Olaf's words were doom-laden, and Leofric spared a thought for his sister.

It had been bad enough when Hrani had first come to Mercia. With Earl Sweyn close by, he couldn't imagine his sister wanting to remain at Deerhurst no matter the close ties with the church where their parents and brothers lay buried. Perhaps he should even suggest she move away. Maybe if the words came from him, it would be easier for her to explain the decision than if he said nothing.

'I can't argue with your statements. Earl Sweyn can only be the worst possible choice out of all the available options. It'll lead to problems with Mercians, even the Danes. They see Lord Godwine, with his pretensions to being a true Dane, and they despise him. And, well, I can't even consider what will happen with the Welsh kings. I'd be surprised if Godwine had the expertise to handle those prickly upstarts.'

'Perhaps the king wishes to go to war? I can't think why else he'd have done what he has.' And Ælfgar threw his hands in the air as he spoke. As if matters could get any worse, his wife chose that moment to join them.

Lady Godgifu leaned to kiss her husband's cheek, but her lips were tight, the action more akin to being stabbed than a show of affection.

'A pity King Harald died in the way he did,' was her opening comment as she settled in an elaborately carved chair facing towards the hearth. The memories of that night immediately flooded

Leofric's mind—another foolish boy who'd not considered that being a king couldn't protect him from all enemies.

'A pity King Harthacnut died so young,' she continued, settling her hands demurely on her lap. Her rigid pose spoke of her fury. 'And both of them without adult heirs to rule after them. One from Cnut's line would have been preferable to the return of King Æthelred's get.' Leofric watched as Godgifu's vehemence dragged Ælfgar from his own fury, and he fixed his mother with a calculating stare, which she met, eyebrow arched high.

'And what would you suggest we do?' Ælfgar demanded.

'We need to do nothing but simply wait for the catastrophe to happen. The king will rue his decision when Sweyn's true nature becomes apparent. It's all well and good, Lord Godwine thrusting his son on the king, but the two men are so unalike, I can't see them ever managing to work together, not even for the good of their family. Sweyn is a selfish fool. He'll quickly unravel his father's skills in getting him the earldom. He's more likely to be banished for some as yet unseen crime than he is to remain the earl for long years. It's impossible to countenance now, but this won't be forever. I'm sure of it.'

'How can you be so confident?'

'Have I not just spoken of foolish men who became king and died young? It's the same with earls. Mark my words, whatever Earl Sweyn manages to accomplish, it'll not save him when he miscalculates. King Edward will regret his decision, and then, my boy, you'll be ready and waiting, the very epitome of what it means to serve and to rule. I assure you, in good time, you'll be an earl, and it won't be because of your father's death. And then, the two earls of the House of Leofwine will rule with their king, and all will be well.' Her words were filled with assurance, and they surprised him. He'd not appreciated her faith in him until now.

'We've endured, through charges of high treason, the indifference of kings, and the reigns of boys who weren't yet men. I'm adamant that the House of Leofwine can survive the imposition of a buffoon over the people of southwest Mercia.' Lady Godgifu's words rang through the house, her conviction even touching Leofric, causing him and Olaf to sit upright, while Ælfgar stopped his pacing and stared at his mother as though she were a raft to save him from drowning.

7
OXFORD AND COVENTRY, ÆLFGAR

'ÆLFGAR,' THE ROAR OF HIS COUSIN'S VOICE ROUSED HIM FROM SLEEP, Elgiva mumbling, 'Get rid of him.' And Ælfgar was minded to do just that; only Wulfstan crashed into his sleeping quarters.

'What's all this?' Ælfgar exclaimed, reaching for his trews and sliding from beneath the fur. A hint of daylight infused the room with warm light, but the expression on Wulfstan's face was murderous.

'What?' Ælfgar asked once more when Wulfstan still didn't speak, his eyes looking anywhere but at the sleeping Elgiva, her hair spread around her on the pillow.

'Fucking Earl Sweyn.'

Ælfgar considered returning to his sleep, after all, this wasn't the first time Earl Sweyn had incensed his cousin in recent weeks, but Wulfstan's demeanour spoke of something much, much worse than in the past.

'Come on,' and Ælfgar stalked beyond his cousin, waiting for him to exit before carefully closing the door behind him to not wake his exhausted wife. Morcar had grizzled for much of the night. Even he felt sick with exhaustion, and he'd managed far more sleep than Elgiva.

'Tell me?' he demanded again.

'He's seized uncle's lands in Shropshire.'

'The ones he left to you in his will?'

'Yes, all of them, not just one place, but every single one. While I've been away on business in London, he's installed reeves acting in his name and no other. I returned last night, only to be denied entry to my home.'

Ælfgar swept his hand through his unruly hair, his mouth hanging slack with shock as he attempted to order his thoughts. The bequests of Uncle Eadwine had royal agreement and had done for nearly four years. What could have happened to make those charters invalid?

'On what grounds?'

'On the grounds that he's an arse, who believes he can do anything he bloody wants.'

'But he can't. There are charters. There's the will. They all make it clear that the bequest was for you. The king has ratified them.'

'I know that,' Wulfstan all but roared, and Ælfgar moved to lay a calming hand on his shoulder, only for the older man to shake him loose.

'Your mother warned he'd cause problems. Well, now he truly has. Those territories aren't all profitable farms to be exploited for their wealth. Some of them are directly on the border opposite Gwynedd. Gruffydd Ap Llewelyn will attack as soon as he realises it's not the House of Leofwine in command there. He'll know there are easy pickings. Earl Sweyn has no military reputation to his name. Gruffydd probably doesn't even know who he is.'

'We need to inform my father of this development.'

'Ælfwine has gone to him at Coventry.'

'Then we should follow on,' Ælfgar announced. 'We need to decide what to do.'

'We need to wrestle those lands back from him. They aren't his to just take.'

'I know that, Wulfstan, but we need advice from my father. We can't march in there fully armed. As you say, if Gruffydd got wind of what was happening, he'd be there in a heartbeat. We need to act sensibly.'

'Well, if we're acting sensibly, then you probably need to know that Lady Gunnhild has made it clear she'll rise against Earl Sweyn. I understand she's sent her oldest son, Hemming, to seek out King Magnus. She intends to invite him to England. She'd rather have Magnus than Edward as her king.'

'You're sure of this?' Ælfgar challenged, the news unsurprising for all it was unwelcome.

'As sure as I can be when the information comes directly from Ælfwine. He happened to overhear the conversation between two of Gunnhild's lithesmen being sent to Norway with Hemming.'

'This is madness,' Ælfgar exclaimed, bending to thrust his feet into his boots. It was barely daylight outside, but he'd already lingered too long.

'Come on, Wulfstan. We must make our way to Coventry. My father ought to be informed about these developments. No doubt, one of us will have to notify the king about what's happening, even as the others must defend your landholdings in Shropshire.'

By now, the heated discussion had roused Elgiva and young Burgheard, and they both padded into the main hall. Burgheard watched his father with sleep-addled eyes, one of the hounds circling him, ball in his mouth, ready to play despite the early hour.

'Come here, young man,' Elgiva called to Burgheard, bending to scoop him into her arms, even though he was a hefty weight. 'Your father needs to go and see your grandfather, but we don't need to be awake yet.' A sleepy nod from Burgheard and Elgiva placed a soft kiss on his rough cheeks, the hound moving away to settle beside the hearth, chastised as well.

'Have a care, my lord husband,' but she offered no other words.

Ælfgar was grateful she didn't try and remind him of his duties for the coming day. The shire court would have to wait. There was something much larger at stake. He was sure the men and women who demanded justice would understand.

'I'VE SENT OLAF TO THE KING AT LONDON,' WERE THE WORDS THAT GREETED Ælfgar before he'd even dismounted in the courtyard of his father's home close to Coventry. 'I know the king will be slow to act. Better to send Olaf than one of us. He has courtly manners that might desert us all, although, well. It's too late now. Olaf has set off and will reach him as soon as he can. I've assembled my warriors. We'll ride out once all is ready.'

'Will it be war?' Ælfgar asked.

'Against Earl Sweyn? Perhaps. We'll have to see what we find when we arrive. I imagine Earl Sweyn will be absent. I predict he'll already be by the king's side making his petition. It doesn't matter. We must travel to Shropshire, remove the reeves from your settlements, restore confidence in you as the rightful lord, and then when that's done, we can inform the king of what we've accomplished.'

'And as for Lady Gunnhild, I don't believe that's our problem. But I hope her son doesn't encounter King Magnus. I wouldn't like his eyes to be cast this way. Not at the moment, when everything is such a mess.' His father's voice filled with frustration.

Ælfgar watched his cousins speaking to each other. They gesticulated wildly to one another. Not for the first time, Ælfgar felt the pang of being an only child. He'd never been as close to someone as Ælfwine and Wulfstan were to each other. He'd never been understood as quickly as the two knew each other. They might well bicker and argue, but that was between themselves. If someone attacked them, they were united in their resolve to combat the opposition.

While his marriage was happy, and Elgiva knew him well, he appreciated that the marriage bond wasn't the same as that of brothers.

At least, he realised, his children wouldn't share his affliction, and he knew it had been God's will to make him an only child. He could never blame his mother and father. He was only too aware they felt the sting of their failure.

'When do we leave?' Ælfgar demanded of his father, taking the time to look at him. His father was well into his fifth decade now, yet Ælfgar detected no lessening in his resolve and commitment. He'd lost none of his warrior's build, even if it had slowly started to lose the definition of a man who trained each and every day. Certainly, he was not like Earl Godwine. That man was on his way to becoming corpulent, and it wasn't an appealing look.

'When we're ready,' his father called over his shoulder, busily ensuring his saddle was placed comfortably on his mount. The animal, a fine, high-stepping black stallion, seemed as poised as his father. That beast would gallop as soon as he was released beyond the gates of his father's home. If they were lucky, they'd arrive late that night, and if not, it wasn't as though they'd be left without a roof over their head. The family had any number of manors where they'd find shelter as they made their way to Shropshire and the settlements that Sweyn hadn't dared to usurp.

But it wasn't the worry of where they'd sleep that drove Ælfgar to discard his favoured mount and replace it with one that hadn't already travelled vast distances that day. No, he feared what they'd find when they arrived in Shropshire.

Damn, Earl Sweyn. He was a greater fool than Ælfgar feared. Ælfgar bit his lip in anger, determined not to give voice to the furious voice in his head that demanded answers to questions that he'd only receive at the end of their journey.

THEY WERE ALL SULLEN AS THEY SET OUT FOR THE WEST. HIS FATHER LED THE way, back rigid, the stinging words of Lady Godgifu driving them all on.

'And tell the damn man that being an earl doesn't mean he owns all of bloody Mercia,' her face had been almost puce. For a heartbeat, Ælfgar had thought his mother might demand to accompany her husband, son, nephews and the household troop as they rode out to counter Sweyn's pretensions. And it wasn't as if she hadn't acted in such a way before. The memory of what she'd done in Coventry to make her fury evident at the king and his taxes were too vivid to forget.

But they made good time as the afternoon slowly wound its way towards sunset. The well-known roads disappeared beneath the horses' hooves, the landscape familiar to them all as they travelled along Watling Street, heading for Lichfield and then onto the west. Ælfgar's anger simmered, but he found his thoughts cast back to memories of his uncle and that terrible battle that had left him dead four years ago.

A solitary tear shimmered down his cheek, his head bowed in remembrance of one of the men who'd been like a father to him. And now bloody Earl Sweyn thought to steal land that wasn't his, and worse, land and settlements that were the property of the House of Leofwine. The actions were shocking because everyone acknowledged the House of Leofwine as the true owners.

Many of the places had once fallen under the reach of Ealdorman Eadric Streona and his family. After Eadric's death, his grandfather had quickly moved to secure the properties. In time, as part of his reparations to Leofwine, King Cnut had confirmed them to Leofwine, who'd then secured them in the name of his youngest son.

Only as darkness covered the land did his father halt their forward momentum.

'We'll rest for the night. Begin again at first light. Better to arrive alert than exhausted.' Ælfgar appreciated his father's wisdom even as he railed against the delay.

'My lord,' the reeve at Bradley bowed low to Leofric. 'I confess, I expected your arrival.' Around them, the household servants moved to take away the horses and to offer drink and food.

'Is it truly so bad?' his father demanded to know of the man.

'It would seem so. There have been some bloody altercations. I fear a man has died at Ditton Priors.'

'And Earl Sweyn's men have remained behind to hold the properties?'

'Yes, my lord, they have, although I don't believe they have the force you do.' Ælfgar watched a tight smile form on his father's lips as he observed the conversation.

'Then at least we can evict them easily, and hopefully, without more lives being lost. The bloody fools.'

From outside came the noise of the rest of the household troop riding into the enclosed gates, dismounting and calling one to another. It sounded as though they were riding to war, and for the first time, Ælfgar appreciated that was what they were doing.

They needed to stop Earl Sweyn's pretensions, or he might take it upon himself to usurp more and more of their properties. Sweyn probably wouldn't restrict himself to those on the periphery of Mercia, but perhaps even Coventry or Oxford and Deerhurst certainly wouldn't be safe from his grasping reach.

Not for the first time, Ælfgar questioned the king's decision to make Sweyn an earl. Did he intend to cause such chaos, or was he so naïve that he didn't realise what would happen when planting a son of the ambitious Earl Godwine in the heartland of Mercia? In the heartland of allegiances that looked to the House of Leofwine first and foremost, and only then the king?

8

BRADLEY AND LONDON, LEOFRIC

Leofric woke early and prepared for the day ahead.

He was a man more accustomed to the order of the court these days, but if need be, he would fight for what was his. He realised that killing for it would bring him no great unease, although the real culprit was beyond his reach.

Damn the king.

Damn Lord Godwine.

And damn his bloody son.

All these years, Lord Godwine and he had manoeuvred around one another, aware of the threat the other posed but somehow managing to keep it almost civil. He didn't see how that would continue now, not with his son deciding that stealing property was acceptable behaviour for one of the king's earls.

The sound of the river outside permeated his senses, quickly drowned out by his waking household warriors. He spared a thought for them. They were as keen to counter Earl Sweyn's pretensions as he was, but he didn't want anyone injured. He'd known many of his men for nearly two decades, some longer. While he wanted to offer a show of strength, he also knew that risking the lives of others over something that could be solved in the king's court, eventually, was irresponsible. He wasn't about to do so unless there was no choice.

He wanted to go to Ford from Bradley, where they'd stopped overnight. Not the most westerly of Wulfstan's possessions, but the closest of those that were. He held out half a hope that Earl Sweyn wouldn't have bothered himself with taking Ellesmere, not when the other manors were so much closer together. Along the way, he'd be able to call a halt at Emstry and begin removing Sweyn's squatting reeves.

Not for the first time, his fury burned through him, almost making him gasp with pain. This wouldn't be allowed to stand. Earl Sweyn would pay for his outrageous exploits.

'Come on,' he called to the rousing men. 'We have a full day ahead of us.' As he spoke, bread and cheese were brought for them all, and he hastily grabbed a chunk of each, filling his water bottle from a waiting jug.

He caught sight of his nephew, Wulfstan, in a fierce debate with the reeve. The property was now Wulfstan's, and Leofric suspected he was offering his support to the reeve. The man had served Eadwine for years. He knew the property and the people intimately, and it was evident that he spoke on their behalf.

They'd mourned for the loss of their oath-sworn lord, but Leofric also suspected they enjoyed the more dynamic leadership of his nephew. It pleased him to see what a good lord he made, even as he wished he could do more for his fatherless nephews.

But, they both refused to marry, much to their mother's sorrow and without a good marriage, Leofric could only do so much for them. Maybe in time, they'd change their mind. He certainly hoped so. And it wasn't as though there was a lack of potential wives. Their father's disgrace had long worn off, even if they were overly conscious of it.

It had rained during the night, although Leofric had slept through the downpour. Puddles had formed where the gates opened onto the main track that quickly led to Watling Street, and the air seemed to steam. Already, he felt hot and uncomfortable, and that was with the sun still barely visible on the distant horizon.

It would be another warm day, a worry for the coming harvest coming on the back of the previous year's failures. Leofric doubted tempers would be any cooler, not when he came face to face with Earl Sweyn's men.

Before they reached Emstrey, Leofric could see where Earl Sweyn's men had struck the settlements. The waft of smoke reached his nostrils just before the buildings appeared. He quickly noticed the burned ruin of one of the grain stores. His ire grew, even as he raised his voice to caution his men.

'Be ready, but only resort to violence on my express command.' Leofric took the time to meet the gaze of his son and two nephews. For them, the order needed to be reinforced. He could tell, in the set of their faces, and the way their hands clamped tightly over the reins, that they were struggling to contain their fury. For a moment, he wished he'd sent them to the king, keeping Olaf with him. Olaf could be relied upon to carry out his orders. He wasn't so sure about his son and nephews.

The new reeve had heard the thunder of hooves, and they were greeted, while still on the roadway, by a large man, his hands balled into fists that rested on his expansive waist, keys clearly showing on his belt that strained in place.

'Earl Leofric,' his voice was rich with derision.

'And you are?'

'My name's Eadwig, sworn man to Earl Sweyn Godwinesson. I had no notice of your arrival. Why are you here, on my lord's land?' Eadwig's voice was too loud and filled with conviction.

Behind Eadwig, Leofric caught the frightened eyes of women and children. Two of the men he could see carried wounds, one to his face, where a welter of blackened greens surrounded his left eye, while the other limped, an upturned branch supporting his body as he couldn't place any weight on his foot.

'I'm here to ensure the people of Emstrey are well. These are dangerous times. The threat of Gruffydd Ap Llewelyn can never be underestimated. But tell me, why are you seeking shelter at Emstrey? Did you come to protect my people against an attack from across the border? I see the grain store has been destroyed.'

'No, I'm the new reeve here, as ordered by Earl Sweyn.'

'But Earl Sweyn doesn't own this settlement or have the oaths of the men and women who live here. His lands are in Hereford, alongside his earldom.' Leofric furrowed his forehead, pretending to his confusion.

'No, my lord. Earl Sweyn has asserted his right to this hamlet by right of conquest.'

'Right of conquest?' Leofric mused. 'How can that be? There's no war here, not amongst the English.'

The large man shrugged his shoulders, although his eyes widened in shock as the remainder of the household troop came into view around a small bend. Eadwig still stood alone, but Leofric couldn't imagine he was the only person left to defend the settlement. Well, if he was, it spoke of Earl Sweyn's over-confidence and arrogance.

'He burned the grain store,' the limping man called, adding a 'my lord' into the ringing silence.

'He came here with a group of warriors, about fifteen of them. They cut down the old reeve when he tried to deny him. Old Bryhtnoth hasn't regained consciousness from when they kicked him into the mud.'

'And how many of those warriors remain?'

Leofric kept his gaze on the limping man, all but ignoring Eadwig, whose face was sheeted in a fury.

'Just him.' The news stunned Leofric, even as it made his next decision more straightforward.

'Well, I think it'll be simple to remove the unwanted infestation,' Leofric menaced, reaching for the seax on his weapons belt. It was a ceremonial item most of the time but sharpened just that morning, the edge keen and eager to sate a thirst that had long been denied.

Only now did Leofric turn his attention to the upstart, and at the same time, the sound of swords and seaxes being drawn rang through the suddenly still, humid air.

Leofric didn't take much pleasure in watching Eadwig swallow thickly, realising that he stood no chance against so many. But he respected the man when he bowed his head low in submission, intelligent enough to realise that only his death could result from continuing to deny the rapid change in his circumstances.

'Have him bound,' Leofric called to Ælfgar. 'And mounted up. We have other settlements to visit today. We'll ensure not one of Earl Sweyn's men remains in Shropshire on land owned by the House of Leofwine.' Those words were greeted with a subdued cheer from the people of Emstrey.

As Ælfgar rushed to contain Eadwig, Leofric dismounted, Wulfstan joining him. Wulfstan moved quickly amongst the men and women, and Leofric realised he knew them all by name. His nephew was an excellent oath lord. But, sometimes, it was necessary to remind everyone he was a member of the House of Leofwine.

'Goodman, you have my thanks,' Leofric stated, standing before the limping man, a quick hand preventing him from tumbling to the ground.

'My lord,' the man looked shocked now by his outburst.

'You need to sit,' Leofric turned, relieved when a small child brought such an item for the man to settle on. He smiled at the child.

'My thanks,' he said. The young lad shrugged, but his eyes were alight with mischief.

'I keep telling 'im to sit down,' he confided.

'Perhaps he'll listen to you now,' Leofric offered.

'Doubt it. Doesn't listen to anyone. Stubborn, that's what they call him.'

'Stubbornness can be a virtue,' Leofric laughed while the child shook his head in disgust.

'Tell me, other than more grain, what will you need? Was anything taken?'

'The best ox and the ram,' a female voice commented acerbically beside Leofric. 'And the cheese. They all ate like pigs, and he's done nothing but fart, eat and drink since the rest moved on.'

'Then make sure your lord knows of the lack. He'll ensure it's all returned to you, but we'll need a record for the king.'

'The king?' The woman raised her eyes high. 'Why will the king need to know?'

'Earl Sweyn shouldn't have been here. His men had no right to take what wasn't there's. Earl Sweyn will find his riches a little lighter when I finish with him.'

'Well, in that case, we need wood for a new grain store and the wergild for Bryhtnoth if he doesn't wake. It'll make it easier for his family if they have some coins to help them.'

'And if you realise anything else is missing, add it to the list.'

'Very well, my lord,' and she dipped the briefest of curtsies before hurrying away, scattering children and animals in her wake. Leofric watched her go before he turned back to ensure Ælfgar had Eadwig trussed up on a spare mount.

'We travel to Ford now to do the same. If you have visitors from any other settlements, assure them we'll attend to them soon. I'll not leave a single one of Earl Sweyn's men in command of property that belongs to the House of Leofwine. Tell everyone. I would have it known.'

Returning to his horse, Leofric glanced at the apprehended man. Sweat beaded Eadwig's forehead, and he refused to meet his eyes. Leofric nodded. As he'd thought, Earl Sweyn had gathered men to his side who enjoyed the thrill of having the upper hand. They had no answer when the roles were reversed.

Arriving in Ford somewhat later in the day, Leofric found a similarly bombastic man placed there by Sweyn. Only when the man caught sight of the bound Eadwig did he capitulate. Leofric decided they could journey to High Ercall and onto Crudginton before darkness fell with two prisoners to his name. At each village or manor, he found the same, a lone member of Earl Sweyn's entourage imposed over the occupants. The audacity of the man amazed Leofric. Was he truly so arrogant that he expected a single person to hold out against the might of the House of Leofwine? He'd have some harsh words for the young upstart when he next saw him.

TWO DAYS LATER, LEOFRIC RODE INTO DODDINGTON, EIGHT OF EARL Sweyn's men, now his captives, to be met by Olaf.

'My lord,' his face was impassive, and that warned Leofric that not everything was well.

'What is it?' he demanded to know, watching as Ælfgar took the submission of yet another of Earl Sweyn's men.

'The king never believes the actions of Earl Sweyn are legal?'

'No, my lord. The king is furious with Sweyn, but that's not the problem. It's a minor inconvenience.'

'To what?'

'To Lady Gunnhild.'

'Her son made it to Norway, unfortunately. He's returned with news that King Magnus plans to attack when he can.'

'How does the king know of this? Surely, it should be a secret.'

'And when has Lady Gunnhild ever managed to keep a secret?' Olaf huffed with annoyance.

'The king wishes you to join him in London as soon as possible. Lord Ælfgar can remain behind and finish the task.'

'Yes, he can, but it's a pity. I was rather enjoying myself,' Leofric almost joked, turning to glare at the captives in his care, enjoying the feeling of righteousness that removing them from Wulfstan's property had given him.

'No one else is, and the king is most displeased.'

'I'll set out tomorrow,' Leofric decided. 'For tonight, we rest here. Tomorrow will come soon enough, and we could make it to London before night falls. But tell me, does the king not wish me to bring Lady Gunnhild?'

'No, not at this time. But he said little else.'

Leofric nodded. Less than a year as king and everything seemed to be falling apart for Edward. It wasn't a good start.

Leofric arrived in London as the sun set in a welter of oranges and reds behind him. His gaze was focused on the spread of the vast settlement before him, the smell of smoke having infiltrated his senses for many miles.

He shook his head. He wasn't in the right frame of mind to force his way through the crush of humanity that would be thronging the streets. Neither did he relish the thought of finding an angry king or a disgruntled Earl Sweyn. There were occasions when he wished not to be held to account by anyone, and this was one of them.

'Nearly there,' he offered the words to his horse with a gentle slap to its right shoulder. The animal had been hard used these last few days. Perhaps, he should have chosen another mount, but he and Oswald were old men attuned to the thoughts of each other. To change would be unwelcome, making the journey even more fractious than it needed to be.

'The king resides at Westminster?'

'Yes, he does,' Olaf confirmed. They rode with only five of his men, Godwulf, Winhus, Scirwold, Cena and Æthelheard. Leofric was comfortable with the men, while the rest of his warriors had been left with Ælfgar and his nephews.

The king's directive wasn't to be disobeyed, but it could have come at a better time. Perhaps Edward didn't truly realise what Earl Sweyn was planning. Maybe he believed it was a trifling matter, quickly resolved. But with the manors so spread out throughout Shropshire, it hadn't been a quick or easy task to remove Sweyn's men from Wulfstan's properties.

'Is Lord Godwine attending upon the king?' Only now did Leofric consider what he'd say to the other man.

'He's been summoned. He was at his properties in Kent, I believe.'

'Then maybe we'll have arrived before him.'

'It's to be hoped,' and Olaf didn't even attempt to keep the sourness from his voice.

'And Earl Sweyn?'

'He was in Hereford, as I understand it. The king wanted to muster him, but I don't know if he'll have done so, not when his mind is so focused on Lady Gunnhild and the worry of a coming war.'

'Then the king really wishes to speak to me about the problem,' Leofric sighed. He and Edward were not the firm allies he'd thought they'd become. But, in his moment of need, perhaps that was about to change. Maybe.

As full darkness descended, lit only by the odd candle visible through open doors and the glow of some braziers left out on the street corners, the press of people, carts and animals had subsided enough that it was almost too easy to make his way to the king's hall in London.

The scent of the river wafted through the air, not quite drowning out the smoke from household hearths, and Leofric held his lips tightly together. He'd grown up next to the river that ran beside Deerhurst, and yet, in London, the experience of living beside a river was overwhelming and often unpleasant.

Leofric handed Oswald to one of the waiting stable boys, having obtained entry behind the walls of the king's abode. He took the time to brush the horsehair from his tunic before seeking admittance, Olaf at his shoulder. Only moments later, he was bowing before King Edward and being instructed to join him to sit before the low flames of the hearth.

'You made good time,' Edward said with approval.

'My lord king,' Leofric was unsure how to respond. They'd hurried because the king had demanded it.

'Earl Sweyn will be reprimanded. Produce a full account of the damages, and it will be settled. Also, have charters drawn up to reconfirm the arrangements. I'll not have the same thing happen again in five or ten years.' Edward's voice was filled with resolve, yet Leofric detected his frustration in how he ran the hem of his ceremonial tunic through his fingers. The stitches hadn't frayed, not yet.

'And now to Lady Gunnhild.'

'Tell me more,' Leofric asked when Edward lapsed into silence. He took the time to examine the king. Edward's fury showed in the shadows beneath his eyes, which kept flickering away from Leofric to focus on something behind them.

'Lady Gunnhild's actions speak of a lingering unease with my kingship. Earl Sweyn has only me to thank for his elevation.' Leofric nodded. The king was perceptive to see that there were different motivations at play.

'But, I don't believe King Magnus will ever come to England, not while problems persist in Denmark. And they do persist. Did you know I met Lady Estrid once, Svein's mother?'

'No, my lord king, I was unaware of that. How did that come about?' Leofric felt his forehead furrow in confusion.

'In Normandy, when she was supposed to marry my uncle. I was a young man. Angry at what had happened in England, determined to undermine King Cnut, if only I had the resources to command, but she was a pleasant woman. I came to respect her, and I still do. I know she and my mother have never shared an amicable friendship. I find that Lady Estrid is a discerning woman.' Leofric dare not speak at the king's derisive comment aimed at his mother.

'Yet Lady Gunnhild, while I understand her, perplexes me. She's been the wife of two powerful men and still doesn't understand the way politics works.'

'Both of her husbands died too young, Earl Hakon when his ship sank, Lord Harold was murdered in Denmark, although there are precious few details as to why. And she has two sons to support in the future. It can, perhaps, force a woman to do things she might not normally consider.'

'Ah, Leofric, you allude to the mysterious Lady Ælfgifu, King

Cnut's first wife. She had a powerful name and family to support her.'

'She did yes, and the fact that her father was assassinated on the orders of a king and her brothers blinded always helped her. Lady Gunnhild doesn't yet have the same level of influence, but I fear the thirst for it blinds her to the more practicable problems of what she wants.'

'What, do you suggest I reward her for such efforts in trying to have me removed from a kingdom I've only just been able to name as my home once more?'

'No, my lord king, of course not. I am, as you know, aware of her ambitions. I confess I'd expected her to relinquish her hopes with time. No doubt, the imposition of Earl Sweyn has redoubled her resolve rather than reduced it.'

Leofric watched his king carefully, keen to see how he would react to such criticisms. Given the decisions the king had made of late, which had been detrimental to Leofric's ambitions, he expected the king to laugh aside his worries or perhaps accuse him of jealousy. But he did neither of those things.

'When Earl Godwine arrives, I'll have him bring his son to order. You'll be tasked with watching Lady Gunnhild. At the first sign of trouble, she'll be brought to trial for treason. I'll not have such discord in the kingdom. Men and women will not toy with others lives or the kingdom's safety while I'm the king. The focus should be feeding every man, woman and child and surviving the terrible harvest.'

Leofric inclined his head at the words, relieved to hear one of England's kings worry about something others might have believed was mundane. Without the thegns, kings-thegns, farmers and craftspeople, there would be no wealth with which England could trade. Perhaps Edward was finally the king that England had needed for long years.

9
NOVEMBER AD1043, WINCHESTER, LEOFRIC

LEOFRIC TRIED TO SUPPRESS HIS RAGE BECAUSE HE KNEW IT WAS DOING HIM no good. But it was almost impossible.

It didn't help that Lord Godwine was so joyful, so keen to go along with the king's wishes. If Leofric didn't know better, he'd suspect Godwine of having more to do with the current shit-storm than could be possible.

Lady Emma! Why? He couldn't understand her antagonism towards her son or even why Edward insisted on being infuriated by his mother. Couldn't he have simply banished her, as King Harald had once done? Or even better, ignored her and allowed her to get on with whatever stirring kept her happy. It wasn't as though others would support her, not now people realised how distant the king and his mother were. No rewriting of her great work by the monk from St Omer could right the wrongs that kept Lady Emma and Edward from reuniting.

Edward rode before his earls, his back rigid. He didn't so much look from side to side, only forwards. His huscarls cleared the roadway in front of him, the Foss Way, that ran from Gloucester southwards. Only then would they turn along London Way to take them to Winchester. Leofric knew that few would have dared stand in the way of such an impressive gathering of horsemen anyway, but of course, the king had standards to maintain.

King Edward had left him with little choice but to agree with his plans for Lady Emma. He'd ventured to Gloucester to win his support rather than summoning him to London or Winchester. Leofric couldn't help but be relieved that the king hadn't acted without his agreement. He could easily have told him nothing, as when Sweyn was made an earl.

All the same, his agreement had come grudgingly. It would have been awkward to gainsay the king. He couldn't put Lady Emma's future before his own, not anymore, and not with Lord Godwine sniffing around the king as though he were a prized tree against which to direct his stream.

No matter that Sweyn had been humiliated by the king for his attack on Wulfstan's properties in Shropshire, Lord Godwine still felt emboldened because his son was one of only four earls. In any vote, Godwine could be assured of half an agreement without even opening his mouth to voice an argument.

Still, having given his agreement to the king, it didn't make the king's intentions palatable, and fury burned with each and every jolt on the road as Oswald rushed to keep up with the other horses.

Bloody Lady Emma. What had she been doing, allowing Bishop Stigand to act with such disregard towards the king? Had she meant to antagonise her oldest son, or had she merely been seeing how far she could push him, expecting him to acquiesce to some of her demands in exchange for a quieter life? Once more, Leofric was amazed at how poorly Lady Emma understood Edward, even now, after they'd been reunited for a few years.

Edward was threatened by enemies from overseas and trying to contain Lord Godwine and all she could do was think of herself. Had she truly been the wife of two kings and the mother of another and not realised that her position wasn't as influential as she believed?

King Æthelred had side-lined her into being little more than a mother. King Cnut had given her more leeway but had still removed all the children from her care with no thought for her wishes.

King Harthacnut had barely tolerated Lady Emma. And King Edward, well, no matter how much he tried to disdain the notion, Edward blamed his mother so virulently for the events that had befallen him before becoming king that he was prepared to accept Lord Godwine's support to overthrow her.

Lord Godwine was just as much to blame for Lord Alfred's death as Lady Emma.

But there was no point in arguing with Edward further. He was England's consecrated king, and Leofric was compelled to obey him. And for once, he could see no way of refusing or even lessening the coming punishment for Lady Emma. She'd be shocked and horrified, yet she was entirely to blame for what would happen.

His horse's gait was steady beneath him, despite the road's poor state so late in the year. It was winter, the air threatening to turn ever colder the further south they travelled along the road, with cracked puddles of icy water showing that others had already ridden in front of him.

Leofric expected them to arrive in Winchester later that day at the current speed, provided they could see when darkness swept the land once more. They'd set out as soon as there was light enough to see.

He shivered beneath his thick cloak, pulling it tighter to his body. It was too damn cold, and Leofric felt all of his years. Yes, the king was less than a decade younger than him but he was filled with the fire of revenge. Leofric had only the cold, hard reality of Lord Godwine's unstoppable resurgence for a companion.

'Lord Leofric,' Earl Siward called to him, and Leofric lifted his head to meet the other man's eyes, noting how the earl angled his hair to cover his receding hairline, although he still wore it long down his back.

'Lord Siward,' he directed Oswald closer to the other man, even though he didn't slow the animal. He didn't want to allow the king or Lord Godwine out of his sight. Leofric was astounded that Godwine could keep up with the king's pace. He pitied the poor horse forced to take the corpulent man's weight.

'I would speak to you about the Welsh kings,' Siward surprised Leofric. Although, Leofric reconsidered, perhaps it was only to be expected. They could hardly discuss their current predicament when the king could hear everything they would say, and if not the king, then Godwine and Sweyn.

'The Welsh are content to bicker amongst themselves,' Leofric offered blithely.

'Perhaps they are, but I hear that Gruffudd Ap Rhydderch means the king ill, and I think you should take greater precautions.' The implied criticism set Leofric's teeth on edge. But he found a tight smile for the other earl. It wouldn't do if he alienated all three of Edward's earls.

'And what of Mac Bethad Mac Findlaich in the land of the Scots?'

A flicker of unease covered Siward's face, and Leofric appreciated that the man was trying to distract from his own problems.

'For now, there's peace. I can't see it lasting, but at least the war has been delayed for another year. It's easier without the Earl of Bamburgh interfering.' His deep voice made a mockery of the words and Leofric only just bit back his complaint at the reminder that Siward had murdered the Earl of Bamburgh. Instead, he fixed Siward with a wary glare.

Siward had been a long-time favourite of King Cnut and Lady Estrid. Entrusted with the family's secrets, he'd shown complete devotion to King Harthacnut. But all the same, Leofric couldn't condone what he'd done to poor Earl Ealdred. It had made Harthacnut little better than his young and impetuous father, who'd had his long-dead brother, Northman, executed without a trial.

Sometimes Leofric wondered why he continued to serve England's kings. They were all corrupt in their own ways. Even

Edward was showing himself to be the same in his treatment of his mother.

'I've left my son, Osbjorn, in command of the north. He's a keen warrior. He'll know what to do, but I don't foresee any issues for the next few months.'

'But you think there'll be problems with the Welsh kings?'

'I don't see how there can't be. Gruffydd Ap Llewelyn was keen enough to take advantage of the unrest under King Harald. I'm sure he'll continue now, especially with Edward vulnerable to attack from King Magnus.'

The problem of King Magnus was vexing. In Denmark, the kings needed to be voted for by the freemen, but Magnus of Norway had come as a military victor on the death of Harthacnut. He'd been voted as Denmark's king because not accepting him would have restarted the war, which had only recently rumbled to a halt between him and Harthacnut.

Leofric found his gaze resting on the king's rigid back. Edward had previously led military campaigns in Normandy for his uncle, the Duke. Well, not military commands but naval expeditions. If Magnus mobilised to claim England, as Lady Gunnhild had requested he do it would be the ship army that would make first contact.

And Lord Godwine had been astute enough to realise that Edward fancied himself as a skilled tactician. Why else had he attempted to buy his way back into the king's good graces with the gift of a dragon-prowed longship? He'd completed the offering by supplying it with treasure and equipment for a hundred and twenty warriors consisting of a helmet, hauberk, spear, sword, shield and Danish axe.

The ship was also magnificent, perhaps even more richly endowed than the one with which Lord Godwine had attempted to buy Harthacnut's good wishes. It hadn't been the same ship, but it had far from beggared the earl.

Leofric eyed Godwine with narrowed eyes. Godwine didn't ride alone but was accompanied by Sweyn and Harold. For a moment, Leofric thought he should have insisted Ælfgar accompany him, but his son was in Shropshire, helping Wulfstan to right the wrongs of Sweyn's infiltration earlier in the year. Not that the king's intervention seemed to have greatly cowed Sweyn. Leofric anticipated that Sweyn was far from done with his interfering ways.

But he was pleased Ælfgar wouldn't witness the king's coming actions against his mother. If, or rather, when, the king repented of his actions towards his mother, Ælfgar would be free from the stain. It was a pity he wouldn't be.

Neither of Godwine's oldest sons was married yet, but Leofric had heard rumours that Harold had a young woman he kept, almost as his wife. Leofric thought the arrangement was a result of Harold's half-Danish upbringing. There was no impediment to bastard sons inheriting property in Denmark. Why would Harold make a marriage when he hoped for a better, more political match due to his father's and brother's positions?

Harold need only consider King Magnus. He was the son of the dead king of Norway and his English concubine, not his wife. His wife, Lady Astrid Olofsdottir, had given King Harald a daughter but never a son. Yet, Lady Astrid supported Magnus, as did her brother, Anund Jakob, the king of the Svear.

His thoughts return to Lady Emma. He'd extracted a promise from Edward to allow his mother to remain in England. King Harald had banished Lady Emma, and she'd gone to Flanders. Even now, Leofric was suspicious of the political intrigue she'd engaged in there. No, he'd informed the king, it was better to have Lady Emma where a careful eye could be kept on her. After all, she'd proven irrational and dangerous in the past when thwarted. He could only think of her desperate attempt to get Edward and Alfred to England when Harthacnut had lingered in Denmark for too long and Harald had threatened her survival. He didn't want her to risk the lives of others.

He realised he'd not responded to Siward, but it didn't matter because Siward had moved away.

The view before them levelled out. In the far distance, out of sight, would be the south coast. But soon, they'd turn aside and make their way directly to Winchester. He considered whether Lady Emma would have prior warning of Edward's intentions. Was there anyone who would have thought to send word? He couldn't imagine there was, not when he'd had no time to do so.

His eyes settled on the road before him. It glittered with the shine of frost, despite the number of horses before him. Why had the king waited until now? Couldn't he have done this during the summer months when the weather was more temperate, and there was no need to shiver inside his cloak?

Leofric blanked his thoughts, focused only on guiding Oswald, not even listening to the conversations being shouted from one to another by the speeding Godwine and Harold. While the last light of day still lit the sky, the horizon shading to pale tones of purples and pinks, he realised they weren't far from Winchester. He risked a glance at Edward, but he still rode rigidly. Evidently, he had no intention of changing his mind about his mother. Leofric appreciated just how obstinate the new king could be.

Coupled with the early glow of sunset, Leofric noticed the pall of smoke that overlays a sizeable settlement. He risked a thought for Lady Emma and reconciled himself to focus on his king's commands. The time to argue was in the past. The possibility of preventing the coming altercation lay not with him but with Lady Emma herself. She'd been a poor mother to Edward, and no one could deny that.

Up ahead, Leofric caught sight of the defences surrounding Winchester; the west gate lit with many brands to guide home those caught out by the premature winter sunset that promised the impenetrable blackness of a long night. With a clatter of hooves and creak of wooden gates, their party gained admittance into Winchester itself through the closely guarded gateway.

He'd lost count of the number of times he'd visited Winchester. While it was the home of the king's treasury, it hadn't always been where Æthelred, Cnut, Harald, and Harthacnut had based their kingship. Certainly, he was no longer awestruck by the place, not even when he stood before the impressive New and Old Minster. The buildings had been constructed so closely together Leofric considered why they'd not just used the one wall to hold them both upright. The stink from the dead birds and wildlife that rotted in the tiny gap had led to small children being enticed to slide between the two walls to retrieve the detritus. They were rewarded handsomely by the bishop and his monks.

Leofric didn't listen to the conversation between Edward's huscarls and the guards as they rode inside Winchester. Instead, he took the time to ready himself for the unpleasantness to come. He could already imagine the look of outrage on Lady Emma's face and also the hurt. He thought it his curse that he'd known her long enough to see through even her court façade. Certainly, Edward wouldn't realise.

Curious eyes glanced at the sight of so many men on horseback. Some mothers called to children to be careful, but Edward had no intention of harming anyone other than his mother. He'd already cautioned his huscarls to forge a cautious path.

Leofric met the eyes of those who looked up at him, mostly children, who bowed or offered a hasty curtsey as they recognised their king. He nodded, a tight smile on his lips. His breath bloomed before him. It was turning even colder inside Winchester than on the road.

His horse kept pace with the other animals, and he made no movement to get closer to the king. He was content, for now, that Lord Godwine rode as near to the king as possible. When the king repented of his actions, and Leofric was in no doubt that he would, it was better if Lord Godwine was the one to remind him of what had happened.

More and more brands were being lit along the street, driving back the encroaching darkness, but Leofric didn't need the flames to know when they'd arrived outside Lady Emma's property. It had been hers since she'd married King Æthelred, admittedly with a few years' absences. Yet, even when she'd been in Bruges, King Harald hadn't moved to confiscate it from her. Even he hadn't been that petty.

It was a large property surrounded by sturdy gates, thick bushes, and trees. The king was hailed by the waiting guardsmen, who readily opened the double gate to allow admission into the large courtyard. At its heart sat a well-maintained and comfortable home, built half of stone and half of wood, the roof, crowned with tiles that would flash red under bright sunlight but didn't do so now, instead glowing white with the promise of another cold night.

There were also many other buildings, a stable, a grain store, homes for the men and women who served Lady Emma on a day-to-day basis, and even a small pond, home to the fish that would be served for meals.

It was strikingly similar to Deerhurst, for all, it was an urban property and not a rural one. Leofric caught sight of Edward, eagerly dismounting. The door to the main building was thrown open. He swallowed thickly then. He was unsurprised that Lady Emma hadn't chosen to answer the door herself. She'd be settling herself inside, perhaps suspecting this was a less-than-friendly visit from her son because it was unexpected.

He followed the king, relinquishing his mount to a waiting groom, and stepped close to the king, Lord Godwine, Sweyn and Earl Siward. Harold Godwinesson stood aside with the grooms. Leofric couldn't hide, not in such a small space.

Edward strode inside, ducking his head below the low door lintel, even though he wasn't tall.

'Here we go,' Earl Siward whispered, his voice reflecting unhappiness, as he followed the eager steps of Sweyn.

'It's only right,' Godwine retorted quickly before lowering his head and entering Lady Emma's home as well.

'Cock,' Siward all but spat, and Leofric felt a flicker of warmth for the man. Sometimes he forgot that he wasn't the only one to have no love for Lord Godwine.

'After you,' Leofric offered Siward so that by the time he'd made it inside, it seemed that the king and his mother were already arguing.

'You'll relinquish your hold on the king's treasury and also your personal belongings.'

Only now did Leofric catch sight of Lady Emma. He then suspected that she'd had some warning of the king's intentions because he was convinced she didn't spend all her days sitting around in such a richly embroidered gown, flashing with gems and golden thread. He surmised neither was her hair usually so carefully concealed beneath a wimple. He'd never thought she'd take to the fashion, but perhaps vanity had forced her to cover the greying mass of her hair.

'And where will I live?' Lady Emma demanded to know, for all her voice was only just loud enough to hear. 'How will I live?' she continued.

'It's not my concern. You and your bishop, Stigand, have caused enough problems. You refuse to obey your king, even if he happens to be your son. For that reason, you'll lose access to all the wealth and, by association, the influence that has made you such a powerful woman within England.'

'My lord king,' and Leofric was horrified to watch her take to her knees, head bowed, hands crossed over her chest. 'I implore you not to humiliate your mother in such a way.' Her words were shrill, not as calm and assured as she'd always been.

'I'll have the key to the treasury,' Edward demanded over her words. 'I'll have them now, Lady Mother. It's beyond the time you relinquished your hold on them. If you accept your fate, I'll ensure you have a small stipend to live on and maintain a modest property. I'll not leave you to starve in the streets. Even if you would have done that to me to ensure you remained queen of England.'

Leofric wrenched his eyes away from Lady Emma and focused instead on the men and women witnessing the king's interaction with his mother. He was sure that rumours would have already infiltrated Winchester. Depending on their true feelings, there would be gossip, either agreeing with the king or showing sympathy for Lady Emma's plight.

In no time, the news would leave England, perhaps make its way to Bruges or Normandy. No doubt, there would be letters and embassies sent to the king on Lady Emma's behalf. She wasn't without international help, even if she stood alone in England.

Some looked scared, and three women were weeping, even as three servants moved to provide the king and his entourage with food and wine, bowing courteously, perhaps not even in the room when the king made his demands.

'We'll not be staying,' Edward broke from his conversation with his mother. 'But you have my thanks, all the same.' Edward tempered his voice to show he wasn't angry with them.

'But, we must discuss this,' Lady Emma was stoic in her defence, even as she remained kneeling with her head lowered.

'There's nothing to discuss. Now, hand the key to me.'

For a long moment, Leofric thought that she'd continue to argue, but then her hands slipped to her girdle, and she began to remove a long key from amongst the collection of five that nestled there.

'This is,' she began, but Edward snatched the item and was already turning to leave.

'I'll be carrying out a full inventory,' Edward called over his shoulder. 'If there's anything remiss, it would be better for you to admit it now and certainly before the catalogue is complete.'

Lady Emma's gasp of outrage cut through Leofric, and instead of turning to follow the king as he strode once more into the dimming day, he remained behind, hoping to catch Lady Emma's eye. She continued to kneel, although two weeping women had gone to her aid, their wails drowning out whatever Lady Emma was doing. She struggled to her feet, the remaining woman almost blubbering in shock. But before Leofric could incline his head to her as she met his gaze, his name rang through the open doorway.

'Earl Leofric. Today, please. There's still much to do.' And he was left with no choice but to obey the order from his king. His gaze lingered on Lady Emma for just a moment, and it told him all he needed to know.

Lady Emma stayed defiant, no matter her son's actions towards her.

Leofric felt a slither of unease. Had the king acted wisely in making his mother one of his enemies? It was impossible to know.

10

WINCHESTER, LEOFRIC

MOUNTED ONCE MORE, THE HORSES PICKED THEIR WAY THROUGH THE deserted street. Leofric felt as though they'd been inside Lady Emma's home for a handful of moments, but it was the time of year when darkness fell between one blink and the next.

Not that it was difficult to see. There were braziers and lamps every few steps, and light spilt from shop fronts that were closing for the day. And anyway, he knew the way well enough. It was difficult to get lost in Winchester when there was no need to go anywhere but along the main street before turning to the left.

The treasury was housed close to the twin minsters, the Old and the New, and Edward had ensured he had his scribes and clerks ready and able to carry out the accounting of his treasure store. Leofric offered a swift prayer that Lady Emma wouldn't have been foolish enough to steal from her son. If anything was found to be missing, he could only imagine how furious Edward would be, and he dreaded to think of the punishment that Lady Emma would face.

Once more, he handed his mount into the waiting hands of a stable boy and followed the king into the building, ducking beneath the lower door mantle. He could already hear Lord Godwine speaking to the king, his delight at the downfall of his one-time ally evident in the joyous tone he was using. Despite the seriousness of it all, Godwine couldn't help but luxuriate in what he perceived as a triumph. It was one of Godwine's least appealing traits.

Lamps brightly lit the way as they wound deeper and deeper into the building. It was one of the oldest in Winchester, constructed of thick slabs of stone and cold no matter the time of year. Right now, Leofric's breath was visible before him, and he wished himself beside a hearth, not inside the damp-smelling building. If anything, it was colder inside than out, and that just wasn't right.

The treasury had never fallen victim to an attack unless that by King Harald was counted when he became king of all England. But in all honesty, Leofric refused to do that. Harald had been the rightful king. He'd had as much right to the vault's contents as Edward did now. Lady Emma should have given up the key willingly to Harald and Edward.

He was slightly too far back to watch Edward pull that key from his belt and thread it into the heavy black lock, but he could hear it all the same. The ancient oak door swung open with a groan of outraged hinges, which Leofric interpreted as a statement on the many acts it had witnessed throughout its long existence. Leofric smirked at his folly and then cleared his face before the king noticed it.

'Come, my earls, you must witness this,' Edward instructed them all, and Leofric pushed forwards. The ceiling overhead, crisscrossed with arches more likely to be seen in the crypt of a church, was low, for all the room extended far into the shadowy distance.

Leofric risked looking around. This was the king's treasury. The existence of this vast collection of coins and treasures underpinned the rule of the kings of England. He couldn't imagine having so much wealth at his fingertips, and he'd always been a fortunate man. He'd never known starvation or poverty, but the wealth contained inside the treasury beggared him.

'These will all need to be counted,' Edward pointed to a collection of vast chests, banded with wood and iron carefully placed against both sides of the room, that had their own locks and continued into the darkest reaches of the room. 'A tally must be made and correlated with the tally from when the chests were filled, sealed and placed within the treasury.' As he spoke, Edward turned to the side and used a different key to open another chest. When he straightened, he held two key rings, both filled with keys, evidently to open the chests.

'My lord king,' the head of the king's clerics bowed low as his underlings filed into the room, following his instructions. They moved quickly but carefully, trying not to disturb the king and his earls as they settled before one of the chests.

Leofric knew that the cleric had made detailed plans for how the treasure would be counted. It would still be a tedious business and one that he'd have been content not to witness. Only he knew better. If he weren't there to attest to it, Lord Godwine, or potentially even the king, would find it too easy to make ill-founded allegations against Lady Emma. It seemed he was there to ensure she was treated fairly once more.

'No one else is to enter,' Edward demanded stringently. 'Have chairs brought for us to sit on and food and ale delivered to the door. It will be a tedious night, but everything must be tabulated, and I will watch it. All of it. And so will my earls.'

So speaking, Edward turned to stand on the opposite side to where the clerics had bent to open the chests. Even though Ælric was in command of the count, Edward moved to check each and every chest as it was carefully unlocked, the lock laid to one side, and then the top lifted open with a squeal of protesting hinges.

Leofric felt his eyes grow huge at the amount of portable wealth displayed as he followed behind the king. King Cnut and his father, King Swein, and before them both, Olaf Tryvggason, had believed England to be rich beyond their wildest imagination. The assumption had been correct.

Although Leofric settled for a time on the offered chair, taking his fill of the meat and bread provided, the wine as well, he soon found himself transfixed by the coins on display. It was evident that there were chests containing coins that had never had the image of King Æthelred on their surface recast, and he'd been dead for over twenty-five years. Leofric considered why Cnut had never had them melted down and re-forged. Perhaps he'd not know of their existence, or more likely, he'd wanted to hold onto them, a tangible reminder of his foe.

And Leofric wasn't the only one entranced by them. Edward had picked up a handful of the coins, a quizzical expression on his face.

'I'd always thought it something of a tale that my father had coins carrying the image of the dove of peace in an effort to drive King Swein away from England's shores.'

Edward spoke softly, perhaps not wanting the other earls to hear.

'No, your father tried everything to keep England whole.' Leofric remembered the coinage. Somehow, Æthelred had thought his God would protect his country with such a show of subservience. It hadn't worked, far from it.

'Apart from going to war?' Edward commented derisively.

'I don't believe your father was ever going to be a battle commander. If he'd realised sooner and made use of your brothers, he'd never have needed to, not in the end. Athelstan and Edmund were both fine strategists. He shouldn't have wasted his time with Eadric Streona; his sons and Ulfcytel of East Anglia, your brother by marriage, would have worked together to defeat Swein. But of course, that's in the past.'

For a moment, Leofric thought Edward would remain silent; only then he pierced Leofric with his gaze.

'You're very quick to criticise my father,' the edge to his voice was impossible to ignore. 'And yet you protect my mother.'

'I've had time to consider your father's actions. In light of what happened, in the end, I can be both kinder and more critical than I could be at the time. I was merely a young man, unsure of what would happen. My father understood your father well, but then, my father was an ally of your grandmother, Lady Elfrida. And she was an extremely sharp woman. She missed nothing and understood her son's motivations better than anyone. Despite the rumours about her now, my father always held her in high regard.'

'And as to your mother. We all do things we regret in the end. No man or woman is born complete and without the potential to act irresponsibly. It seems that she's yet to learn that lesson.'

Edward nodded, even as he handed the dove of peace coin back to the cleric, counting the contents of that chest.

'It's hard to see the past as you do or the present.'

'Some would call me too forgiving,' Leofric acknowledged, with a dip of his chin, pleased that Godwine and Sweyn couldn't overhear their conversation and that Siward was speaking to two clerics further away. 'I am. I won't deny that. But I'm also an honourable man. I've upheld all my oaths, even those gained from me under trying circumstances. But I've been lucky in many respects. I've never had to sacrifice my family for my survival, and I believe your mother had to do so. But her later mistakes aren't mine to justify. I was with Lord Alfred after his kidnapping. I know what happened to him.'

'And now?'

'I can't say, my lord king. I have no illusions about what she's capable of, but I wouldn't like to decide whether she's a traitor to you. I think she forgets her place. I also know there are others keen to exploit any discord between the two of you, and that person is not to be wholly trusted either.'

Leofric glanced to where Lord Godwine sat on his chair, head resting on one of the double-stacked chests, heartily snoring, having consumed a great deal of wine far too quickly.

'I take your caution as it's offered,' Edward stood stiffly, his tone far from reconciled. 'But, you're my earl and England's earl, not my mother's. You'd do well to remember that.'

'My lord king,' Leofric bowed his head low as he watched Edward meander his way along the row of chests under examination until he stopped and spoke to Siward. So far, at least fifty chests had been counted, but there were many more to go. As quickly as the clerics worked, there was no chance that ten men could complete the reckoning quickly.

Leofric remained where he was, aware of the cleric's scrutiny. He offered the man a smile of encouragement. He was finding the process quite soothing. So far, there had been no inconsistencies, and while Leofric knew there was still time for some to be found, he could already tell that the king was feeling less anger towards his mother. She might have been interfering in matters that didn't concern her, but she'd not stolen from her son.

It would be good if it lasted.

Later, after another two hundred chests had been reconciled with that recorded as being stored inside them, Leofric found it impossible to stay awake. It seemed the king felt the same.

'We'll rest now and resume later today before darkness falls. My thanks to the clerics for their accurate work. Finish the current task, and then we can seal the chests.'

Leofric listened to the sound of silver coins and treasures being carefully returned to their home, but he focused on Lord Godwine. There was something about the self-satisfied smirk on the face of the waking man that worried Leofric. Surely, Godwine wouldn't purposefully implicate the king's mother? Yet, the pair had a chequered history, which ran back through the years to the beginning of Cnut's reign. And one thing was for sure. Should the situation be reversed, Lady Emma wouldn't have thought twice about doing the same to Godwine.

Leofric cautioned himself to linger, to be one of the last to leave, ensuring Lord Godwine was gone before him.

He wasn't about to risk his future on gainsaying Lord Godwine if he accused Lady Emma, but he would certainly speak to the king about the potential for Godwine's snooping. He hoped it wouldn't be needed, yet Leofric understood Godwine too well. Godwine had survived by being a wily bastard, and also by ensuring there was always someone else to earn the king's enmity. Lady Emma might just give him another way of regaining the king's good graces. Leofric couldn't allow that to happen.

HE WAS DIRECTED TO A ROOM WITHIN THE TREASURY BUILDING AS THE FIRST rays of a late winter morning began to shade the sky. The room was comfortable, and with extra coverings on the bed to drive back the stone's coldness, he slept soundly throughout the busy daylight hours. When Leofric woke, a gentle hand on his shoulder, he felt disorientated and unsure of where he was until he glanced at the ceiling above him. Then, it all came rushing back to him.

'Is the king awake?' he asked the servant sent to wake him.

'He's being woken, as per his instructions,' the man offered quickly, in response to the sharpness in Leofric's voice, as he bowed.

'My thanks,' he offered more gently. 'And lord Godwine?' For a moment, there was a flicker of unease on the servant's face, quickly smoothed away because he was conversing with one of the king's men.

'Earl Godwine has been awake during the day but now sleeps deeply.'

'What was he doing during the day?' Leofric asked, unaware his words were spoken aloud.

'He ventured out into Winchester itself. I couldn't correctly tell you where he went.'

Leofric startled at the reply but forced a tight smile for the servant.

'You have my thanks for waking me. Now, I'll dress and join the king.'

The servant bowed his way from the room as Leofric reached for his tunic and trews and only then his boots. He couldn't deny that he'd slept too soundly, and now his back ached from all the riding yesterday. He'd have liked nothing more than to pull the furs over his chilled body and sleep the night away. But he couldn't.

Maybe one of the men who'd escorted him would have been awake and followed Lord Godwine into Winchester. They all knew to be wary of the earl. As they'd not been called upon to watch the count taking place in the treasury, they'd have been able to keep to a routine, sleeping during the night and awake during the day.

As Leofric entered the small communal area in the treasury building, a servant rushed to prepare food and ale for him, and he accepted what he was offered, his stomach growling gratefully. He sat close to the hearth at the centre of the room. He almost considered calling for his outdoor cloak to drive away the cold, only then the king arrived.

Edward moved purposefully, his movements more fluid than Leofric's, but then, he didn't carry quite as many years.

'Good day,' King Edward called to Leofric, his eyes peering into the darkened corner of the room as though he might find Earls Siward, Godwine and Sweyn there as well.

'You're the first awake?' Edward asked, his tone rueful.

'I believe so. Although, I hear that Lord Godwine hasn't slept as long as we have. It seems he had business in Winchester itself.' The news didn't upset Edward, yet Leofric detected a slight narrowing of his intelligent eyes. Did he suspect the other earl, even as he relied on him? It was an impossible situation for the king to find himself in. On the one hand, he needed his earls to support his kingship, but did he require Godwine amongst that number?

King Harthacnut had been adamant that the earl should have no more influence within England, but his death had allowed Godwine to regain his lost power. England might benefit from Edward as her king, but would it if Godwine continued to recover his previously held position?

'Well, we can only wait for so long. I must have the scrutinisation completed today. I don't wish to linger in Winchester longer than I must.' Edward's lips curled as he spoke, no doubt considering the next part of the task he'd set himself—first his mother, and then Bishop Stigand.

As though conjuring the missing earls, Siward and Godwine entered the room, looking sleep-rumpled, even as they spoke quietly. The sight of the two great earls of England talking so conspiratorially together caused Leofric some concern. Now, what were they planning, if anything?

'Where's Sweyn?' Godwine demanded to know, as though it was his king's responsibility to keep track of his son.

'I believe he still sleeps, but I don't know,' Leofric offered, sparing the king from having to answer such an abrupt question.

'Lazy boy. I'll wake him immediately.' Godwine swept from the room once more.

'I pity the man,' Siward grinned, striding to join them by the hearth.

'The man is an earl,' Edward commented, his tone betraying his unease at Godwine's behaviour.

'Well, he still needs his father to wake him,' Leofric commented, trying, but failing, to mask his unhappiness. Sweyn shouldn't have been made an earl, not yet, but it hadn't been his choice to make. It would have made far more sense for Ælfgar to be proclaimed as earl in place of Hrani.

Siward chuckled at the statement, his eyes alight with the ludicrous situation, while Leofric kept himself busy spooning food into his mouth. It was a strange time of day to be breaking his fast, and he wasn't sure that the meaty pottage was quite what was needed but couldn't deny that he was ravenous.

'Have the clerics discovered any discrepancies?' Siward asked between mouthfuls of his pottage.

'I haven't been informed of any, but, neither have I asked. I'm content to wait until the examination is complete before I make any statement.'

'There's certainly more coin than I expected there to be,' Siward continued, a glint in his eye. Leofric was surprised by the admission. Did Siward not understand the wealth of the English kingdom? He'd served Cnut's sister in Denmark before earning his earldom from

Cnut. But then, Siward had probably spent so much of his time north of the River Humber that he was ignorant of such basic information about the king's taxes.

'I think we forget how large a single coin can be, let alone many thousands of them. It certainly takes up more room than you might imagine,' Leofric explained.

'Yes, it does, and it makes me appreciate why the treasury is such a large building, not that most people realise quite how big,' Edward offered conspiratorially.

Siward quirked an eyebrow at Leofric, and then Godwine was back, blowing into the room like a winter storm, his face furious.

'Sweyn's not here.'

'And he should be?' Edward asked. Leofric enjoyed the wrathful look of the king, tempered only slightly to take the edge from it.

'Yes, my son should be here. He's one of your earls, and he must witness this.'

'Then, I suggest you find him because I'll not wait. It's up to you, Earl Godwine, as to whether you run around after your son or witness the examination of the chests.'

Edward sped from the room, his intentions to begin straight away clear. Leofric wanted to follow the king, but something made him linger.

'Damn the bloody boy, always wandering off without informing me. And the king. Why is he suddenly in such a rush? Last night he called an end to the proceedings, sighting exhaustion, and now it must be done.' Lord Godwine sounded beyond aggrieved, but Leofric had no sympathy for him. 'If it were Harold who was the earl, I'd not need to run around after him as though he were a child.'

Without waiting for any sort of response from Leofric or Siward, Godwine again left the room, a servant waiting, head bowed, with a bowl of pottage in his hand. It seemed it wasn't needed.

'I wouldn't be surprised to discover Lady Emma had something to do with this,' Siward mused, but he expressed no sympathy for

Godwine. Leofric couldn't find it in him to pity the other earl either. Once more, it made him question the king's choice of Sweyn.

Siward and Leofric made their way to the treasury and found the king before the vault's sealed door, surrounded by the clerics from the day before. Some of them yawned, and Leofric stifled his yawn.

'Good,' Edward announced on seeing them. 'We can continue with all haste.' He pulled the familiar black key from beneath his cloak and opened the vast lock as he spoke. It gave a reassuring clink as it fell open, and then the heavy door was once more pushed inwards so that all could see the space hadn't been disturbed in the intervening time.

Edward stepped inside first, followed by his clerics, who knew where they were next to direct their attention as soon as they had the required key. Leofric and Siward entered behind them all eyes keen, but without Godwine and Sweyn there, the endeavour proceeded far more quickly. Leofric was convinced that even the king enjoyed the absence of the two earls.

Godwine didn't appear throughout the night, and Leofric was delighted at the turn of events. It only intensified when the final chest was resealed, and the clerics bowed to the king before filing from the room. It had taken much of the second night, but at least it was finally done.

'I don't yet have all the details tallied, but it would appear as though there's no discrepancy, not even a single coin extra or under,' the head cleric sounded impressed. Edward nodded.

'Good. Then we'll seal the door once more. I'll have another key made. One will remain in my possession all of the time, and the other will be handed to the keeper of the treasury to keep secure for when I'm absent from Winchester.'

'Very well, my lord king,' the cleric bowed. The king hesitated, and Leofric stood on stiff legs, hoisting his chair, made to leave the room, Siward trailing behind him.

'I'd expected the worst of my mother, but perhaps she's not as malevolent as some would have me believe.' Leofric heard the words, even though the king spoke softly and seemingly, only to himself. It didn't take much thought to determine whom the king was referencing. Damn Godwine. He was so good at sowing discord because he had so much experience being the one causing the problems. It didn't promise a peaceful future. Far from it, in fact.

11

WINCHESTER, LEOFRIC

'MY LORD KING, I MUST APOLOGIZE FOR MY ABSENCE,' IT WAS THE NEXT DAY, and the king had retired to his palace at Winchester, taking his earls with him in order to rest before the next part of their journey. Earl Sweyn bowed low before the king, his furious father right behind him, seemingly prepared to force his son to show the correct subservience, if needed, with a firm hand on his back. Leofric could tell that the two had argued, and recently. The pair shared the same red faces, and Sweyn kept trying to shuffle aside from his father.

'It must have been essential to keep you from performing your obligations to your king,' Edward mused from his place on the dais, only to dismiss the errant young man immediately. Leofric didn't blame his king. He wouldn't have wanted to listen to the ineffectual utterings of the boy either. He'd not been there, as the king had instructed, that was more than enough.

'But, my lord king,' of course, Leofric had forgotten Lord Godwine. 'You must hear what happened to Earl Sweyn.' Godwine held Sweyn's tunic in his hands, preventing him from moving aside as the king had commanded.

'I must, must I? I don't think so, Earl Godwine. I've no intention of listening to some pathetic excuses. I know where Earl Sweyn was. You're not the only one with eyes and ears throughout Winchester.'

Leofric considered keeping his focus on the king but knew he couldn't miss the opportunity to watch Lord Godwine flail once more. With little interference, Earl Sweyn had shown himself to be unreliable. The king would remember. He seemed to have perfect recall, even for events that had taken place many years before.

And Leofric wasn't to be disappointed.

Earl Godwine continued to arrest his son in place. They were almost mirror images of each other if you could factor in thirty years of over-excess around Godwine's waist, with the wrinkles to show. They both wore ugly scowls, even in the presence of the king. Leofric again was incredulous that Sweyn had been raised to an earldom while Ælfgar had been overlooked. It wasn't just fatherly pride that made him appreciate how much better prepared the one was for the task.

There were already problems in Sweyn's earldom, and it didn't help that people sought Leofric's assistance when they were unhappy. It wasn't the first time such had happened to Leofric. It had been the same when King Cnut assigned his Danish earls to their border earldoms. The problem had never really gone away. Even under Earl Hrani, some Hereford men and women had sought Leofric's advice.

Still, Lord Godwine seemed determined to argue his son's case.

'My lord king. It wasn't my son's fault. You must know what happened.'

'As I said, I'm fully aware of what waylaid Earl Sweyn. If he found the matter worthier of his attention than his king, then that was his decision. He made his choice, and Earl Godwine, it was his choice to make. You can't make excuses for the fact he chose poorly after the event.'

Leofric knew the king was incensed by the scene Sweyn had caused the previous day. He also appreciated that Godwine was furious with his errant son. Not that Leofric could help it if he'd tracked down Sweyn, whereas Godwine had accomplished little but frantic pacing while he'd sent the king's servants hither and thither to find him. Neither was it Leofric's fault that his men had hunted down the missing earl and informed Leofric of his location when the count was complete, allowing Leofric to witness what was happening with his eyes.

It had been far from a pretty scene. Sweyn, thinking to slip away from the king and his father, had returned to Lady Emma's house, having spent much of the day drinking his courage. Leofric had walked in on a raging row between the two of them.

Lady Emma had barely noticed Leofric's arrival, but he knew she'd noted it. Not so Sweyn.

The younger man, all puffed up and pretending to his nobility, had sprawled himself in the chair closest to the hearth, while Lady Emma, clearly summoned from some task outdoors, was rosy-cheeked and still wearing her outdoor cloak. The smell of ale and wine seemed to infuse the room, and Leofric had wrinkled his nose.

'Ah, my lady mother,' Sweyn had begun, his voice a drawl, the words elongated. Leofric had heard the hiss of outrage from Lady Emma's attendants at such an outrage.

'You do your mother no good service when you name me as such.'

'Well, of course, I know my mother, Lady Gytha, birthed me, but I named you as my mother because you were my father's wife then.'

'You do King Cnut no honour when you name him as your father, for he was no such thing.'

'Ah, Lady Emma, dearest mother. My father, King Cnut, is long dead. His four acknowledged children are also no more than ash and bones. It's time you acknowledged me as his only surviving child. If you backed me as your candidate as king of England, we could rule together. Just think of that. You could hold the key to my treasury, and your bishop could run amuck in East Anglia.'

A flash of fury on Lady Emma's flushed face, and Leofric could deduce that the thought wasn't quite as unappealing as she meant to imply.

'My son, King Edward, son of King Æthelred and I, is England's anointed king. He can't be cast aside. Not now,' she added more quietly.

'Then I could be named as his brother and heir, just as Edward was declared Harthacnut's brother and heir.'

Leofric had kept his eyes on Sweyn's back, not wishing to see the spark of ambition on Lady Emma's face. After all these years, he'd expected her to be better at masking her emotions. But then, King Edward had humiliated her only the night before. Perhaps she welcomed the means to gain some revenge on him, to embarrass him and his ambitions.

'You're the son of your father, Earl Godwine, and his wife, Lady Gytha. You're not my son or King Cnut's son. You can never be declared the king of England or even the king of England's heir.' But, Leofric was disappointed by the lack of conviction in her wavering voice. In fact, he was honest enough to know that if he'd not appeared, but Lord Godwine had tracked down his son instead, the conversation would be taking an entirely different route.

'Come, lady mother,' and Sweyn's voice remained oiled and oozed with charm, even as he slurred his words. 'There's no longer the need to pretend to my birth. King Cnut and Lady Gytha shared a brief romance when Earl Godwine was away in Denmark. I know the truth about it. The whole court knows the truth about it. If he could have two wives simultaneously, then a casual liaison wouldn't have been much cause for concern.'

'King Cnut had only one wife, and you know that well. The other boys weren't Cnut's. He never claimed them as his own.'

Leofric hadn't needed to be looking at Sweyn Godwinesson to know how much he was enjoying upsetting Lady Emma. Perhaps, now that Edward had humiliated her, Sweyn had decided the king's mother was open to further affronts. It was a strange way to win her as an ally, but then, Sweyn didn't truly seem to be thinking at all.

He'd had only one real purpose in approaching her, to get her to admit that Cnut had been his father.

'I was born in 1020. Earl Godwine wasn't to realise that King Cnut had taken his pleasure with my mother when he was absent.'

Leofric watched the revulsion playing over Lady Emma's face at Sweyn casually mentioning her beloved second husband's amorous ways.

'No doubt, you were round with child, unable to offer him what he needed. It's nothing about which to be ashamed. Men will be men, and wives must do their duty to their husbands.' The condescension in Sweyn's voice had boiled Leofric, but he'd held his tongue.

'Earl Sweyn.' Lady Emma's voice had been calm. His appeal to her vanity might have flourished for a heartbeat, but it wouldn't work, not when she'd had a few moments to truly consider what he was suggesting.

'I'll not have you speak about my husband in such a way. Cnut was your king. He highly regarded your father and your mother. He wouldn't have done such a thing, and you would do well to remember that.' Leofric had allowed himself to relax only to realise that Lady Emma's fury hadn't been as intense as she'd wanted him to believe. She'd seemed to be trying to tell Sweyn something, the way her chin had jutted out, and she'd angled her head.

As Sweyn had turned to gaze at him, a contemptuous look on his face, Leofric realised that Lady Emma didn't quite believe her words. Was it possible that once more, she'd cast Cnut's reputation aside just to ensure she remained relevant and essential?

'Earl Sweyn, the king has missed you. He requests that you join him immediately.'

'Ah, yes, the king, my brother. Please inform him that I'll be along shortly. And now, Earl Leofric, you're most unwelcome here. I order you to scurry back to the king. I must speak to my mother.'

Leofric had paused, considering whether he'd wanted to make Sweyn more of an enemy than he already was, trying to determine what Lady Emma might have been thinking by even entertaining such a notion. But, she was a courtier of old. She'd know very well how the passage of years could rename even the most heinous treasons into some minor upset.

'My lady, my lord,' and Leofric had bowed his way from their presence.

'My lord king,' now Lord Godwine tried to win the king around with a whine to his voice. Leofric considered why he bothered. If Sweyn was so convinced that Cnut was his father and not Godwine, why keep him by his side? But, of course, such things were never as simple. There was power in the idea that Sweyn might be Cnut's natural-born son.

'Earl Godwine, Earl Sweyn, I'll discuss the matter no further. My lady mother has displeased me with her meddling with the bishops, and now, despite her humiliation, she means to do me yet more damage. It will be proclaimed that she's no longer my close confidant. People will heed her words with extreme caution. They'll interpret your claim as it should be identified, as an even more desperate bid to a position that's not yours to have.'

And the king was far from finished, even as his words cut with the sharpest blade.

'England has known more than enough upheaval since the days of King Cnut's conquest. I may well be King Cnut's step-son, but my ancestry is older than that. I'm a member of the ancient and long-lived House of Wessex dynasty. I claim descent from King Alfred and the mighty King Athelstan, who united our kingdom, the English kingdom and fought England's enemies at the famous battle of Brunanburh. No one will want a man who's achieved so little as their king. I'm a naval commander, a tried and tested statesperson, and more importantly, the ordained king.'

'Remember, King Cnut acknowledged all of his children when he knew his death was imminent. I'm afraid I don't recall your name mentioned alongside that of the others.'

The pronouncement made, King Edward settled himself in the chair on the dais.

'And now, we'll return to the matter that concerns me, that of the royal treasury.' The air was heavy with intent. Leofric considered that Sweyn might well push the king further. Some previously unseen intellect forced Sweyn to silence, but Leofric knew that the matter was far from at an end. The king might think it concluded, but he knew the ambitions of Godwine and his family from long experience. This might just be the beginning of Sweyn's attempts to win the kingdom for himself, or at least to be named as an ætheling.

12

NOVEMBER AD1043, BURY ST EDMUNDS, LEOFRIC

IT WASN'T THE TIME OF YEAR TO BE TRAVELLING, FAR FROM IT. THE JOURNEY from Gloucester to Winchester had been bad enough. Leofric cursed Lady Emma again as his horse moved to avoid another muddy pool spread from one field, all across the track, to another. This area might be cut off if it didn't stop raining soon.

The journey had been beset with problems, wheels lodging in deep puddles filled with half-frozen water, horses going lame, and through it all, the king had kept up his relentless pace. Leofric was unsure why there was such a rush but knew he'd find out eventually.

Now as they travelled along Icknield Way on what he hoped would be the final part of the journey, the clouds overhead promised not just rain but perhaps even snow. The temperature had dropped significantly since they'd overnighted in London. Leofric shivered inside his thick cloak and called himself all sorts of names.

He should be at home, in Coventry with his wife, preparing for the end of the year for the Yule celebration and not riding through layers of filth and mulch that lined the roadways, and caused everything to feel gritty to the touch.

One of the horses had slipped only that morning, breaking a leg.

They'd been forced to wait while it was put out of its misery. The mood was sombre amongst the huscarls and those forced to accompany the king. Earl Siward travelled with them, but it was almost on his way to the north, so that made sense, and he'd leave them and continue to Bamburgh when the king was finished with him. Lord Godwine and his son had slunk back to their respective earldoms, the king's fury at Sweyn's actions making it imperative that they spend some time apart.

It made the task ahead more pleasant, even as he realised that Lord Godwine didn't want to be associated with what was about to happen. The man never stopped thinking of ways to distance himself from an act that might turn unpleasant.

Beorn and Ralph had joined the king. Ralph could account for his presence as it was on a slight detour from his mother's possessions, but Beorn, still without any land to call his own, remained entirely dependent on the king's good wishes. He went wherever the king went.

Perhaps Beorn was safer in England. In time, Leofric felt sure that the king would feel secure enough in his new position to start rewarding his loyal allies. He no longer needed to be a solitary figure. Leofric believed the move against his mother and Bishop Stigand would be the beginning of a swathe of changes. It was just a pity that Sweyn had been named as earl while the king had felt vulnerable and needed Lord Godwine's support.

The sound of a heaving river snapped him from his reverie. Leofric detected the welcoming sight of burning brands in the distance, the aroma of smoke making him shiver. He'd appreciate being out of the rain, even if it meant the king and Bishop Stigand were closer to their altercation.

Yet, it wasn't Bishop Stigand who greeted them in the damp courtyard of the monastery, but rather Abbot Ufi, agitated at having the king appear with little notice, his robes trailing in the water pooling all around them.

Leofric gratefully dismounted, handing his horse to a sombre-looking monk, his face entirely hidden beneath his cowl in an effort to keep warm. He turned to rush beneath the thatch of the main building, the open doorway glowing with the promise of light and warmth. Edward had already gone inside, Beorn and Ralph with him, encouraging Abbot Ufi to no longer linger in the rain.

Leofric could barely see anything around him. The early winter night had drawn in even more quickly because of the black rain clouds. Perhaps he'd see more in the morning. If it ever stopped raining.

Eagerly, he shrugged out of his dank cloak, handing it to a waiting servant with an apology and stamping the mud from his boots in the rushes close to the door so that he wouldn't drag more of the mire inside the clean hall.

The fire roared at its centre, the warmth almost making Leofric moan with delight. While the king and the abbot spoke away from the hearth, Leofric made his way to it, smiling grimly at Ralph, who clapped his hands together, no doubt trying to drive some warmth back into his blue hands after he'd tugged his gloves aside.

'Filthy weather,' Leofric offered. No one had spoken for much of the journey. It hadn't been possible to pull back cloaks without being covered in a deluge. He eagerly took a steaming beaker from another servant. Abbot Ufi might be raising hell, saying he'd not known of the king's arrival, but he'd had some notice, or they were just well prepared.

'Is Bishop Stigand not here?' he asked Ralph in an aside when there was still no sign of the tall man.

'Yes, he is. But he's refusing to leave the church. He says he must pray with the brother monks.' Ralph spoke with assurance. He was becoming used to being one of the king's closest allies. He might not benefit from an earldom, which he might have expected, but his clothes spoke of a man growing in stature. Even the gloves he'd yanked from his hand were rimmed with expensive fur.

'Well, at least he's here. I wouldn't have been surprised to learn that he'd escaped.'

'That would show his guilt, surely? This way, he gets to pretend he's done nothing wrong.' Ralph's lips turned downwards as he spoke, no doubt thinking of the coming confrontation.

'Indeed,' Leofric nodded, sipping the too-hot fluid that seemed to scorch all the way into his belly, and yet the heat was welcome.

'Will this pestilent rain never stop,' Earl Siward was the next to join the impromptu meeting, Beorn not far behind. While they shed cloaks and made small talk, they all kept a firm eye on what was happening between the king and Abbot Ufi. Leofric watched the abbot's outrage as he gesticulated wildly. Edward's countenance became more and more furious as well.

By the time Bishop Stigand streamed back into the hall, amongst the monks of the abbey in their sodden clothes and trailing mud from across the courtyard, Leofric had warmed up and found himself a chair to settle within that allowed him to keep much of his body warm. There was a fug of dampness in the air, the hint of horse the riders all carried, mildly unpleasant.

Bishop Stigand immediately went to greet the king, although it was clear he was reluctant. Perhaps only the fact that so many watched made him stand firm and take those steps towards Edward.

Stigand bowed low, keeping his eyes focused on the king's feet. Leofric wasn't surprised when Edward didn't indicate that Stigand should stand. He was making his displeasure felt in the smallest and meanest of ways, those that were often the most effective.

Now, while the monks settled to a meal laid out on a long table to the far side of the hearth, all eyes on the events playing out before them, the king finally indicated that Stigand could rise. King Edward settled himself into a waiting chair, the abbot at his right shoulder, Ufi's face more composed than it had been throughout his discussion with the king.

'I've come to deprive you of your bishopric, Stigand. I know of few who've held their position for as short a time as you and caused as many problems for the communities they're supposed to protect.' The words were sharp, loud and allowed no objection.

Bishop Stigand's entire body quivered at the words. Even Leofric was surprised by the ferocity of the king's decision, and he'd expected it to be severe.

'The abbey will be given its liberty. The vill of Milenhall will also form part of the abbey's lands from now on. The burial place of the holy St Edmund will not fall into your hands again. It's for the abbot and the monks to use, not a too-ambitious bishop with thoughts of their benefactor at the forefront. You'll return to Winchester with me and resume your position as one of the royal priests.'

Edward fixed Stigand with a steely stare, expecting him to argue. It appeared that might happen, only the bishop deflated before them all. He bowed his head once more, accepting his punishment.

'As you will, my lord king. I'll have it known that no harm was intended. All I did was for the glory of the church.' Those words rang sourly around the hall. Edward dismissed him with a curt nod of his head, and the moment was over.

Leofric expelled a breath he hadn't realised he was holding and gratefully went to join the monks at their meal. His belly growled angrily, and he eagerly tore into the bread that was offered to him.

But the king hadn't finished his announcements.

'Tomorrow is St Edmund's feast day, and we'll remain here, offer our prayers at his tomb. Many miracles have been recorded here since the Danes cut him down in the prime of his life. I would honour him.'

Leofric almost choked at the words. While he'd expected Edward to turn this into a pilgrimage, he'd not realised his objective. The need to rush made sense now. Immediately, his eyes flashed to Beorn, trying to determine what the Danish man thought of the king's intentions, but he'd clearly been prepared for the announcement and merely ate his fill.

Leofric cast his head downwards, hiding the hint of a smile that played around his lips.

The king never failed to surprise him. Here, at a place that his mother's bishop had tried to steal away from the monks of the abbey, a place where King Cnut had made overt signs of his patronage as a Danish king come to heal the wounds of the long-running wars between the English and the Norse, Edward had made a clear statement. He was an English king, and he would not only revere a man murdered by their old-time enemy but also endow the monastery to make it far wealthier than in the past.

Leofric doubted that this would be the last of such displays from the king.

Later, when the king summoned them to attend him beside Edmund the Martyr's tomb, Leofric went eagerly enough, watchful that Earl Siward and even Beorn were reluctant.

The king, Leofric decided, was astute enough to play both sides to ensure that he won, and it was a skill Lord Godwine had yet to realise Edward possessed. Perhaps witnessing the king's triumph had been worth the sodden and uncomfortable journey after all.

13

OXFORD, ÆLFGAR

ÆLFGAR WATCHED HIS FATHER, MOUTH GAPING OPEN IN SHOCK, EVEN AS HIS oldest son, Burgheard, clambered for his attention. Outside the wind howled, and the patter of rain on the roof fluctuated to the occasional roar before dying away once more. His father was returning from Bury St Edmunds and had come to Oxford to inform his son of events there.

'Sweyn Godwinesson intends to press the point?'

'He does, yes, and I think Lady Emma will encourage him. It'll embarrass both the king and the earl. She must be enjoying it. As if she hadn't caused the king enough problems with this business with the bishop.'

Ælfgar allowed himself a moment to truly detest Sweyn. Ever since he'd been named an earl, he'd done everything he could to torment Ælfgar about being overlooked by the king. His attempt to take control of Wulfstan's properties in Shropshire had been his most blatant attack, but there were other, more insidious slights, and they burned, just as intended.

'It's a pity that Sweyn only made his assertion so well-known now.'

'Yes, it is,' Leofric confirmed, encouraging Burgheard to his side. The youngster needed minimal persuasion. Ælfgar held his amusement in check at the huge grin on his father's face. He was a natural with his grandchildren. A pity his mother wasn't quite so enamoured of them.

Burgheard was a tall child for his age, but the hound beside him, a direct descendant of Hunter, if his aunt had correctly traced the bloodline, just about topped his head. Certainly, Ælfgar thought the hound intelligent enough that it could have helped a half-blind man such as his grandfather get about otherwise unaided. Not for the first time, Ælfgar wished his memories of his grandfather were more than just a hazy recollection.

'Well, he has his earldom now. Edward has wavered between his four earls so much that it's impossible to know whom he favours and whom he doesn't. Until now, you would be forgiven for thinking that Godwine had wormed his way back into the king's affections. Now, he might have to decide between his son and his earldom. Perhaps Lady Emma has done us a favour in refusing to do more to rubbish Sweyn's outrageous claims.' Leofric laughed as he spoke, the thought just occurring to him.

'Do you think she'd do that for us?' Ælfgar asked, his forehead furrowed with thought.

'Of course not. She'll merely be stirring up trouble.'

'What does Sweyn truly intend?'

'I honestly believe he thinks himself the son of Cnut. He's seen Swein Cnutsson rule in Norway and Kings Harald and Harthacnut rule in England. I imagine he wishes to do the same. And, there are those who'll support him?'

'Who would encourage him?'

'Anyone who still has loyalty to King Cnut and his family, rather than King Edward. King Harthacnut was disingenuous when he declared his half-brother as king. No one truly believes the untruths, or rather, slights of hand, that he employed in declaring Edward as his brother and by association, Cnut's son.'

'I had hoped that the years of upheaval might be over with Edward crowned as king.'

'Ah, I don't believe that ever truly happens. If I look back on the years that Æthelred and then Cnut reigned, I thought there were moments of calm when there were none. You, son, are learning the disadvantages of hindsight.'

Ælfgar chuckled at his father's rueful tone.

'Any other news?'

'Not really. Again, there are rumblings from Denmark. King Magnus is a stubborn individual. He might try to push his claim to England as well, not just because Lady Gunnhild has been begging him to do so.'

'And of course, there'll be those prepared to support him.'

'There are always men and women who see their star rising with some new king. Edward has been cautious. Other than appointing Sweyn, he's done little to offend those who currently hold sway in England. But it'll not always be like that. I'm sure that in time, both Ralph and Beorn will have their earldoms. Such promotions will bring about changes, and I can't imagine they'll be the last that the king makes. He feels more secure now. His actions against Bishop Stigand and his mother speak of someone with greater confidence than ever before. Our king is making his own decisions.'

'And what of my earldom?' Ælfgar felt stung into asking, even though he was intelligent enough to realise that his father was warning him that transformations would be made within Mercia.

'There'll come a time when the king must promote you. I can't foresee the future, but I see his regret about Sweyn. I doubt he'll be keen to advance another of Lord Godwine's sons, even if Harold is far more sensible than Sweyn.'

'Then, I must wait?' Ælfgar regretted the petulance in his tone.

'Yes, you must. Either that or you must bring about my death. But impatience was never one of your traits.' His father chuckled as he spoke, his eyes remaining on Burgheard even as he spoke about matters of politics.

'No, it isn't,' Ælfgar sighed. 'But, I should like to stand at your side, with more authority than just that of being your son.' Ælfgar didn't even wish to consider what would happen when his father died. He might want more clout, his own position, but he didn't yet want to be responsible for so much. His father handled matters efficiently, was quick to listen to all sides, and was slow to offer resolutions, ensuring any decision was reasoned and fair, even to those who lost out. Ælfgar didn't believe he possessed such wisdom yet. Perhaps he never would.

'Mercia is held together by our family,' his father's keen eyes raked his face, seriousness touching the lines and shadows that revealed the passage of years. 'Your uncle is an important man, your cousins as well, but you and I stand as the figureheads alongside your mother. She has quite the reputation now, after Coventry.' His father's face softened as he spoke. His mother had surprised them all, and now she was widely regaled and sought for assistance with all manners of things.

She'd begun endowing some small religious establishments, but now she did much more. Lady Godgifu's reach was extensive, and Ælfgar admired her. She was a woman with a husband who was an earl, but only now did he feel that others appreciated her the way he always had. Certainly, Elgiva was in awe of her. Elgiva had already begun trying to make her place in Mercia in mimicry of Lady Godgifu.

'My sister continues to hold Deerhurst, although I don't think she will for much longer. Time has perhaps come when a new incumbent should be found if Earl Sweyn is to remain close, as seems probable.'

'It may seem,' and again Ælfgar felt the full force of his father's attention, 'as though the House of Godwine is everywhere, but they aren't. Not really. I'm not saying they're not our equal or that the king won't further reward them, but we need to keep some perspective. It's Mercia that matters to our king and us. What Lord Godwine does in Wessex isn't our concern. Not now the king has oversight of all he does.'

Ælfgar nodded, but it hurt him. He couldn't deny it.

He felt a weight on his shoulder, his father's warm clasp.

'Son, politics is never easy. None of it is. You learn to forge a path through it all, and determine what's important to you. My father believed in honour and keeping his word, no matter what the kings did to him. Yes, King Cnut nearly broke him, but he rallied and recovered. I've tried to do the same. I feel I've been less successful, yet my reach is vaster than that my father could claim. As we've seen, kings come and go, but the House of Leofwine remains steadfast.'

Ælfgar met his father's eyes evenly. There was reassurance in them and also understanding. King Cnut had repeatedly thwarted his father. He knew that. Cnut had seemingly toyed with his father, advancing Earl Godwine without question, forcing Leofric to find a way of working with the Danish earls sent to guard the border with the Welsh. On occasion, it had been as though Cnut had punished Leofric for not being his father. Yet, Leofric had his family spread over much of Mercia. Not even Earl Hrani had left anyone behind to rule in his stead.

It had been a knee-jerk decision by Cnut. It must have been an attempt to impose a military solution over the troubled border regions. Like Cnut's northern empire, it had not lasted beyond his death.

'So you believe the king will reward Beorn and Ralph with earldoms?'

'I do, yes, but not just yet. This year he brought his mother and Bishop Stigand under control. Next year he'll continue the task he's begun in rewarding his loyal supporters from Normandy. I expect to see new faces at Edward's side.'

'But he elevated Earl Sweyn,' an arch of his eyebrow and Leofric nodded and then smiled, although there was no humour in it.

'Even kings make mistakes. I believe Edward will rue this one for many years to come. Unfortunately, Sweyn has been given Hrani's old earldom. He'll cause more chaos and carnage, perhaps inciting war with Gruffydd. But, that's no bad thing, and sooner he risks his life and his men than we do ours.'

A swift flicker of fury on his father's face was the only indication of his hatred of the man who'd killed his brother, but it was enough.

Ælfgar nodded. 'So it's a blessing?'

'No, never that, but we can live with it. For now. We've managed it before, and Ealdorman Eadric Streona was much worse than Sweyn. Let's hope that Sweyn's loyalty is more secure, although I doubt it. Not with his insistence that he's Cnut's son.'

THE ANGLO-SAXON
CHRONICLE ENTRY FOR 1043

(C - Abingdon)In this year Edward was consecrated king at Winchester on Easter Sunday with great ceremony and Easter was on 3 April. Archbishop Eadsige consecrated him. Stigand the priest was consecrated bishop of the East Angles. And soon after this the king brought all the lands his mother owned forcibly into his own control and he took from her all that she owned in gold and silver and things beyond description, because she had withheld it too firmly from him. And soon after Stigand was deprived of his bishopric, and all that he owned was placed in the king's control because he was closest in his mother's counsel, and because, as was suspected, she did as he advised.

(D - Worcester)In this year Edward was consecrated king at Winchester on Easter Sunday. And this year, a fortnight before St Andrews Day (30th November being St Andrews Day), the king was given advice as a result of which he rode from Gloucester together with Earl Leofric and Earl Godwine and Earl Siward with their retinue to Winchester. And they came unexpectedly upon the lady (Lady Emma) and they deprived her of all the treasures which she owned and these were beyond counting, because she had formerly been very hard to the king, her son, in that she did less for him than he wished both before he became king and afterwards as well. And they allowed her to stay there afterwards.

(E - Peterborough) In this year Edward was consecrated king at Winchester on Easter Day with great ceremony. Easter was then on 3 April. Archbishop Eadsige consecrated him and gave him good instruction before all the people, and admonished him well for his own sake and for the sake of all the people. Stigand the priest was consecrated bishop of East Anglia. And soon after this the king brought all the lands his mother owned forcibly into his own control, and he took from her all that she owned in gold and silver and things beyond description, because she had withheld it too firmly from him.

14

AD1044, COVENTRY, LEOFRIC

'THERE ARE RUMOURS.' LEOFRIC WATCHED HIS SON IN CONSTERNATION AS HE strode into the room, aware his eyes rolled upwards in exasperation, but Ælfgar pressed on regardless. He brought with him the sharp bite of a crisp day. Leofric huddled into his cloak, pleased not to have to move from his warm spot by the hearth.

'That King Magnus of Norway, and Denmark, intends to mount an expedition to take England this year. Lord Svein Estridsson has been forced to capitulate to him or risk being killed.'

Leofric groaned at the words.

'I thought your arrival would concern the Godwines, not King Magnus. I would name Lady Gunnhild a pestilence, but we both know that Magnus needed no true encouragement to turn his gaze towards England.'

'It never rains, but it pours,' Ælfgar offered, although there was no lightness to his voice.

'And what does the king plan to do about it?'

'He's decided to mount a counter-attack. He's calling together the lithesmen and the ships. King Edward has no intention of losing his kingdom again.'

'I imagine Lord Godwine is filled with encouragement for the scheme.'

'Of course, he is. After all, he's given the king a fabulous ship, and now it will be used.'

Leofric stood from his place close to the hearth and began to pace.

'I'm not against the king defending his kingdom, never think that.'

'But Earl Godwine can happily drown,' Ælfgar interjected.

'He can, yes. I would have no problem with that, even if I've never sought to gain at the death of another.'

'There are those for whom it's impossible not to wish ill upon.' Ælfgar was bending low, working to remove his boots from his feet. Leofric startled. He'd not even welcomed his son to his home. Luckily, his servant knew him well, and quickly wine, bread and cheese were brought for them.

'My thanks,' he offered, smiling at the older woman. She offered a dip of a curtsy and hustled away to be about her usual business. Leofric appreciated once more that he was blessed to have such fiercely loyal servants. He didn't know what he'd done to earn such respect from them.

'And the king orders us to join him?'

'The king is keen to be seen as the military leader he claims to be, unlike his father, and in the guise of Kings Cnut and Harthacnut.'

'He's full of contradictions,' Leofric mused unhappily. The thought of another war for England's kingdom filled him with foreboding, even if the chance to sail once more would be welcome.

'The king means to attack Norway?'

'No, the king means to oppose the attack with his fleet. He wants King Magnus to face him at sea but with England close enough to see while still being out of reach. It's Sweyn who's truly keen to go to war. It seems that upsetting the Welsh kings isn't enough for him. He means to make an enemy of everyone.'

Leofric reached for his wine and drank sparingly. It was too early to imbibe much, but the fluid's tartness awakened him from the lethargy these fresh problems induced.

'One of us will need to join the king if not both of us.'

'Don't tell me that Lord Godwine will venture into a ship?' Leofric couldn't keep the incredulity from his voice.

'Well, he bluffs about it, but I'm sure he'll find an excuse not to when the time comes. Harold will no doubt go in his stead.' A slither of hope entered Ælfgar's voice at the possibility.

'So, how will we ensure that happens,' Leofric asked. 'If I say I'll join the fleet, then no doubt, Lord Godwine will determine to go, and if I send you in my stead, then he's likely to go just to prove he's the more loyal.'

Ælfgar laughed softly at his father's reasoning.

'I'll leave that for you to decide. But, do you truly think King Magnus will attempt to claim England? Surely he's just all bluff.'

'We can hope Lord Svein keeps him and his forces busy in Denmark. That way, like Harthacnut before him, he'll not be able to take the risk that abandoning Denmark will lose him the kingdom.'

Ælfgar grumbled at his father's succinct summation.

'I still don't believe King Magnus has any true claim to England. It wasn't Harthacnut's to offer, no matter that he was England's king.'

'You know how these Norsemen are. They're all ambitious and will use the most fragile pretexts.'

'I thought Lord Svein would become king of Denmark on Harthacnut's death. Beorn assumed the same.'

'I don't believe Svein has quite the support he needs, not with a wrathful Magnus on the warpath. I'm sure, and I certainly believe, that he'll be proclaimed king in time. Just perhaps not yet. In all honesty, the longer he can cause problems for Magnus, the better for England.'

'So, the fact that Magnus might be heading for England would speak of his triumph over Svein?'

Leofric considered the logic of that.

'Sometimes, I wish that the raging seas didn't separate us, but other times, I'm grateful not to be embroiled in the wars of the Norse. So, when does the king mean to assemble his fleet?'

'June.'

'Then we have much to arrange,' Leofric confirmed. His thoughts went to his father's ship. Admittedly, it had been repaired so often it could hardly be called the same boat as the one bequeathed to him by King Æthelred when he was to travel with Olaf Tryggvason to Norway. It still thrilled him whenever he saw it, even though it was few and far between. His lithesmen spent most of their time in London under the strict guidance of their commander.

Sometimes, Leofric felt he did little but pay the bills and advance money for repairs, but there was an honour in owning such a vessel. It drew gasps from those who'd never seen it, and while the sail had been remade countless times over the years, its bright colours made it instantly recognisable.

And, of course, it tied him to his father just as much as the hounds that categorised his family. It was a part of who he was and what his family represented. Continuity, often re-forged, but continuity from King Æthelred and by association, his only remaining son, now king of England.

No, Leofric considered, it would be an excellent means of reinforcing his loyalty to the king, as well as his longevity. Both were something that Lord Godwine and his horde of sons couldn't claim.

'Wulfstan and Ælfwine should be there as well,' only Ælfgar was opening his mouth to argue against the necessity.

'I don't mean to thrust them in front of the king in the hope he'll honour them, but instead because I thought they might enjoy it.' Immediately, Ælfgar reconsidered.

'A good idea,' he confirmed quickly.

The possibility of some excitement, and hopefully not war, would drag his nephews from the rumblings within Mercia itself. Earl Sweyn was ensuring he caused ructions wherever he went. Leofric dreaded to hear of his next outrageous claim.

. . .

THE RIVER THAMES STRETCHED AWAY BEFORE HIM. LEOFRIC NOTED THE HAZE
of the sun glinting on the vast expanse. From here, it seemed to be a
river of silver running far out of sight, but it was none of those things
up close. No, it was a fetid swamp filled with the detritus of the city's
denizens. When he'd pulled King Harald's body from the depths into
which it had been cast, it had not been the most disgusting and
disquieting item he'd found.

'You can smell it from here,' Ælfgar muttered at his side. They
were mounted on the rise just to the west of London. Leofric
chuckled.

'And that shows you as a countryman. Not for you, the hustle
and bustle of city life.'

'Not for me, the smell and the lack of privacy,' Ælfgar's lips
turned down as he spoke.

'There,' Leofric pointed. 'I can see her, even from here.'
Indeed he spied his father's old ship, the deeply burnished
wood of the hull was unmistakable, the red and gold of the sail,
a welcome splash of colour amongst the shimmering silver of
the distant Thames. Somehow, in the many years since his
father had taken possession of the ship, no one else had
thought to polish their craft to such a high sheen. It was a
source of pride for the men who crewed her, even if they
resented the imprecations of Commander Eowa each and every
winter when the ship was brought ashore for necessary mainte-
nance and repairs.

Not that his craft was alone in the Thames. No, it was busy, and
he counted at least sixteen vessels. No doubt, the remaining ships of
the king's fleet had begun to make their way to Sandwich or had yet
to leave the quayside and take to the open water.

Leofric couldn't deny that it gave him a thrill to see the boats. It
was rare that the king's fleet was assembled and ever more atypical
that the sight of sails didn't foreshadow a threat from some distant

enemy. In the past, it had been Olaf Tryggvason, King Swein, Thorkell the Tall, Cnut, and Harthacnut.

If Magnus were to attack, he'd face staunch resistance. Indeed, no one other than Lady Gunnhild would be offering him England's crown, not when she already had an anointed monarch. And Edward was not his father. He wasn't too terrified to counter the threat.

'She looks magnificent,' Ælfwine offered the praise as he brought his mount to a halt beside Leofric.

'She always does,' Wulfstan responded dryly. Away from the stresses and strains of the ambitions of Earl Sweyn, his nephews seemed to have lost the heavy worries they'd been carrying. Leofric knew he'd acted correctly in demanding that they travel with him, no matter their arguments to the contrary. Lady Mildyrth and Lady Godgifu would be more than a match for anything Sweyn attempted in their absence.

'I'll race you,' Ælfgar called to his cousins, already encouraging his horse onwards. Leofric shook his head at their antics. It was as though they were small boys once more.

Olaf joined him as the three raced away down the long slope.

'I wish I had the bloody energy,' Olaf complained, content to travel at Leofric's pace, as he rubbed his back with his right hand. Leofric noted the grey tinging his brother by marriage's thick hair, the grey stubble on his stubborn chin.

'I'm sure we were their age once, although I don't recall.'

'Bloody hell, you sound as old as the venerable Wulfstan before he died. You're not quite that old yet.'

Leofric arched an eyebrow. 'You're the one moaning about your age.'

'I'm just saying, I wish I had the energy.'

'So, it's not because you're an old git then,' Leofric mocked.

'No, not that. Never that,' Olaf reassured, still rubbing his back, wincing with the movement.

Ahead, they could see the young men hurtling towards the gates that allowed access into London at Newgate. It reminded Leofric of so many journeys he'd made this way that it was impossible to put them all into the correct order. Some stuck more firmly in his mind than others, and as often the case, his thoughts turned to Northman, and that headlong dash he'd made to London to prevent Northman's execution. A journey that had ended with the worst possible outcome.

But what would his brother have made of this new development? Leofric had no idea. It had been so many years now, and yet there were times when he still poignantly missed him. It should have been the four brothers securing Mercia in the name of the House of Leofwine with his sister's aid. Now only he and Godwine remained, and they weren't getting any younger.

'Are we going straight to the quayside?' Ælfgar asked his voice light with the exhilaration of his mad dash onwards. When he finally caught up with them, Leofric didn't know which of the three had won. He doubted they even knew. It had just been about feeling the rush of the wind in their ears as they raced. The winning was irrelevant.

'Yes. Better to see with our own eyes what's happening down there. I'm sure Commander Eowa will be full of complaints.' Leofric spoke the last sentence softly. It was fine to joke about the man, but not in front of others who might inadvertently inform Eowa.

Inside London, the streets were busy, clogged with the day-to-day traffic of men and women about their business, hawking their wares or just trying to get from one place to another. By the time they arrived at the quayside, Leofric was tired of always forcing his horse aside to avoid oblivious foot passengers. It reminded him why he preferred staying away from such a busy place. Certainly, Oxford was never this busy.

'Hail,' he turned his head and immediately caught sight of Commander Eowa at the prow, the ship slowly coming into the quayside, the oars raised as it glided into place against the coils of rope to the side meant to prevent the ship scraping against the wooden quay.

'Here,' and Leofric handed the reins to Godwulf. The man quickly took them and turned to lead Oswald to a less busy area, away from the slap of the water against the quay.

'How is she?' Leofric asked when he was face to face with the wind-roughened face of Eowa.

'Good, not that I can say the same for your shoddy shipmen?' Eowa roared this part of the sentence over his shoulder. 'Lazy bastards,' he finished, and Leofric grinned at the equally foul-mouthed responses muttered by the grinning men as they primed the ship.

'No, my lord, I assure you she's well prepared for whatever might come, her crew as well. We'll honour you and the English when we join the rest of the fleet. I believe the king has command of twenty-five other ships, the rest are under the king's command but financed by the earls and king's thegns.'

'I've brought some more crew for you,' Leofric indicated his nephews and son with his chin, who'd joined him, and now assisted the men on board by taking hold of ropes and barrels.

'I never say no to strong arms,' Eowa commented easily, a hint of mockery in his voice as he watched them work. Leofric nodded, looking away so no one would see his smirk of amusement or arched look that Eowa shared with him.

'It'll do them good to be out there and for the king to see them.'

'I understand, my lord. I hear that Earl Godwine has outfitted two ships and means to have Earl Sweyn on one of them and Lord Harold on the other.'

This was news to Leofric, yet he was far from surprised. At least Godwine wasn't planning on going himself.

'Neither of them will be as good as ours. She's the envy of all. I'm always surprised that Lord Godwine takes so little interest in ships. After all, his father was a great commander, but I hear he leaves that side of the business to his Danish wife.'

'Well, he was, until he wasn't,' Eowa offered, his words edged with derision. Leofric chuckled at the tone.

'The lads and I will endeavour to make you proud. I give you my oath.'

'You don't need to do that. I just need you to stay safe and come home alive.'

'Do you think there'll be a battle?' His voice lowered as he spoke, as though it were a secret only they could share.

'I just can't see it, I confess. I believe King Magnus is busy in Denmark. I've certainly heard nothing to the contrary.'

'Me neither. The few trading vessels I've seen hailing from Ribe or Roskilde say the same. The only ship army under Magnus' command is encamped on mainland Denmark. They say that Lord Svein has been proclaimed king by the Witan there. Magnus has vowed to outlaw him.'

'Well, if that's the case, I don't foresee a war. But, I imagine that might not please the king. He's probably keen to show himself as a warrior in the mould of his predecessors.'

'But not his father?'

'My father once told me of the battle in Strathclyde. He said King Æthelred managed well. Perhaps not the highest words of praise ever to be heard, but not the worst.'

'Aye, my lord. Well, whatever we encounter, I guarantee the lads, and I will return safe and well, having shown some of these arse-holes the skills needed to sail a vessel on the Whale Road.' While Eowa spoke, a loud, screeching noise filled the air. As one, every eye on the bustling quayside turned towards the sound.

'Bloody hell,' Eowa complained, already springing back to the ship.

'Easy now, lads, but we'll move her back into the channel. That's not going to end well,' he added scathingly.

Leofric squinted against the sun's brightness, his hand above his eyes, but knew that Eowa was correct, moving to add his weight to those trying to force his father's ship away from the quayside.

One of the other ships was careering too quickly towards the quay. Already, it had run through the bow of one of the tethered vessels, and it still hadn't slowed enough.

'Bring that craft under control,' Leofric roared, watching the men on board trying to follow their commander's instructions, running one way and then another when all they needed to do was dip their oars deep into the churning water to bring it to an abrupt stop. And then Leofric groaned.

Of course, it had to be, didn't it?

Earl Sweyn was in personal control of the craft, a man who was undoubtedly the rightful commander shouted strident instructions to his crew as he attempted to bring the ship under control. The shipmen didn't know whose orders to follow – their liege lord or commander.

Leofric risked glancing to where Eowa was hauling on the steer-board as the men dipped their oars into the murky water. He was reassured to see the craft slipping into the faster-flowing water. The same couldn't be said for the small fishing vessel that dipped below the water as the hull of Sweyn's ship slid over it, or of the trading ship, in the process of being unloaded, which was going to be sunk next.

'Bloody bollocks.' Leofric felt the rush of men and women sprinting towards the stricken vessel, even as another ear-splitting screech of wood on wood filled the air. The cries of dismay added a discordant sound to that of the imminent disaster.

If there were someone who was going to cock up docking, it would be Earl Sweyn. It wasn't even as if the quayside was particularly full, not with so many of the king's ships having already left.

'Arsehole,' Wulfstan stated flatly, and Leofric couldn't argue with his nephew's assessment.

'He'll have to pay for the damages. It's not as if there's a lack of witnesses to what he's done.'

'He can certainly afford it,' Wulfstan grumbled.

With a thundering crash that reverberated through the wooden quayside, the ship finally came to a stop. The trading craft was just about afloat, although with a massive tear in its side into which water was pouring as the crew hurried to fill the hole.

'Earl Leofric,' the voice calling to him was imperious. 'You'll stand as my witness that these ships purposefully impeded one of the king's ships.'

A collective groan echoed from the crowd, frantically trying to save the caskets and barrels from the stricken vessel.

Leofric shook his head as he sought out the man.

'I'll do no such thing, Earl Sweyn. I'll stand as witness to the damages that you've inflicted. I'll ensure you make good on the required reparations. You should have had someone with more expertise take over. Now, your vessel will need to be checked. You can't go to sea in a leaky boat.' Leofric's voice was edged with displeasure as he met the eyes of the aggrieved earl.

'Now, Earl Leofric, it's always your way to take the side of the merchants and fishermen, as you did in Worcester. I know the king will see things my way.' The public argument elicited another gasp of outrage from those listening.

'The king will ensure the law is adhered to, Earl Sweyn. He has no regard for the social standing of those involved. I assure you that it would be better to simply settle the matter now. I'm happy to witness the payments you must make to those affected by your calamitous attempt at sailing.'

Sweyn's face was slowly turning a deep shade of puce. Leofric knew that any moment now, the earl's notoriously short temper would be ignited. He found it would be rather welcome.

'This has been designated the king's quay. These people,' and he spat the word 'people', 'shouldn't even be here.' Sweyn flung his arm outwards to indicate the men and women on the quay.

'This isn't the king's quay,' Eowa called from a safe distance away, still within earshot. 'The king's quay is the next one down,' and he pointed to where five of the king's ships could be seen bobbing in the water.

Earl Sweyn turned confused eyes to where Eowa pointed, and

Leofric enjoyed watching the flurry of emotions cover the young man's face as he realised that there was no one to blame but himself.

For a heartbeat, Leofric thought he might still try and deny responsibility, but then he sighed, his shoulders deflating.

'My apologies,' he swept a deep bow, placing a rueful smile on his young face. 'It seems I'm not quite the sailor I believed myself to be. I'll make restitution, and Earl Leofric will witness them to ensure all are satisfied. As you're not on board, Earl Leofric, can I ask you to take the names of the people involved? I must join the rest of the ships, but I don't wish to abrogate my responsibilities.'

And like that, Sweyn had won the crowd over to him.

Leofric inclined his head, agreeing to Sweyn's terms, even though he, too, had places to be.

A handful of men and women came hesitantly towards Leofric, and he dredged a welcoming smile in encouragement. Out of the corner of his eye, he watched Sweyn and Eowa taking their ships down to the king's quay. Eowa, he noted quickly, had put Ælfwine and Wulfstan to work, returning to the quay to allow them to clamber on board. Ælfgar was also on the ship, but he and Eowa spoke earnestly beside the steerboard, heads bowed low.

Olaf assisted Leofric as they inspected the damage and determined the correct level of recompense for those affected by Sweyn's terrible sailing ability. The fishing vessel was lost forever to the murky depths of the Thames. The man who claimed the ship was a swarthy man, with bulging muscles showing on his arms and a perplexed expression on his lined face.

'I don't know what I'll do,' he huffed. 'How will I fish? There's no one available to construct a new ship for me. Every ship-builder is working on the king's fleet. It's been in my family for two generations. How will I feed my family?'

Leofric considered.

'I can demand recompense for your lost profession, and, for now, I can find you a position with the king's fleet. You'll be paid until you can get a new ship made.'

A flicker of delight touched the man's eyes.

'My name's Dunston,' he offered, holding his hand out to seal the agreement with a vigorous arm clasp. 'I should like that,' he confirmed. 'The chance to be a part of the king's ship army. No man could ever decline such an opportunity.'

'Then, inform your family, and gather your possessions. Make your way to the king's quay. In the meantime, your family will survive on the compensation owed by Earl Sweyn for the damage he's caused.' Leofric reached for the small bag he carried that contained enough coins to survive while away from his home.

Carefully, he found five of the heaviest silver coins with Edward's image struck onto them and placed them into Dunston's hand. It was more than enough for his family. Perhaps more than he'd have ever seen. Maybe he should have offered the payment before suggesting the man join the king's shipmen.

Dunston didn't even glance at the coins but gripped them tightly, his eyes sweeping to the king's quay.

'I'll be as quick as I can,' he confirmed before disappearing into the milling crowd.

Leofric made short work of completing his task, handing out more coins to men and women affected by Sweyn's over-enthusi-asm. He kept a detailed account of precisely what Sweyn owed him. He would undoubtedly argue the values, but Leofric wasn't going to leave any man or woman without the means to feed themselves. Especially not with the cost of wheat as high as it currently was.

'Damn fool,' Olaf grumbled as they mounted and made their way to the king's quay.

'A young, damn fool,' Leofric agreed. Not that he'd never been young. Not that he'd never made mistakes, but Sweyn did little but make mistakes.

'You know you'll never get all your money back, don't you?' Olaf commented conversationally.

'I know I did the right thing. If Sweyn makes a fuss, I'm content to make it a matter for the king to resolve again. I'm sure he won't want his time taken up with a tedious argument about a fishing vessel's true cost. He'll order Sweyn to pay, as he did with the attack on Wulfstan's properties, but it'll probably be sensible to keep the matter between the two of us.'

'Maybe, but he already takes what he wants, without considering the consequences. I wouldn't encourage him further.'

Leofric held his tongue. Olaf was correct to caution him.

THE FOLLOWING DAY, WITH SWEYN STUDIOUSLY AVOIDING HIM, LEOFRIC watched the rest of the king's fleet stream along the Thames, heading for the open sea in the far distance. The tide was running well, and the ships were all powered by their sails, not their oars. It made his heart soar to see the sight, and indeed, much of London had lined the riverbank, eager to watch the departing king's fleet.

Leofric looked at the crowds, appreciating how important London's loyalty was to England's king. For years against King Swein, London had held out, only capitulating when it was impossible to continue the defence. London had been the centre of Harald's kingship as well.

And now London cheered for King Edward, and Leofric doubted that it had ever done the same for Æthelred. No, Edward was determined not to make the same mistakes his father had. Only time would tell if he would fulfil his desires.

15
ÆLFGAR

HE'D TAKEN HIS PLACE ON THE ROWING BENCH, BUT FOR NOW, THERE WAS NO need to manoeuvre the oar in his hands into the brown sweep of the Thames. A fair wind blew, driving the ships towards the expanse of the open sea, taking the stink of fetid water with it, and then to Sandwich, where Edward had ordered his fleet to meet.

He'd left his father in London and now demurred to the instructions of Commander Eowa. Unlike Earl Sweyn, he wasn't about to make a fool of himself before so many. He wasn't the ship's commander. But he was prepared to honour his king by taking his place amongst the men who owed their allegiance to him.

He tried not to watch the antics of Earl Sweyn, but it was almost impossible to ignore the scene playing out before his eyes. Not content with damaging two ships already, Sweyn was now trying to follow the example of the experienced men and their crews, making him a laughing stock.

While his father's Mercians were doing their best to ignore the spectacle, the laughter of others rippled across the water. There was no way that Earl Sweyn couldn't hear it and know it for what it was.

Sweyn would be furious when he finally, or rather, if he finally made it to Sandwich. At the moment, it was doubtful.

'Damn arse. And to think, he comes from such fine stock. His grandfather would be furious.' Eowa's words were only meant for Ælfgar's ears, and he was grateful for that. After all, he would have to face Sweyn, and none of the others would, and certainly not under the king's scrutiny.

'There's no dishonour in deferring to someone who knows what they're doing.' He grinned as he spoke, and Eowa grunted. He wasn't an easy man to compliment.

'Perhaps. But his family have more than enough ships. I don't understand why he's never learned. They sail to and from Dublin often enough.'

Ælfgar's lips turned as Eowa spoke. Besides all the other arrogances of Godwine and his family, the fact they were embroiled in the buying and selling of slaves, making money from other's misery, was just another reason not to esteem them. He was aware that Lady Gytha made much of her money from the slave trade. Surely, as the wife of one of England's premier earls, she could have amassed wealth from elsewhere? The argument that it was her dead brothers' business made no impact on Ælfgar, or the oft-quoted phrase that it was better she did so than other, less scrupulous men and women.

'So, will there be a battle, Lord Ælfgar?' Eowa's piercing gaze almost cut Ælfgar with its intensity

'I can't see it, and neither can Earl Leofric and yet, we must prepare, all the same.'

'I imagine we should. After all, we've not sailed in any sort of formation since it was feared King Harthacnut would arrive from Denmark with eighty-five ships. And, of course, he did arrive, but by then, he was England's king, and our task was merely to welcome him to England. And, of course, to pay the costs he'd incurred.'

'I'm sure we'll discover more when we reach Sandwich,' Ælfgar mollified.

'Hopefully,' and Eowa went about his business while Ælfgar

pondered his words. How many years had it been since the ship army was put to any significant use? A few, certainly, and yet, it was impossible to consider England not having ships to protect her.

King Magnus might not attack this year, but there was no guarantee that he wouldn't next year or even the year after that. Like his father, King Olaf Haraldsson, Magnus was determined to forge an empire out of the northern kingdoms. King Olaf had become some sort of saint in Trondheim after his death. Men and women revered him, and miracles were reported to occur at his graveside. Ælfgar would sooner dismiss such notions, but the dead's power to cure the living was well-known, and the Holy Church certainly believed it was possible. Who, then, was he to mock the notion?

Ahead, Ælfgar could scent the change in the wind and the smell of the water. No longer sludge-filled, the bite of the sea air tanged on his lips, and he gazed out towards the expanse of the sea. For a moment, he pictured it filled with ships, a ship army and an ambitious king leading them. And then he shook his head.

England hadn't been attacked since King Cnut's invasion over two decades ago. He felt confident that his father was correct in his assertion. There'd be no battle. Not anytime soon.

As they entered the sheltered bay at Sandwich, Ælfgar's eyes roamed the quayside. Many of the king's ships were already there, sails stowed, oars stored down the centre of the boat to either side of the mast. Yet there was a sense of anticipation in the high voices of those who took hold of ropes and helped the ship moor next to their own.

It was already too busy for each craft to have separate space in the harbour, but it was possible to clamber ashore side by side, even if it meant crossing another craft. Planks of wood were laid across the ships, and Ælfgar scrambled landward, unsurprised to find King Edward there, Ralph and Beorn in close company, as so often the case.

Not that the king was alone apart from the two other men. No, it was almost too busy, as men and women hurried to prepare the ships for a voyage out to sea, bringing barrels and chests filled with supplies.

'My lord king.' Ælfgar made his way to the king, his cousins behind him, and all of them bowed their heads in a show of obedience.

'Ah, Lord Ælfgar,' even the king had flushed cheeks. It seemed he was as excited as the rest of the shipmen. 'You've arrived, and with more of the London-based ships. And your father?'

'He means to come via land. I'm sure he'll reach us shortly.' The king seemed to be expecting the news.

'Excellent. We intend to leave the day after tomorrow, provided the winds are kind and the rest of the ships have assembled.' And then Edward peered over Ælfgar's shoulder, his lips pursed.

'Did Earl Sweyn not join the flotilla?' A gentle snigger from behind him, and Ælfgar cursed his cousin for his lack of etiquette.

'Yes, my lord king. Earl Sweyn was in control of his craft. I believe he'll be along in good time.' The king fixed him with a firm look, the flicker of amusement evident in how his lips quivered.

'You're truly a man of the court,' the king flattered him, his voice filled with appreciation.

'My lord,' and Ælfgar bowed again and moved aside to be greeted by Lord Harold. They were uneasy allies, yet Ælfgar was still pleased to see him.

'My lord,' Harold bowed to him, and Ælfgar mirrored the movement. They took pains to ensure they never slighted one another, if not because it concerned them, to prevent their families' complaints.

'Harold, have you a ship to lead?'

'No, I have a ship on which I'll serve and fight if necessary.' There were elements of strain in his voice, and it surprised Ælfgar.

Ælfgar thought he'd say nothing further, and his next words surprised him.

'Walk with me.'

'Of course,' and Ælfgar turned to his cousins, but they were busy talking to Beorn and Ralph, so he left them.

Quickly and without speaking, the two men walked along the quayside. The closer they got to the huddle of buildings, the fewer people there were, and when there was almost no one around them, Harold stopped abruptly.

'Tell me, what has my arse of a brother been up to now?'

Ælfgar considered denying it but realised he'd rather know if the situation were reversed. Sweyn was proving to be an embarrassment.

'He crashed into two ships in London. He sunk a fishing vessel, tried to blame the people involved, and only then realised that he was at fault because he was in the wrong place.'

Harold's face, so like his father's, with his long hair and black beard, tensed with a flicker of annoyance in his hazel eyes. He was tall, a sensible cloak flung around his shoulders to keep the sea breeze from chilling him.

'And he made restitution for the damage?'

'With some encouragement, yes, he did.'

Harold offered nothing else, and Ælfgar felt uncomfortable as the silence stretched between them.

'I'm an ambitious man,' Harold finally said. 'But I'm not a fool. Remember that, my lord,' and with that, he gave a quick bow of his head and strode away, his steps clipped. Ælfgar watched him go, noting the assured stride and how he kept his head up, taking in all of the frantic activity on the quay. It was evident that Ælfgar wasn't alone in feeling overlooked by the king. It was a far from pleasant feeling.

THE SEA STRETCHED BEFORE HIM, BLUE NOW, SHADED WITH DEEP GREENS, the sky overhead nearly cloudless. His long legs were stretched before him, his eyes almost half-closed. They'd been at sea for three days, or rather, they'd left Sandwich as the horizon tinged grey for the last three days and returned just as the sun set far in the distance.

They'd seen nothing, but the king had divided the thirty-five ships that had massed into three groups, and each day, they'd been led to a different location. Ælfgar was unsure what marks the commanders were using, but he was content to know that they were familiar with the waters. They knew what they were doing, and he was in safe hands allowing Eowa to order the shipmen.

Today, it was their flotilla's turn to run further from Sandwich, out into the deep expanse of sea that divided England from the shores of the much larger land-mass, divided into myriad petty kingdoms, where Denmark's shoreline on the far horizon lurked.

None of the flotillas had encountered more than a handful of ships, all busy trading, all keen to hail the commanders and announce themselves as friends, not foes.

The wind blew just enough to fill the sails and guide them onwards so there was no need to row, and there hadn't been since they'd left Sandwich.

The shipmen, more accustomed to such journeys, had busied themselves with games, conversation, songs, and even some midship training, in which Ælfwine had fallen flat on his arse, and Wulfstan had excelled. The two cousins were currently studiously ignoring each other, and Ælfgar felt no compulsion to intervene. They'd sort it out, eventually.

He gazed all around him, relishing the sound of the open sea. Beneath the occasional creek of the ship's wooden strakes, he could hear the water as it crested and dipped, the movement perceptible but not unpleasant. Overhead, a flock of sea birds had followed them, perhaps hoping for some fish entrails. They didn't know that these were crafts for war, not fishing.

Ælfgar felt at peace. Perhaps, after all, he should have become a ship man. Maybe he'd have enjoyed life at sea rather than as a member of the king's court. Perhaps.

'Ship ahead,' Eowa's voice cut through his musings, and Ælfgar peered across the vast expanse of rolling waves, keen to pick out the craft as it came into sight. Eowa's vision was excellent, and it took longer for Ælfgar to focus on what he'd seen.

Only, it wasn't a single ship.

'Ships,' Ælfgar called to Eowa, standing to walk towards the other man where he stared out from his position at the steerboard.

'Aye, ships, about twenty of them, I'd say.' The words were spoken with a hint of trepidation.

'Do you recognise the sails?' Ælfgar demanded to know.

'Maybe. I don't know.'

Eowa had been leading the fleet, it being his turn to direct the other crafts towards their intended target. As Ælfgar turned to check that they were all still in one group, he realised that all had sighted the other ships.

The ship closest to them was busy sliding oars into the water, and they weren't alone.

'Get back to your bench,' Eowa instructed, jutting his chin towards the vacant bench before turning to holler at the rest of the crew.

'Oars, and now. Be prepared for what might happen. Have weapons to hand.'

Ælfgar rushed back to his rowing bench and grabbed the waiting oar, held aloft from the water by an innovative lever in the oar port. His hands, not used to the movement, were already rubbed raw from the activity, but that wasn't what worried him. Now, it was the maroon sails of the ships they'd spied and which had changed direction to meet them.

Eowa snapped his instructions, and the ship lurched to the left, the oar vibrating painfully against Ælfgar's hand as the water battered it from a different angle. He risked looking where they were going, the sails of the other ships much easier to see.

While the king's fleet all had the same sails, emblazoned with the House of Wessex's wyvern emblem, the ships that the earls owned and crewed, the bishops and archbishops as well, all had individual sails. It meant the fleet looked disjointed from a distance, making it easier to determine who was on board which craft. But these vessels all showed the same emblem: a black raven on a bleached-white background. Ælfgar feared they'd found King Magnus' shipmen.

Abruptly, all joy in the expedition faded, and Ælfgar decided the sea was suddenly dark and foreboding rather than looking peaceful and inviting. Even the sea birds' cries were edged with sharp fury, promising they'd be there to pick at the eyes of the dead and dying, should it come to that.

He swallowed down his flicker of unease, refusing to consider what might befall him here. He didn't miss that they were outnumbered and more, that at least half of the ships were not crewed by the king's shipmen, or that amongst their number was Lord Sweyn.

The easily recognisable twang of a bow roused Ælfgar from his thoughts. His head whipped from side to side, searching for an arrow. Only the soft shushing noise and the small disturbance on the surface of the sea showed him where the arrow had gone, disappearing beneath the menacing water.

With growing dread, he followed the trajectory he believed the arrow had taken, and his eyes rested on the steady eyes of a warrior, bow in hand, gazing out at the king's ship army from the prow of one of the enemy ships.

His arms, bare to the shoulders, were covered in the inkings that the Norsemen took so much pride in, and Ælfgar understood, without doubt, that these were Magnus' shipmen.

'Shields,' Ælfgar hardly needed the instruction from Eowa, as he fumbled for the discarded weapon and slid it into place along the shelf that ran along the ship's edge. The manoeuvre was well-practised, and the action was quickly completed. But, it left Ælfgar unable to see as much as he'd have liked. Instead, he had to rely on Eowa's directions from his place beside the steerboard, and they were quick and fast in coming.

'Arrows,' Eowa yelled, and four men took to the centre of the ship, bows in hand, and the sound of more missiles flying through the air, whispered loudly. There were so many arrows that Ælfgar had to assume the other ships in the king's fleet were mirroring Eowa's actions.

He braced for an impact, for the sound of the enemy trying to board them, but it didn't come. Instead, there was the tell-tale sound of arrows hitting their shields, his quivering so much that he was sure he'd had a lucky escape.

The enemy were expert marksmen.

Eowa instructed them to row faster, and Ælfgar realised that Eowa was keen to engage the enemy, not run before them. With his hands busy on the oars, Ælfgar could not check that he had his weapons close to hand and had to console himself that they'd been there earlier. There was no need for them to have moved. If it came to man-to-man combat, he was well-prepared. He trusted his skills, even if they'd not been employed on many occasions.

He spared a thought for Elgiva, his four children and only then considered his father. Whatever happened here, he must stay alive. His father needed him to stand against the might of Earl Godwine and Sweyn.

'What's he doing?' the aggrieved call reached Ælfgar as sweat beaded his brow, the action of rowing grounded him to the battle, as opposed to the fear of a watery death.

Ælfgar groaned. He was sure that Eowa spoke of Earl Sweyn.

Despite his mistakes to date, he'd still not relinquished the control of his craft to the commander of his men. Instead, Sweyn had continued to cause problems, at one point, even forcing his men to row in a tight circle rather than admit he'd given an incorrect instruction and made a mistake with the steerboard. Ælfgar understood that even his shipmen had been laughing at the earl. He wasn't surprised.

Ælfgar risked rising slightly from his bench, ensuring he could still row, to angle a view over the rim of the shields, and his breath left his body.

Sweyn, rather than staying with the fleet, had directed his men toward the lead enemy vessel at speed, every oar sliding in and out of the waves with impeccable timing. The earl was determined to make a name for himself by ramming the enemy ship and earning glory in battle.

'Back in your seat,' Eowa yelled, and Ælfgar thudded down, his back straining, his arms aching, as the ship finally completed the manoeuvre and Eowa ordered them to row forwards. He was going after Sweyn.

Ælfgar ventured a glance behind to see what the other vessels were doing and appreciated that every craft seemed frozen in time. Eowa was by far the quickest to react.

As they came closer and closer to Sweyn, the sea swell seemed to work to drive the ship back, not forwards. Ælfgar struggled to hear. The cries of Sweyn's crew and Magnus' men filled the air, akin to a roar of thunder.

Ælfgar felt sweat dripping down his face, but Eowa wasn't about to call a stop until they were in place and could assist Sweyn's ship.

Once more, the shush of arrows filled the air, and Ælfgar ducked, even though he couldn't see the missiles. A resounding thud close by assured him he was right to do so. The high-pitched scream of one of the shipmen filled the air, and Ælfgar closed his eyes and offered a swift prayer that the wound wouldn't be fatal but only excruciating.

When Ælfgar opened his eyes, the black raven on the front enemy ship seemed to be leering down at him as the sound of timbers scrapping over timber permeated the air. The shriek of buck-ling wood set his teeth on edge. He gritted them together, all the time rowing, following Eowa's howled instructions.

And then the sound he didn't wish to hear percolated his consciousness; the tell-tale sound of men in the water, slapping it with their flailing arms, calling for aid. What struck Ælfgar was that the voices were all speaking English.

16

ÆLFGAR

'Bring it round, round,' Eowa was screaming at his men, not with fury, but with surety. His eyes were focused on the disaster unfurling before them, and Ælfgar realised that all the shipmen had their eyes trained on Eowa. They trusted him. Implicitly.

The older man's neck was tense, veins showing against the white of his flesh as he hauled on the rudder, directing the ship to where he wanted to go. Only now did Ælfgar hear the shouts of men in the other vessels in Edward's fleet. He also caught sight of sails. It seemed they weren't the only craft coming to the aid of Sweyn and his craft, but they were still the closest.

Ælfgar tried to row, but the oar suddenly felt weighed down, and he worried that it might be wrapped around a piece of debris from the floundering craft.

A cold, clammy hand slapped the side of the ship closest to Ælfgar, and he grasped that his oar was being used by one of the drowning men.

'Help me,' the words were garbled, filled with water.

Without considering whether he should, Ælfgar released the grip on his oar, allowing it to drop into the water. The sinking man cried out in fear. Ælfgar stood, towering over the shield that ran along the length of the craft, quickly moving it to one side with one hand as he reached down to offer his help to the man below.

Panicked eyes looked his way, flashing the brightest blue Ælfgar had ever seen. The man's fierce grip almost tumbled Ælfgar into the crashing waves, but he steadied himself, offering both hands.

He heaved, and the man scrambled with his legs, trying to find purchase for his feet against the strakes of the ship. The man weighed three times more than usual, perhaps even four, and his arms shook with the exertion. But then, with a mighty effort, they both tumbled into the stinking bilge water. Ælfgar concentrated on breathing, as he looked upwards, gazing at those same birds overhead, their cries raucous.

'Get back to it,' Eowa's voice boomed, and he scrambled to his feet. He reached for the shield, only before he could insert it back into place to counter the continuing threat of the arrows, which still fell sporadically, he caught sight of the scene before him.

The water boiled with fury. Three of Magnus' ships surrounded the ruins of Sweyn's craft, and yet, Sweyn and his men, on board those parts that still floated, fought with any weapon they could find, oblivious to the broken ruin of the ship they were still within.

At least two-thirds of the shipmen had been up-ended into the water, and some of them tried to swim while others clung to anything they could find. All the time, Magnus' shipmen jabbed down, some hanging so low over the sides of their crafts they were almost in the water themselves.

'Arrows,' Ælfgar bellowed, hoping the men would heed his instruction. He pointed to where the English shipmen were most at risk and was rewarded with the whistle of arrows flying through the air. No ship carried many arrows, but they were invaluable if caught in a sea battle like this one.

'This way,' Ælfgar reached down, thumping the head of someone in the water just in danger of being sucked beneath the ship. Frightened eyes looked up.

'English,' he expelled, trying to explain he was an ally.

Comprehension was quickly followed by yet more cold hands reaching for Ælfgar. This time, he was prepared for the extra weight of sopping clothes. He braced his feet against the ship's side, heaving with all his might.

'Help them,' Eowa had seen what Ælfgar was doing, and now he called more of his men to join in what was becoming a rescue operation.

Ælfgar didn't dare look to see what was happening with the other English ships. He could only hope they weren't pulling men into the dubious safety of their craft just to have them attacked by another of Magnus' vessels.

With another drenched man onboard, shivering and shaking next to the first man, Ælfgar turned again to the scene before him.

Sweyn, red-faced and half-sodden by the sea, seemed oblivious to the stricken nature of his ship. His focus, and that of the shipmen who stood with him, even as the water flooded into the shattered remnants of their vessel, only on killing Magnus' ship-men who attacked them.

'He'll die,' Wulfstan spoke into Ælfgar's ear, the sound only just audible above the crashing and screeching of the battle as they worked together to rescue the stranded. Ælfgar had never appreciated the awful sound wood made in distress.

'He will if he doesn't retreat,' Ælfgar huffed. Another floating body swirled in the churned water, and Ælfgar reached down to get the man's attention. But there was no response as he struck the man's head.

'Help me,' he instructed Wulfstan, and together they reached over the side of the ship, trying to find the means to haul the man inside the boat.

Not that they were alone, not now. More and more of the rescued shipmen had climbed to their feet and tried to retrieve their stricken comrades even as they juddered with cold. Ælfgar was aware that Eowa had abandoned his attempt to attack the vessels loyal to Magnus in favour of helping the wrecked English shipmen.

There were more than enough ships for others to oppose the attack. Bad enough to lose a battle, so much worse to return to England with many of the shipmen missing and presumed dead in the impromptu strike.

Ælfgar was sure that this hadn't been Edward's intention in calling the ship army together. It had been envisioned as a show of strength, he was sure of it, not an exercise in revealing their weaknesses and lack of skill. Well, for some of them.

He couldn't understand why Sweyn had acted so irrationally. Well, he could, but he didn't want to believe it was possible.

It was chaotic, and Ælfgar couldn't keep his gaze from flicking, time and time again, to where Sweyn battled against the enemy shipmen.

Three ships had almost encircled the floundering craft. Yet Sweyn fought on, as did those at his side who remained. Sweyn's face dripped a strange shade of pink, a cut somewhere beneath his hair merging with the saltwater. Ælfgar appreciated that it would sting like a bastard. And, Ælfgar could grasp that Sweyn wasn't without ability. Even now, it seemed possible that he'd board the first craft he'd engaged in the attack as he tugged on his foe and pulled him into the roiling water below them.

'Watch what you're doing,' Wulfstan's angry words forced Ælfgar to concentrate on what was happening nearer to hand. One of the retrieved shipmen, face almost blue with cold, had grabbed Wulfstan's seax, and thrust it against one of the other shaking men. The other man didn't seem to notice until the last possible moment, and then he swung his hands upwards, and luckily the seax blade slide into the gap between his hands.

'What's going on?' Ælfgar waded through the bilge water, his feet so cold he couldn't feel them, determined to force the men aside.

'He's one of the bloody enemies. Kill him,' Ælfgar's gaze was drawn to the cowering man. He noted then that he wore a single arm ring of silver, high up, almost on his shoulder, and that he had a bloody gash running down his side, visible because the water beneath him was a dirty red.

'Leave him,' Ælfgar roared, even as the ship lurched precariously from side to side.

'Spread out, you damn fools,' Eowa bellowed above the cries of his shipmen and the battle that raged beside them. Ælfgar saw the danger immediately, even as he reached for the seax in the man's hand. Too many of them were on the far side of the ship, and it threatened to tip.

'This side,' he raised his voice to join Eowa's. 'Split yourself, come to this side, but not all of you.' Eowa had already turned aside, eyes focused on cleaving a path through the floating debris so that they could scoop up as many of the sea-tossed as possible.

'He's one of the enemies,' the man all but whined as Ælfgar grabbed his right hand and wrestled the seax from it so that it tumbled into the bilge water. It was far easier than he might have thought, but they were all cold and wet.

'He's our prisoner,' Ælfgar huffed into the other man's face, noting his wide-eyes, pain-hazed expression and how his left hand was clamped to his chest.

'Show me,' he demanded. 'Show me your wound.' While he shook his head, Ælfgar was aware of Wulfstan bending to speak with the enemy prisoner. He could hear their voices rumbling as the man he talked to peeled up his saturated tunic and revealed a deep cut, blood oozing slowly.

'It's stopping,' Ælfgar confirmed, bending to rip the lower half of his tunic free so that he could bind the wound. 'Here, we need to tie this tightly. And you need to keep still. It'll need stitches when we get back to Sandwich.'

But the man didn't hear him, still gnashing his teeth at the enemy.

'What's your name?' Ælfgar demanded, trying to get the man to focus on him and not the enemy amongst them. Belatedly, Ælfgar was aware that battle cries were starting to falter, but he didn't risk looking. Not yet.

'Brihtric, my lord.' Brihtric had come to his senses enough to realise who was helping him.

'Well, Brihtric, you're lucky to be alive, and I'm going to make sure you remain that way, but leave our enemy alone. He'll be invaluable if we can get him back to England. The king needs to know what King Magnus has planned. This will be the way we find out.'

With a none-too-gentle yank on the linen from his tunic he was tying in place, Ælfgar satisfied himself that he'd done all that could be done for the time being.

'Now, can I trust you to watch our enemy and make sure no one kills him while I go back and help others.'

'Yes, my lord. Yes, you can.' Brihtric vigorously nodded as he spoke, and Ælfgar hoped he spoke the truth but didn't have the time to be sure. Others required rescuing and one of them was now Earl Sweyn.

Three of the English ships had managed to manoeuvre into such a position that they could attack the opponents from the other side of the triangle they'd made around Sweyn's floundering craft, but it could be too late.

Even as Ælfgar watched, the men supporting Sweyn were forced to turn aside as the pieces of the wrecked ship they'd been standing on succumbed to the pull of the ocean's ravages. They had no choice but to discard swords and war axes to the depths or risk sinking with them. Ælfgar hardly dared look because it left only Sweyn as the others attempted to swim clear. The enemy, well, those not countering the threat from the other English ships, were all focused on Sweyn.

The only advantage for Sweyn was that there was so little of his craft remaining to stand on that none of his foes dared risk leaving the relative safety of their ship. It meant that only one, at most two, of them could even attempt to land a blow on him.

Ælfgar watched in shock as Sweyn, unaware of what was

happening around him, fought against the enemy. He held a war axe in one hand, and in the other, a seax which he used to stab upwards even while the war axe came down. It was the most ineffective technique that Ælfgar had ever seen, and he was sure that if it weren't for the rising and falling of the water below Sweyn, not one of the blows would have landed on the enemy.

But, the swell was helping Sweyn, and the sound of the axe striking the side of the ship clanged loudly, even though so much else was happening simultaneously.

'He'll not last long,' Ælfwine was the voice of reason, and Ælfgar agreed.

'We need to get him to come here before it's too late and he drowns. I don't want to tell his damn father that.'

'But how?' And that was the problem. There was a small gap between the triangle of ships, but it was only enough to catch sight of Sweyn occasionally and through which the other men had swum for survival. Those shipmen who'd been forced to abandon their lord had made their way to one of the waiting English ships because there were now four of them beside Eowa's, but it was inevitable that Sweyn would be lost to sight as Magnus' men shouted one to another.

All was in disarray, and Sweyn couldn't be rescued. Yet, behind the enemy ships trying to attack Sweyn and the English ships trying to attack the enemy, Ælfgar could see that the rest of the crafts weren't engaging. If anything, they were preparing to escape.

Ælfgar chanced to glance along the ship's length, at the Mercians keeping the vessel steady with their oars, at the men rescued from the icy grasp of the sea, at Wulfstan as he worked to provide what dry coverings he could for the shivering men. Only then his eyes met Eowa's, and he knew the commander was thinking the same as him.

They shared a look that said more than could ever be communicated with words. Was it worth the risk? Could they put so many people in danger? Would the ship even withstand what was to come? Ælfgar swallowed heavily, the mantle of responsibility settling heavily on him. But really, there was no choice, and there had never been.

'Oars,' Eowa's bellowed word was echoed by Ælfgar as he scrambled to retake his seat, wedge the shield back in place, and work to free the arrow caught in the cloth of the weapon. He tossed it into the belly of the craft, knowing such should never be discarded, focusing only on what had to be done.

He was drenched from the seawater, the feel of clammy hands working their way along his arms and exposed belly, teeth gritted, wondering why the fuck he had to be the one to make good on Sweyn's failings.

'Stop,' Eowa's sharp word was immediately obeyed, the shriek of timbers echoing through the air, the craft shuddering even more than the half-drowned men. Once more, Ælfgar swallowed down his apprehension.

'Stow the oars,' Eowa roared. Ælfgar reached to grip the golden-hued wood and pull it towards him, even as the bow of one of the enemy ships reared up before him. It would be close, but just in time, the oar was entirely on board, and they glided beyond the enemy. A squeak of surprise from the ship man at the rear of the foe ship assured Ælfgar that their actions had caught them all by surprise.

He saw the Mercians doing the same, their opponents oblivious to what they were doing to the far side.

'Grab him,' Eowa commanded with a shouted bark. Ælfgar leapt to his feet, hands reaching for Sweyn. If they didn't get him if the ship was just too far away, it would be too late, and Sweyn would die, or worse, be taken captive by King Magnus' men.

Ælfwine was at his side, both of them looking for Sweyn in the claustrophobic space of too many ships. Ælfgar leapt forward, knocking the shield aside, and his hands closed on Sweyn's left arm as he flailed at one of the enemies with the axe.

'Get in,' Ælfgar roared, even as Sweyn's body convulsed in shock. With a flick of a blade, Ælfgar had to relinquish his grip or risk being sliced by Sweyn, who believed they were the enemy.

'Get in,' Ælfgar tried again, but Sweyn was too caught up in fighting for survival.

As quickly as he could, Ælfgar laid hold of Sweyn again, this time on the right side of his body, and still, Sweyn bucked beneath him, fighting even though all appeared lost.

'English,' Ælfwine called from beside Ælfgar. 'We're the English, you bloody fool,' and something in Ælfwine's frustrated tone caused Sweyn to cease his attack.

Shocked eyes glanced at Ælfgar from a face that was more fluid than solid, and then Sweyn dropped his weapons. He jumped across the divide, arms outstretched for them to clasp, keen to be inside the ship, even as his two thwarted opponents roared their rage.

'Arrows,' Ælfgar instructed, losing his balance. His cry was rewarded with the sound of two arrows, one after another, thudding into flesh or wood. He didn't look to see because he was once more in the bilge water, Sweyn on top of him, and it was all Ælfgar could do to breathe.

'Get off,' he beat against the other man as the ship veered dangerously to one side, and he got nothing for his efforts but a mouthful of filthy, salty water.

The sound of timbers on timbers shrieked, and Ælfgar appreciated that they'd cleaved a path through the enemy ships. Now all they needed to do was turn towards home. Only, if Sweyn didn't get off him, he'd be long dead by then.

Frustrated and struggling for breath, Ælfgar kicked out with both of his feet, attempting to bend his right knee so he could lever the other man from him. But it didn't work.

Next, he worked his hands between his chest and Sweyn's back and thrust, but the other man's dead weight still didn't budge.

Ælfgar was desperate now.

'Move,' he screamed. 'Get off me,' but then all his air was gone, and he couldn't force more into his mouth because he was choking on water that tasted of too much filth. Ælfgar realised this was it. He couldn't work his chest enough to cough the fluid clear, and he knew he was drowning even though he wasn't in the sea.

And then Sweyn was shoved aside, and Wulfstan grinned down at him, his damp hair stuck to his face.

'Come on, let's get you up.' Behind him, Ælfwine thumped on his chest, and Ælfgar could finally snatch a full breath of air. His hair dripped into his eyes, and he shook, only then realising that he had weeping wounds along his left arm, no doubt from where Sweyn had cut him when he'd thought him an enemy.

'Damn fool,' he mumbled, but Sweyn still hadn't stirred, and he moved to his knees, reaching for the other man.

Roughly, Ælfgar turned Sweyn to him, noticing the dullness of his face and his skin's blueness. Yet, he also saw a flicker on his chest and understood he was breathing, even though he was chilled almost to death.

'Help me,' but Wulfstan had already realised the problem. Together, they dragged the prone body to the rest of the rescued men, well, those who were too exhausted to assist with the oars, which had once more been dipped into the sea.

'Make room for him; keep him warm.' Sweyn was wedged between two men who shared a rough blanket. Neither looked impressed by the imposition until they realised who it was. A flicker of fury touched the first man's face.

'Bastard,' he exclaimed, although he stretched out his arm to ensure Sweyn was fully covered. 'He nearly got us all killed.'

The other man nodded but was too cold to do more, his teeth chattering loudly. He grimaced as he tried to keep them closed.

'Keep him as warm as you can,' Ælfgar ordered, standing to get his bearings.

In the intervening time, Eowa had found the wind, and while the oars were once more poised for action, the hastily released sail dragged them from the sight of the unexpected attack as it filled with a gentle swell.

Ælfgar watched as the three English ships turned to follow, one of the enemy ships floundering low in the water. Ælfgar could see the rest of the foe-ships, running with the wind, away from England in the far distance. He sighed with relief. It was over, but in his heart, he knew it should never have begun.

What would the king say when they returned to Sandwich?

And what of Earl Sweyn? As he eyed the son of Godwine, he couldn't help but consider why he'd risked his men and his life to rescue a man who caused them nothing but problems.

17
LEOFRIC

HE'D BEEN SUMMONED TO THE QUAYSIDE AS SOON AS THE FIRST SHIP HAD returned with incomplete tales of what had happened.

Since then, he'd stood, barely hoping that his son and nephews would return to him. Why had he not gone himself? It would have made more sense. He was an old man, his life nearly over anyway. Far better that he'd found a watery grave than his son and nephews.

The king had returned from his expedition while he waited, his keen eyes taking in the sight of the vessels with their missing oars or broken shields. Some men were being led limping from the ships, nursing deep cuts on arms and faces. Holding more wisdom than Leofric believed possible, the king held his tongue, alert to the problem without asking.

Not so Lord Godwine. The corpulent man stood, Harold at his side, muttering to himself, his chest puffed out, his body swathed in a huge cloak for all there was a warm breeze.

'We must go after them,' Godwine had begged the king more than once, yet Edward hadn't responded. Not once. There was no point. The darkness of a night without a moon slowly closed around them. While braziers and lanterns had been lit all along the quayside, a beacon to encourage the straggling ships to return to Sandwich, everyone knew they couldn't risk a night-time excursion into the rapidly rising winds that promised rain from the burgeoning clouds.

The ships would make it home tonight, or they wouldn't. And if they got caught in the storm, it was unlikely that they would. Not with wounded on board and holes in the timbers.

Leofric recalled the farewell he'd flung at his son and nephews that morning, the overriding belief that there was no enemy out there, just waiting to attack. It felt like weeks ago, and Leofric knew he'd aged that day. What would he tell his wife? What would he say to Lady Elgiva? How would he ever face Lady Mildryth?

'Another one,' a keen-eyed youth who seemed to belong to no one but climbed the masts of the ships berthed in the quayside with alarming ease, pointed. Leofric's heart leapt once more. It had been this way with each and every boat that had returned to Sandwich. Yet, not one of them had carried the burnished hue of his father's ship.

Leofric had stopped counting the returning ships, although he knew the king, and one of his clerics kept a close eye. The king only had thirty-five ships, and couldn't afford to lose any of them, not if King Magnus meant to attack England's shores, as now seemed likely.

Fury enveloped Leofric. Why had Harthacnut made such an ill-advised agreement with King Magnus that had allowed him to interpret it so that he believed England was his? Why had Lady Gunnhild compounded the issue by inviting Magnus to take England? And now he feared his son was dead, his nephews as well. Everything he'd worked so hard to achieve would be for nothing. Bad enough to rely on one son to follow him as earl of Mercia, but he might only have three grandsons now, and none of them would be capable of ruling for at least fifteen years.

He might be dead by then, the family of Godwine in the ascendant. But he didn't care about that. He cared about his son and his nephews. His brother had died for Mercia. His son and nephews might die for England. It was all such a waste.

Only then, Leofric truly looked at the ship, and his heart thudded too loudly in his chest. He was sure that everyone must be able to hear it as Harold's face turned to glance at him.

'Eowa?' He found his voice, took a deep breath and bellowed the name as loudly as he could. Yet, it didn't seem to reach the ship. For a moment, he faltered. Was he wrong? Was he seeing his father's boat or not?

'Eowa?' Leofric lifted his voice once more when the wind dipped, pleased when Olaf's voice joined his. Surely it had to be? None of the other ships looked like that. Even in the creeping darkness, she was unmistakable.

'Aye, my lord. I'll be right with you,' Leofric almost collapsed with relief when Eowa's distinctive voice carried across the water.

'Father?' his son, sounding like a small boy and not the lord he'd become, also called to him. Now Leofric did sag, Olaf beside him doing all he could to keep him upright so the king wouldn't note his weakness.

'I'm here,' Leofric called, only for Godwine to interrupt.

'Where's Earl Sweyn? Where's my son?' Godwine had no problem raising his voice to be heard above the wounded's groans and the gusting wind.

Leofric glared at the earl but then relented. It seemed that Lord Godwine would have to wait, for the Mercian ship came alone. Leofric winced to see the scars that had ravaged the sleek vessel, the missing varnish, the broken oars which dipped in and out of the water but with much of the paddles missing. What had happened to them out there?

Now Ælfgar stood, shadowed by the flames on land, and called to those on the shoreline.

'We have Earl Sweyn and other men who require assistance. They're too cold and need to be inside, out of the wind and the rain as soon as possible.'

Leofric peeked at Godwine to see how he absorbed the news that his son survived, but there was only fury on his face.

'Where is his ship? Where are his men?'

'Come, Lord Godwine. Let's see to the men's health first,' Leofric retorted. Already orders were running up and down the landward side, requests for blankets, cloaks and furs, even as a clap of thunder overhead heralded the first raindrops from the menacing clouds.

And then the ship bounced against the quayside, a space cleared for it to dock directly next to the wooden beams. Leofric watched as a flaming brand was passed across. He grimaced at the scene that greeted him. There were too many wounded, the bilge water reflecting a stained pink, but what concerned him more were the bleached faces of the shipmen. Even those from the southern climes had white lips. The ship might be back, but some men might not survive.

Ælfgar and Eowa tried to organise the ship; Ælfgar taking responsibility for those who needed assistance to stand and disembark; Eowa ensuring the craft was safely brought to land. But all the time, Lord Godwine was trying to clamber inside the ship, his baulk surprising him as it prevented his actions.

'Stand aside, Lord Godwine,' King Edward's words snapped out into the lull between the thunder and the thud of heavy rain falling to bounce off the woodwork. 'Stand aside and let them disembark,' yet Lord Godwine was deaf to the request.

Leofric watched as Ælfgar made a snap decision and handed the man he was helping over to the waiting shore people before returning to grab Sweyn.

Leofric shuddered at the sight of his marbled flesh, he looked no better than a day-old corpse, but at least Lord Godwine ceased his struggles. Ælfgar and Ælfwine manoeuvred Sweyn into Godwine's waiting embrace, only for Sweyn to slide to the floor as Godwine failed to grasp how lifeless he was. Harold was more alert, and quickly, he grabbed hold of his brother and just about stopped him from falling back into the cold water, with no thanks for his father's assistance.

'Make way,' Lord Godwine called imperiously, but the king had seen enough.

'Earl Godwine stop making a scene. You're getting in the way of those providing assistance. Move aside immediately, and let others help your son.'

Leofric stepped forward, swirling his cloak from his shoulders and wrapping it around the shoulders of the next shaking ship man. He had a nasty-looking cut above his left eye, and a blackened eye was the only colour on his face.

'Here, take this,' Leofric ordered, turning to escort the man inside. The smell of rank seawater infused his nostrils, even as he pulled one of the man's arms around his shoulder, but he didn't let it stop him from assisting the injured man.

He'd seen what he needed to see. His son and nephews lived, and he wasn't about to make a scene as Lord Godwine was doing.

'TELL ME WHAT HAPPENED?' IT WAS THE KING WHO SPOKE TO ÆLFGAR where he huddled close to the hearth. Colour infused his lips again, and he could talk without shaking. Wulfstan and Ælfwine had found spots to sleep and now snored softly, their rumbles a counterpart to the fervent activity around them. They were oblivious, even when one of the hall's hounds nosed her way between them.

The king had only heard snatches of what had befallen his men until now, and most of that had been from Lord Godwine, keen to declare the expedition a success, even though they'd lost a ship, and everything eluded to the contrary.

Ælfgar rubbed his eyes with one hand, and Leofric noticed the white skin, almost ready to slough from his hands. He'd been in the water for too long. It would take time to dry off and return to its normal texture.

'We encountered a fleet of Magnus' ships—about twenty of

them. Earl Sweyn was keen to engage and promptly did so alone. I can't tell you what would have happened if he hadn't done so. Most enemy ships quickly turned tail and fled, a few remained to fight.' Ælfgar hesitated now, his gaze seeking out someone amongst the flood of sleeping bodies and those who remained awake.

Leofric imagined he looked for Earl Sweyn, Godwine, or his brothers, but content that they were all out of earshot, Ælfgar continued his story.

Leofric listened with disbelief, unsurprised by the king's hisses of anger. Who knew what damage Sweyn might have done. When the ships returned to King Magnus, they would undoubtedly tell him that the English shipmen were ill-prepared. Rather than a show of strength from the English, Sweyn might have achieved the exact opposite.

As Ælfgar finished his account, the king stood abruptly.

'Sleep, my lord. You have my thanks for what you've accomplished today and for bringing me a prisoner, but Earl Leofric, I would speak with you further.'

A look of panic entered Ælfgar's tired eyes for a moment, but Leofric shook his head, reaching out to grip his shoulder.

'Sleep, you've exceeded all expectations, and I'm overjoyed you're safe.'

Ælfgar nodded, although he looked far from convinced.

Following the king, Leofric found himself outside once more. The night was black, lit only by the few remaining braziers and flaming brands. The wind had died away, but the thud of heavy rain echoed all around.

Leofric couldn't see enough of the king to determine his thoughts. He couldn't imagine he was pleased by the events of the day.

'Earl Leofric,' and the king paused before he said more. 'I don't blame you for Lady Gunnhild's actions. Neither do I blame your son for the shit-storm that happened today. It's unfortunate that you and your son never seem far from the troubles that affect my reign.'

Leofric clamped his mouth shut, refusing to make a knee-jerk response that might only cause more long-term problems. He wouldn't be petulant and deny everything.

'But, I can't shy away from giving you an unpleasant task, but it must be done, even if I'd rather not.'

'You want me to bring Lady Gunnhild and her sons to you?' Leofric would much sooner that Earl Sweyn had been given the undertaking, but of course, he would be far too rough with the family. Leofric knew Lady Gunnhild. She'd come with him, and the king knew that.

'Yes, I do, and as soon as possible. I'd also ask you to adopt Earl Godwine's interpretation of today's battle, your son and nephews, as well. I can't have it known that we might only have made it worse, not better.'

'So, you mean to allow Earl Sweyn his moment of glory, even though he lost his ship, and nearly killed half of his shipmen?' Despite the darkness, Leofric saw the king's expression at his words, the flash of white teeth as his lips closed over them, the tension in his shoulders.

'I do, yes. It'll be for the best. For the greater good.' But Leofric was shaking his head.

'I doubt that, my lord king. But, I've always served my kings with loyalty and never refused to carry out a direct order. However, I believe you should think long and hard about this.'

'I have, my lord,' and Leofric realised he'd managed to displease the king with just those few words.

'Then, I hope you know what you're doing,' and Leofric stalked from the king's side and back inside the hall. He was furious and also resigned. He was failing in the oath Harthacnut had forced on him, and felt bitter. It was impossible to deny.

18

ÆLFGAR

'Lord Ælfgar.' He turned, surprised to be hailed by Lord Harold. It was two days after the failed attack against Magnus' shipmen. Ælfgar was still trying to reconcile himself to the king's wishes that it be portrayed as a victory when at most, it had been an impasse.

'Lord Harold,' Ælfgar dredged a smile to his tight lips and slowed his steps to allow the other man to catch up to him on the quayside.

Eowa had already completed the repairs on the ship, and Ælfgar was preparing to return to it the following day. The king hadn't allowed the attack to dissuade him. Instead, he was using it as an excuse to extend the sailing season. While the shipmen involved in the attack had been permitted to excuse themselves for the last two days, those with a ship to sail in were expected to join the expeditions.

Ælfgar waited for Harold to speak, but he didn't, although his steps fell into the same rhythm. Together they strode along the quayside, hailed by those who owed them their oath. Yet, Harold remained quiet, and Ælfgar kept his gaze on the ships and the expanse of sea which glowered below a faint sun, shrouded by clouds.

The days since their return to Sandwich had been fair, perfect for sailing, but a storm threatened now. Ælfgar felt his lips turn downcast.

There had been no new sighting of the enemy, but the king was determined to continue with his vigilance.

'I suppose I should thank you,' Lord Harold's voice startled Ælfgar from his thoughts.

'There's no need to thank me,' Ælfgar started, ready to say more, but Harold, now he'd begun to speak, seemed determined not to be dissuaded.

'I only said that I suppose I should thank you. I'm not going to do so.' His words cracked with fury. 'Have you not considered how much easier our lives might have been had Sweyn not survived? He's a menace. I don't understand why my father extols his virtues so highly. I can't comprehend why the king advanced him. I know you think it was to reward my father for his loyalty, but I think it was for the opposite. The king wants my brother to do nothing but embarrass my family, and he's done so once again. I know it, and so does everyone here. My brother could have died a hero, but now he can live and continue his wave of destruction.'

Ælfgar felt his mouth open in shock, and it was an effort not to turn to the other man, consternation showing on his face.

'You might think me a heartless man, a callous individual, but I know that Sweyn will do nothing but cause problems in the future. King Edward knows it as well. He's only going along with it because it serves his ultimate purpose. The king wants the English to fear the menace of King Magnus. He might have had less experience ruling than you or even I, but he knows there's nothing like a common menace to unite the people behind him. Clever sod.'

'And so, you'd have preferred your brother to die?'

'I'd have preferred him not to be rescued,' Harold hissed. Ælfgar knew there was no difference in the sentiment, yet he held his tongue all the same.

He didn't want to admit that the thought of abandoning Sweyn hadn't even occurred to him. Perhaps he'd been foolish to risk the ship and Eowa to rescue the stranded man, but he didn't think he could have done anything differently. No matter his thoughts and wants.

An uncomfortable silence fell between them. Ælfgar hazarded a glance at the other man from the corner of his eye. Harold's chest was heaving, and Ælfgar didn't know if it was from fury or relief at giving voice to his darkest thoughts.

'I know my sister thinks the same. I'm unsure about Tostig. Although younger, he's as wild as Sweyn, so I'll allow that he might yet change. I can't say the same for Sweyn. I can assure you that it would have been better for everyone had Sweyn died.'

'I think you've probably said enough,' Ælfgar announced. He didn't know what else to say. Certainly, he didn't want to learn more about the rivalries between Godwine's sons, even if it might aid him.

'I'm sure I have, but I thought you, at least, would understand.'

'I would never countenance the wilful death of a brother. I've seen what it does to those left behind.' Instantly, the fury left Harold's face, and he heaved in a deep breath.

'You're right, my lord. I apologise. It's too easy to forget, in the heat of the moment, that there are others who've experienced what I desire and found it to be less than pleasant. But, now that my brother is an earl, he's impossible to control. He believes himself capable of ruling all of England, given half a chance.'

'That sort of ambition isn't to be encouraged. We have our king, and no one desires to return to war.'

Now Harold fixed him with a pained expression.

'We do, yes, but that won't stop him. Not at all. Be warned, Lord Ælfgar, you think my brother has acted irresponsibly in Shropshire and London and out at sea, but I can assure you, this is merely the beginning of it all. My father will do nothing to reel him in. He'll let him do whatever he wants. I know, although I shouldn't tell you, that he already entertains ideas of an alliance with Gruffydd Ap

Llewelyn because Gruffydd toys with him and says he'll accept him as England's king as he's Cnut's son.'

Just mentioning the Welsh king's name caused Ælfgar to splutter with anger. One day, Ælfgar would take his revenge against him for his uncle's murder, and that day couldn't come soon enough.

'I thank you for the warning, and I'll be mindful of it. And you must heed my warning as well. If the king already suspects a rift in your family, and he means to cause more ructions, you must show a more united front. If, and I don't know if he does or not, the king means to punish your father even more for the death of his brother, Lord Alfred, then he won't stop. It might just be that your brother and the king have met their match.'

Harold growled.

'I don't care what the king means to do. My father has more ambition than skill, and Sweyn, well, Sweyn believes himself the son of Cnut and that he should be king. He'll not discard that notion, no matter how much it wounds my mother. Sweyn will do whatever needs to be done to unseat the king. As I said, it would be better had he died, but as he hasn't, we must learn to live with your decision to rescue him.'

With that, Harold walked away, his steps clipped, and Ælfgar watched him go, mouth agape once more.

BEING ON-BOARD THE SHIP AGAIN FELT REASSURING, WHICH SURPRISED Ælfgar. He'd expected to feel some sort of anxiety but didn't. Eowa, as terse as ever, allowed no one to wallow in self-pity, snapping out instructions and sparing no one's feelings when they weren't carried out to his exacting standards.

The king and the remainder of the fleet had been out on patrol the previous two days. There had been so signs of the enemy. Ælfgar wasn't about to be quite as buoyed by that news as others.

There had only been twenty ships. For a sea country such as Norway, Ælfgar was sure the fleet must be bigger. How else would

Magnus have taken control of Denmark with only twenty ships? Not that he was inviting another altercation, far from it, but he wouldn't be surprised if they did encounter more of Magnus' fleet. Either that, or he'd have to question whether they were King Magnus' men or just a flotilla of craft travelling together for safety. Only the fact that they all shared the same sail gave Ælfgar pause.

Maybe it was just that King Magnus was arrogant enough to believe England could be conquered with such a small force, but Ælfgar doubted that. Harthacnut had brought eighty-five ships with him, and he'd had a far greater chance of being accepted as England's king than Magnus.

No, Ælfgar was sure that if Magnus were going to make the attempt, he'd lead the force. As young as Magnus was, his arrogance was immense. He believed in his right to rule Norway and Denmark, and the same surety drove his ambitions toward England.

Overhead, clouds floated lazily by, a gentle breeze making it necessary to row, and Ælfgar welcomed the physical exertion as sweat began to bead his face and trickle down his back. It felt good to be alive, and perhaps better, Earl Sweyn hadn't been included in their flotilla. With no craft to command, Sweyn had been grounded, despite his best attempts to find another ship to take him. But there was a feeling that wherever Sweyn went, disaster would follow, and no one wanted to have such an omen on board.

Not that Sweyn had taken the affront well, not at all. The king had been forced to intervene once more, chastising Sweyn with a royal command.

Ælfgar knew a moment of pity for his father, stranded in Sandwich with a cantankerous Godwine and Sweyn, but his father had endured similar before and always survived. He was sure this time would be the same.

Having Sweyn put aside meant that Ælfgar was, to all intents and purposes, the king's representative on this expedition. It thrilled him, even as a sliver of worry wormed its way into his thoughts. Would he react with more skill if they were attacked? He hoped so, but he knew that men and women could panic in unexpected circumstances, and really, would his ships be that unfortunate as to come into contact with the enemy again? He hoped not.

As the day advanced, Ælfgar was sure he'd get his fervent hope. They did meet other ships, but they were solitary, or in groups of no more than three or four. The ship's commanders hailed them, in English or Norse, explaining where they were going. The shush of arrows fleeing through the air wasn't heard even once, and Ælfgar began to relax.

The wind developed enough to allow them to use the sail, and he welcomed the respite. His back ached from the unaccustomed activity, although nearly everyone else appeared unbothered. Well, all apart from Ælfwine. Wulfstan had been left behind on his father's instructions. Leofric had decided he wouldn't risk all of his potential heirs at sea. Ælfgar could understand the logic, although Wulfstan had been furious.

Not that Wulfstan had ranted in front of everyone as Earl Sweyn had done. No, his complaint had been in private, but no less pained for that. Ælfgar was merely pleased his father had chosen his cousin and not him.

'Bloody hell, my arms feel as though they're shaking,' Ælfwine huffed, sitting beside Ælfgar on the rowing bench so they could both peer out along the unending expanse of water.

There was no sign of an enemy, and the shields that usually lined the ship's side hadn't been forced into place. Above their heads, sea birds called one to another, and every so often, Ælfgar heard the plop of a fish leaving the sea, only to fall back into it. It felt altogether more peaceful than being on land. Yet he didn't allow himself to uncoil completely. And neither, he fancied, did Eowa from his position at the steerboard.

His shipmen might be at their leisure, but the leathery-faced man peered into the distance, hand above his eyes. The sea's dark depths were far from inviting, but the sun glinted over the surface, making it appear as little more than a pond.

The other ships were equally at rest, bobbing on the sea's surface, a handful of shipmen tasked with keeping the vessels in a loose arrangement. They were to wait there for some time and only then return to Sandwich before complete darkness fell. Not that there was any great feeling of concern. It would be a full moon that night and provided the sky remained clear, it would be almost as bright as daylight.

'Over there,' Ælfwine spotted the glint of something far off in the distance.

Ælfgar leaned forward, elbows on his knees, keen to see what it was. He was expecting it just to be another solitary trading vessel, no doubt hurrying from Normandy to England or even to Dublin, but quickly, another sail popped into view and then another. He recognised the colours from the previous confrontation.

'Ships,' he called to Eowa, but the other man had already seen them. His warning cry rang to the next ship and could be heard as an echo passed from one craft to another.

'Shields,' Eowa bellowed, and while Ælfwine hurried back to his rowing position, Ælfgar bent and forced his shield into place. A tremor of unease made his hands shake, but he wasn't alone.

'Bastards,' the man sitting behind him complained, although his eyes were keen, and Ælfgar couldn't help but think he was hungering for a fight.

'Hold position,' again the order echoed back and forth between the ships. Ælfgar reached for his oar but only held it loosely, checking that he could quickly return it to the sea from its current position. Not that he wanted to turn tail and run, but until they knew how many were coming this way, it was impossible to know if it would be possible to intimidate them.

One by one, he watched the white sails flash into view, almost as though they appeared from beneath the depths of the sea, and then popped into sight, wobbling slightly from side to side as they steadied themselves.

He counted each vessel that appeared, and he wasn't the only one.

'Thirty-one,' Ælfgar murmured. They weren't only outnumbered; they were outnumbered by two to one.

Eowa peered at Ælfgar, but the other man knew what the king wanted them to do. Ælfgar knew not to interfere.

'Stand firm and ready the bows,' Eowa called to his shipmen. Eyes focused on the approaching ships, Ælfgar tried to see if he recognised any of them, but it was almost impossible to see anything without standing. He wasn't going to risk that. Instead, he breathed deeply, clearing his thoughts, prepared to focus on what seemed inevitable.

The whistle of an arrow overhead had Ælfgar ducking low, wishing for the comfort of a shield over his head rather than beside him, but there was no such thing.

The arrow landed with a resolute thud in the craft's bow, and Ælfgar braced for more, but none came. Instead, he heard a shouted voice.

'Hail,' the accent was impossible to deny.

'We are the king's fleet. Tell me your intentions,' Eowa's voice was resolute.

'How can you be the king's fleet when your king stands before you.' Ælfgar couldn't help himself, he had to stand at that, or rather squat, peering at the man who spoke the words with such a mocking tone.

Ælfgar knew that King Magnus was young but was still surprised to be faced by such a youthful warrior from the fore of the first ship. He was decked out in a sealskin cloak covering most of his body, although silver arm-rings could be seen on both forearms. Behind him, shipmen held weapons, ready to attack when the order came. Ælfgar felt exposed.

His father had shared the details of his meeting with Olaf Haraldsson, Magnus' father, when King Cnut had sent him to organise peace. Now Ælfgar realised that Magnus must look much like his sire, although without the moustache. It seemed he was too immature yet to have grown something quite as magnificent.

'He was a man with deep green eyes, a huge moustache and a slightly too narrow nose,' Leofric had informed both Ælfgar and the king. 'I remember most vividly that he had thin lips and a booming voice. He was much loved by the people he ruled, although others spoke of his avarice, keen only to gain, and who used his Christianity more as a weapon.'

Not that Leofric was the only man to have met Olaf Haraldsson. After all, he'd tried to meddle in England's affairs before, assisting King Æthelred against Cnut. It seemed his son was keen to forget that fact.

Now King Magnus, because Ælfgar was convinced that was who hailed them, rested his leg on the side of the ship, his appearance casual, although he had the sort of body language that spoke of a desire to pounce.

'King Magnus,' Ælfgar stood, abandoning his oar, hoping he sounded confident because he didn't feel it. 'I'm Lord Ælfgar, son of Earl Leofric. I believe my father once met yours.' For a moment, an angry glint entered Magnus' eyes.

'I hardly knew my father, so your father knew him better than I did.'

The two ships were almost nose to nose, although the rest of Magnus' fleet hovered some distance away, as did the English crafts. While Magnus' arrival might imply a battle, he seemed prepared to converse first.

'Where's King Edward?'

Ælfgar wasn't sure how to answer but knew he needed to say something.

'The king of England is with the rest of his fleet.'

'So, this isn't all of it, then?' Magnus spoke scornfully, his accent hardly evident as he conversed in English.

'Far from it, my lord.' Ælfgar didn't call him a 'king.' He didn't want Magnus to get any ideas.

'I hear there was a clash with the rest of my fleet a few days ago.'

'Yes, I was there,' Ælfgar confirmed. It felt strange to have such a conversation, shouted across the narrowing sea expanse separating the two ships. He could tell that Eowa was maintaining the gap. It was just enough that the shipmen from Magnus' ship couldn't board their own, although it was within easy distance of an arrow shot.

Ælfgar felt relieved that the bow men were ready if needed. He was entirely unsure of Magnus' intentions.

'It's unfortunate that your king isn't here. I'd sooner this was done, and England mine.'

'You mean to attack then?' Ælfgar quizzed.

'That must be evident. I have my shipmen with me, my ships as well.'

'Perhaps, and yet we're here, in the middle of the ocean, talking, not fighting.'

Once more, Ælfgar watched the stain of anger on the other man's face, and he considered what Magnus saw when he stared at him. They were separated by no more than half a decade in age, and yet Magnus was spoken of derisively as little more than a boy playing with his father's toys by the English. Ælfgar might not be an earl, as Sweyn was, but he was a man of power and influence, with four children to his name.

'I merely meant to allow you to declare yourselves for me, preserve your lives. I could make use of loyal Englishmen.'

Ælfgar nodded as though considering his words seriously. He had no intention of turning his allegiance. King Edward might not yet be the man England needed to rule her, but he was a consecrated king with a genuine claim as the true heir. What did King Magnus have? Nothing but some garbled agreement made with Harthacnut? What right had Harthacnut had to barter away England's kingship to a stranger?

'We won't be doing that today. King Edward is our king, our rightful king.'

Something like respect flashed over the other man's face, his green eyes seeming to darken as though with delight.

He offered a small incline of his head.

'Return to your king. Tell him that King Magnus is coming to take his inheritance. I could destroy you now, but I want your king to watch his dreams come to nothing. Now, rush back to King Edward and tell him of our conversation.'

But Ælfgar was already shaking his head.

'I don't believe so, not today,' and from behind him, he heard the shush of arrows flying through the air and the sweep of oars through the water. The fleet was coming to engage the enemy.

Ælfgar took delight in the look of shock on Magnus' face, evident before he began barking instructions in his own tongue, the first of which was to retreat to the main body of his ships. But Eowa understood his intent. As quickly as Magnus tried to move away, he kept pace with the other vessel, more and more arrows flying across the closing expanse of sea that separated them.

Ælfgar rushed back into position, gripping his oar and adding it to the exertions of the rest of the shipmen. Magnus had quite a reputation. Ælfgar sensed his self-belief, but that wouldn't be enough, not against the English fleet. Even as outnumbered as they were, Ælfgar trusted the ships of the king's fleet. They'd trained for this, for years, if not decades, and Ælfgar was happy to consent to the commands of the other crafts, as almost as one they moved into position.

He kept his hands loose on the oar, even as he kept time as dictated by Eowa. He could not see much beyond the back of the man before him. The shipmen had been trained under King Cnut or by men trained by King Cnut's shipmen and were deadly when given the opportunity.

Only now did the thud of returning arrows reach his ears, although the majority seemed to impact the water with a sizzle, before disappearing beneath the white crests of the waves. The ship moved with the water, Eowa rocking with the motion, and Ælfgar found a smile on his lips.

This was what it meant to be a member of the ship army. Not like before, when Earl Sweyn had acted irrationally and without thought for the years of experience the other men had.

Not that it was an easy fight. Ælfgar heard the cries of men in pain, the shocked gasps of the wounded, and he braced himself for when they'd be close enough to mount one of King Magnus' ships. It would then be warrior against warrior, and the unlucky would sink beneath the waves, never to be seen again.

Keeping his eyes forward, he followed every instruction, no matter how strange it felt.

Ælfgar risked looking behind him, the rhythm of his oar strokes disturbed so that it banged against his knee. But he'd seen enough to know what Eowa had seen.

The remainder of the fleet hastened towards them, sails flashing in the bright sunlight. They were no longer outnumbered. He'd not believed they'd lose against King Magnus anyway, and now he was sure of it because it wasn't only the king's fleet that rushed towards them but every ship in England that Edward had called to Sandwich.

The breadth of the sea teemed with ships, sails and oars powering them towards King Magnus and his thirty-one ships.

Ælfgar allowed a thin smile to split his sweat-stained face. Yes, they'd not won yet, but he knew they would.

Only then did he feel the ship knocked by another craft, the thud of wood hitting wood, rocking the craft to the accompaniment of a loud screech. He gritted his teeth, risked reaching for his seax, and waited to be called to action. He'd never fought on a ship before, but he was sure it couldn't be much different to fighting on land. All he needed to do was maintain his balance and not tumble into the sea.

Therefore, they all wore light clothes, just enough to stop the sun from searing their skin. A few wore byrnies, but they were too hot to row in. Ælfgar didn't even consider shrugging into the one he had at his feet, held above the oily bilge water in a small wooden chest that protruded from the overlapping planks of the ship's side.

The oars from the other side of the ship were hastily raised clear from the water, and pulled inside the boat to prevent them from being crushed by the approaching vessel. Ælfgar lifted his oar from the water, to stop the two ships from circling together.

He watched his cousin ram a helm over his unruly hair, a flash of understanding passing between them, a promise that both men would live through this, and then all was chaos. Magnus' men threatened to engulf the ship, yet for every two warriors that leapt the small gap between them, one landed with a loud splash in the sea. Those that made it were all greeted with flashing seaxes, axes and the occasional short sword, although they were not as good for fighting in such a confined space.

Ælfgar waited his turn, trying not to listen to the roars and cries of the wounded until he felt something disturb the shield that protected him from the side.

Eyes wide, he watched as a hand fumbled its way along the side of the ship.

"Ware,' he roared, hoping the shipmen behind him appreciated the danger. He bided his time, pulling his seax into his hand. He wanted the right moment. Maybe when the enemy was at their most vulnerable. The audacity of such a plan shocked him. Magnus had shipmen prepared to risk the icy cold of the sea to gain access to the ship.

He heard the rustle of others readying to attack, and then the time was upon him.

Ælfgar could have sliced the hand, perhaps removing a finger or two, but instead, he stabbed down, spearing the hand to the side of the ship. A shriek of agony greeted his action. Blood fountained into the air so that he had to spit it aside as he reached for his war axe, removing the protective shield in one sweep of his left hand and then hacking across the exposed throat of his enemy.

The move was completed quickly, understanding flashing in his enemy's eyes before he thumped the shield back into place and gripped the seax tightly, releasing the dead man into the water beneath the ship. The warrior made a satisfying splash as he entered the water. Ælfgar panted with the exertion.

He risked a glance towards Ælfwine. His cousin was battling against one of Magnus' men, hammering him so that the man over-balanced and tumbled onto his ship that had managed to pull level with their own.

'Row,' the order came directly from Eowa. Ælfgar released his oar from its rest and dug it deep into the sea, trying not to notice how it seemed to snag on detritus in the water—no doubt one of the dead or soon-to-be dead.

This time, Eowa wanted them to circle, just the one side of the ship digging their oars into the sea so that the enemy ship wedged tightly to them was caught in the same spiral. It made it almost impossible to stand and fight as the ships spun together more and more quickly.

Ælfgar fought back nausea, relieved when the call came to stop.

Again, he watched as the enemy struggled to regain their foothold on their ship, more and more of them trying to return to their places rather than risk fighting when they were so off-balance. Splashes rang through the air, accompanied by the thud of arrows from the other English ships.

Ælfgar could see nothing but the immediate space around him, but he hoped the rest of the English ships were having as much success. Whether Magnus died in this attack or not, it needed to be evident that he'd have no victory against the English.

Slowly, the foe-ship pulled away from their craft, Ælfwine returning to his rowing bench, although he breathed heavily. Ælfgar could see a trail of blood running down his arm. Others seemed less fortunate, and the bench in front of Ælfgar remained empty, even as Eowa called the men together, commanding both sides to row.

Ælfgar looked up, expecting to see the enemy ships' sails, but they were nowhere to be seen in his limited view. Surely, they hadn't gone already? He wouldn't expect someone such as King Magnus to give up this easily.

'Easy,' Eowa's new directive allowed him to suck in much-needed air and to seek out his cousin. Ælfwine grinned at him, his mouth showing a bloody mess of stained teeth.

'Bit my bloody lip,' Ælfwine roared, and Ælfgar grinned at his triumphant cousin. It seemed they'd both taken a kill, perhaps Ælfwine had made more than one killing blow.

'Ready yourselves,' Eowa instructed his shipmen. Ælfgar understood that the battle was far from over; this was merely a respite.

A ripple of movement ran down the centre of the ship, and Ælfgar saw a sail appear before them. He breathed in, his chest filling before he let it out slowly.

There was more fighting to be done.

EOWA DIRECTED THE SHIP BESIDE ONE OF THE ENEMY CRAFT. THE SAIL SLID past them, and Ælfgar was perplexed by the lack of defence from the shipmen on board. He still had no idea how the main battle played out, but Eowa was determined to continue the attack.

This time, his side of the ship bumped against the foe-ship with a familiar grind. He slipped his seax lose, waiting for the command to board. The flight of arrows had long ago ceased to menace the air. After all, only so many arrows could be kept on a ship. The attack would be one on one now, man-to-man.

Ælfgar prepared to pick up the shield to use it to protect himself from the enemy who would be attacking, and he wasn't disappointed.

In one fluid movement, he hefted the shield, holding it in his left hand, as one of Magnus' men almost tumbled into the ship, unbalanced. He must have been leaning on the shield.

Ælfgar sliced down with his seax, drawing blood across the man's exposed neck. Quickly, he reversed his grip and stabbed downwards. A gurgling sound greeted the action, and a fresh wave of blood enveloped his hand. It was slippery, and smelt of rust, but the flash of warmth was almost welcome against the chill of the seawater.

Immediately, he stood upright, seeking out the next enemy to kill. The dead body was an impediment, but moving it with the two ships so closely together was impossible.

Behind the ship they were attacking, Ælfgar caught sight of another two boats in fierce combat, locked together like lovers in the height of passion, even as the shipmen from the opposing sides fought savagely.

A whack on his shield brought him back to the here and now. He lashed out with his seax, only for it to slide harmlessly from another shield.

'Arse,' he complained, sweeping back, aiming once more to smash into the enemy. This time, his seax, dug deep, but it still came away clear of blood. He surmised that the enemy wore a byrnie.

Beside him, his crewmates fought fiercely, the one stabbing above the height of his shield, the other beneath it. Ælfgar licked his dry lips before following their example. He stabbed upwards, missing the enemy shield, as his seax sliced the man's chin. He wore no helm, unlike Ælfgar, and the blow grazed a deep cut on his chin from which blood flowed.

He followed up the move by reversing his seax and using the butt of the weapon to thrust upwards into the man's nose. His enemy's eyes lost focus, and he stumbled backwards, falling into the bilge of his ship. Ælfgar was eager to follow him, but he felt hands pulling him back.

Ælfgar thought to fight back, trying to shrug off the touch.

'Stay in the damn ship,' Ælfwine hissed into his ear, fury lacing his words. 'We're not after bloody heroes here.'

Ælfgar nodded to show he understood and held his place in the shield wall. No new foe stepped into the gap left by the bleeding man. Instead, the enemy ship had decided to row clear from the attack. The remaining shipmen battled against the turmoil of the sea, crammed as it was with other ships and floating bodies. Ælfgar thought it wouldn't get away, but then it did, oars forced between the boats, driving the one away from the other from both ends.

The gap widened between the two ships. Ælfgar felt his rage as he spied his enemy standing on unsteady legs. He'd sooner have finished him, but he knew the risk had been too great. He might have been marooned on the other craft, forced to face an overwhelming number of warriors.

'Oars.' There would be no let-up as Eowa snapped out another order. He was leaning heavily on the steerboard. Ælfgar couldn't see where his gaze was fixed. He'd retaken his seat and now heaved on the oar, concentrating on matching the rhythm of the rest of the men. The ship powered through the water, everyone in time, and Ælfgar felt a broad grin touching his cheeks.

Ælfgar waited to be summoned to wield his seax again, surprised when Eowa bellowed, 'Stop.'

There was no thunk of wood on wood, no cry of the wounded. In fact, for a moment, Ælfgar could hear nothing but his heavy breathing.

His eyes fixed on Eowa; he watched as the ship's commander turned and shrugged.

'Stand down, men. It's over. Look.'

Ælfgar leapt to his feet, finally seeing over the shields easily. To the left, he spied a ship, broken up and rapidly submerging beneath the water. Barrels and chests bobbed in the water, flailing arms reaching for anything they could find to keep them afloat. The white sail slowly collapsed on itself. One ship was trying to haul as many survivors as possible into its belly behind it. Beyond them, Ælfgar could see six or seven boats turning tail and slowly moving away.

There was no sign of King Magnus.

Ælfgar swirled his head to the right, catching sight of the English ships, the king standing high in the prow of one of them, the sail featuring a wyvern hanging taut in the sky, although there was little wind. The rest of the English fleet was spaced out behind or to the king's side, one vessel busily being bailed out, but there were no floundering ships.

Next to Eowa's ship, there were another four ships, all of them with ship-men finally taking a look around them. He could see cuts on some of the warriors, one man with a wrapped tunic around his head, a trail of blood sneaking beneath its folds, while the fabric slowly darkened.

'Is it over?' he gasped. 'Where's King Magnus?'

He couldn't believe that the fearless Magnus had given up so soon. It was impossible, and yet there was no other explanation.

Muffled cheers reached his ears, but Ælfgar felt poised to strike again, the thrum of battle rippling through his tense body. He was ready to continue the attack. How dare the enemy run away when the battle was far from done.

'We won,' Ælfwine's voice was high with excitement as he thumped Ælfgar hard on the back.

'We bloody well won,' he crowed. The other shipmen were also beginning to realise that it was over. Men called one to another, their voices shrill or deep with relief.

'We beat the bastard,' Ælfwine continued, and Ælfgar turned to him, flung his arms around his cousin, and held him tightly for a long moment.

'Wulfstan's not going to forgive us,' he stated, his lips stretched into a smile.

'I hadn't considered that,' Ælfwine retorted, the joy sliding from his face at the realisation.

'He's not going to be bloody pleased with your father,' but he was laughing as he spoke.

19
LEOFRIC

LEOFRIC EYED THE KING WITH A SYMPATHY HE'D NOT EXPECTED. THE YEAR had been tumultuous from beginning to end, and now there was this to contend with.

It wasn't that they'd been unaware of Lady Gunnhild's attempts to betray the king, but it couldn't be denied that none of them had expected her to be so successful. When the king had ordered his fleet to gather at Sandwich, it had been on the pretext that King Magnus might attack. An attack led by King Magnus had been unexpected. But Magnus had grown into a man keen to stake his claim to kingdoms.

And now, men had lost their lives in the sea battle, which had been a victory of sorts for King Edward. But someone needed to be brought to justice for the treason committed.

That person was Lady Gunnhild and her two sons.

They stood now before the king. The sons with their heads bowed. The matriarch with defiant eyes, refusing to show any respect for the man who'd shunned her attempts to make one of her sons an earl. A woman who'd gone so far as to try to remove him from the kingship by force and giving her full support to King Magnus.

'My lady,' the king spoke directly to Lady Gunnhild. His fierce eyes locked with hers, and he refused to be the first to break that contact. 'We've heard from those who escorted your son to Norway. We know that the intent was to bring King Magnus here, to encourage him and the baseless claims he asserts to be the true ruler of England. You've offered no denial, so I am determined to pass a sentence on you for such crimes. Your sons will be included in the sentence.'

It was no secret that the king would banish Lady Gunnhild. If anything, it had come as a surprise to some that the king had insisted on going through with a trial and in having clerics scour the legal texts to determine on what charge she could be sent from England's shores. It was more effort than King Harald had put into his banishment for Lady Emma.

'But, for a final time, I'll allow you to speak to England's witan and to offer some sort of explanation. It might have some impact on my decision. It depends on what you say.'

Leofric observed Lady Gunnhild intently. He and the other earls and bishops had been seated close to the king for the trial. From there, they had a good view of the rest of the witan and of the stubborn cast that soured Lady Gunnhild's face.

She continued to hold the king's eyes, and Leofric suspected she'd only break the look when led away to face her fate. Beside her, Thorkell, shifted, his gaze moving from the floor to his mother's face. Only then did Gunnhild turn away from the king.

Something passed between the son and mother. Leofric watched the effect of it on Lady Gunnhild. Her body had been rigid, her hands held tightly inside one another, bunched in her dress's rich, blue fabric. Her jewels and brooches gleamed brightly, her hair elaborately twisted and braided, and even more gems were flashing in the glow from the many candles used to light the darkening room.

The trial had taken much of the day. It would soon be fully dark outside. Leofric appreciated that he'd not return to Coventry that day, no matter how much he longed to be free from the tense atmosphere of the king's court.

'My lord king,' Lady Gunnhild began, her voice little more than a whisper so that she was forced to stop and clear her throat before resuming.

At that moment, with the lights cast low, and the shadows reaching across the wooden floor, Leofric noticed her steely eyes and light hair colouring. She was the very epitome of a proud Danish woman.

'My lord king. I would beg your forgiveness for my actions that imperilled England and brought a conqueror once more to her shores. And not just any conqueror, but the man who builds himself an empire across the northern sea. I'm a mother with no husband to protect me and my family, who are under King Magnus's control. I risked harming not only England but them as well, and I'm truly sorry.'

'I would make excuses for my actions, but they would sound hollow here, before the men and women who rule England. But I would speak for my sons. As any good children must, they acted only to carry out my orders. I would beg forgiveness for them. Even if it means never seeing them again in this lifetime, I would ask that they not be included in my banishment. They'll be left with nothing, not their father's inheritance, and at the moment, with no hope of finding a home elsewhere, for we wouldn't be welcome in Denmark.'

Silence greeted her words, and Leofric felt as though no one moved in the great hall at Winchester. Lady Gunnhild finally dropped her head in a sign of submission, and Leofric waited. He didn't know what the king would make of such an impassioned speech. There was truth in the words she spoke. Yet, Leofric knew that the king's thoughts would immediately turn to his mother.

Lady Emma had done so many things in her life that she could justify as acting for the sake of her children. All of them had been detrimental to Edward. All of them. Now, she was banished from the king's presence and forced to remain on her property in Winchester. Leofric believed Lady Gunnhild, while being honest with the king, had only served to harden his resolve against her.

'Lady Gunnhild, I admire you in advocating for your sons. But, alas, your justification for inviting an invader to England speaks only of ambition. England could have fallen, many might have died, and all because you were upset that one of your sons, who are barely even men, wasn't named as one of England's earls. Look at the men who serve me if you would, Lady Gunnhild. Earl Leofric's family have ruled areas of Mercia for nearly fifty years, Earl Godwine's family for twenty and Earl Siward for the last decade. Your sons weren't even born when two of my earls earned their positions. No, I reject your demands that your sons not be included in your banishment.'

As the king uttered the word, Thorkell's young shoulders slumped, and Lady Gunnhild expelled her held breath, once more causing the jewels and golden thread that covered her dress to glimmer.

'You'll lose all of your landed properties, although I'm not so cruel as to prevent you from taking your portable wealth with you so that you can at least afford to live elsewhere. You'll surrender all of your landed wealth, and all of your rents will be redirected to the king's treasury. All three of you are banished from England for the rest of your lives.' Having spoken, the king finally tore his eyes away from Lady Gunnhild, turning to peer at his cleric, no doubt keen to ensure the sentence was correctly recorded in the court's records.

The cleric scratched quickly over the fine parchment, the sound resonating through the hall, the only noise to be heard.

'You have a month to gather and make ready. My huscarls will escort you to your home and stay with you before taking you wherever you wish to go, provided it involves a ship.'

Leofric half anticipated Lady Gunnhild falling to her knees, begging the king to reconsider, but she believed herself royal and showed her nature now. A pity she'd not thought to use it before.

Lady Gunnhild dipped low, performing a perfect curtsey. Leofric thought that King Magnus wouldn't have been encouraged to travel to England if she'd only done that in the first place. There was even the slightest chance that one of her sons might have been made a sheriff. After all, the king could now reward those who'd proved their loyalty to him.

Lady Gunnhild strode from the king's presence, her head high, her steps echoing, the huscarls almost running to keep up with her. Leofric watched with wry amusement. He could finally understand how she'd enticed a king to come to England and why Edward thought her such a risk. She certainly had the attitude of a monarch.

In her wake, a low babble of conversation sprang up as though the witan had been concluded, but Leofric knew that wasn't the case. He recalled his previous conversation with the king three nights before, on his arrival.

'Earl Leofric, I know you probably expect me to speak to you about Lady Gunnhild, but it's not she who worries me. There's another matter, and I'd be pleased to hear your advice.'

The king's request had surprised Leofric. He'd believed the only matter to be resolved was that of Lady Gunnhild and some minor issues about taxation and the review of the law codes. But apparently not.

He'd eyed the king. Edward had been dressed as simply as usual, although his tunic was made from the finest cloth, the cut accentuating his good build. Since the sea battle against King Magnus, Leofric had heard rumours that the king had been taking a more active part in the training regimes of the huscarls. The king had enjoyed the experience. But then, it was always easier to revel in something when you were the victor.

The king's eyes had been fierce as he'd settled behind his desk. Leofric thought it had never looked so tidy. Edward was a man who liked order in his everyday life, which extended to the minutiae of being king.

'It concerns the Archbishop, Eadsige.'

Leofric had felt his right eyebrow rise in surprise. Of all the things he'd thought the king might want to discuss, it wasn't the archbishop. Although, well, he had heard some rumours about the man behaving oddly.

'He's asked to retire from his position because of his ill health, or rather, to have another continue with the day-to-day running of the archbishopric. He'll stay as a figurehead. I have a mind to agree. He's become forgetful of late, and although no one must know this, he was found outside, wandering around in confusion, unable to tell the monk who found him his name only last week.'

'Luckily, it was in the enclosed cloister, and only the monk who found him and the infirmary staff know what occurred, but it's quite scared Eadsige. He has vague recollections of something similar happening to his grandfather. The infirmarian advised it could be something that happens in families.'

Leofric nodded. While the king cautioned him to secrecy, some part of the archbishop's problem seemed much more widely known.

'I can't have my archbishop getting lost. If our enemy became aware of it, they might kidnap him, or even worse.'

'So, a replacement needs to be found?' Leofric appreciated that the king wouldn't want Canterbury to fall into disrepute with a forgetful incumbent. Yet, his forehead furrowed all the same.

'Isn't it for the bishops to decide on any replacement?'

'It can be, but this matter must be resolved quickly. I'd not have a man loyal to my mother trying to claim the archbishopric or some unscrupulous foe. And Eadsige agrees with me. He came to me personally, seeking my advice and help. I'm keen to give it. But, I would have your approval before I make the announcement after Lady Gunnhild's trial.'

'And who have you chosen?'

'Abbot Siward of Abingdon.'

Leofric had nodded. He knew of Siward. He'd been appointed to his current position during King Cnut's reign. He was loyal to Abingdon. He was faithful to his kings.

'Will Siward agree? I understand he had no hopes of further advancement.'

'It need not be forever,' Edward stated. 'But, I require someone with his skills and talents for now. It helps that Eadsige esteems the man. I believe there's a feeling of mutual trust and respect between them. It must be similar to when Harthacnut invited me to England – Eadsige preparing his replacement even while he lives.'

Leofric wasn't sure how to respond to the statement or react to Edward's consternation. But the king had the right to it. After all, he'd spent his adult years ensuring Ælfgar would be prepared to become earl in his place when he died.

'I've consulted Earl Godwine and Siward.' Leofric hadn't missed that he'd made no mention of Sweyn. Maybe the king had decided that consulting one family member was enough. No doubt, Godwine would inform his son, anyway.

'Then, you have my agreement. A pity for Archbishop Eadsige, but he deserves our thanks and respect for recognising his problems.'

'Yes, and I'll inform the witan after the trial. I wish to pronounce it as completed and not something to debate. The archbishop will inform Siward or may already have done so. It won't shock him, that's for sure.'

And now the king addressed the members of the witan. Leofric considered what words he'd use to spare Eadsige from further embarrassment.

'I would make a further announcement. On Archbishop Eadsige's request, I'm appointing a bishop to work beside him to ensure that the arduous task of administering the large archbishopric is shared. As such, Abbot Siward, formerly of Abingdon, will become bishop of Canterbury. I'm sure you'll join me in wishing him well with the task.'

Siward stood from his place amongst the abbots as the king spoke, a pensive expression on his face. He inclined his head to the king before turning to do the same to Archbishop Eadsige, who'd also been assisted to his feet.

The comparison between the two men couldn't be more significant. Eadsige was old before his time, his head a tumble of white hair, grown so thin on top that it was possible to see the shape of his skull clearly beneath it. His eyes looked rheumy, a little out of focus. In contrast, Siward had a monk's tonsure, his brown hair glistening brightly in the glow from the candles. His face was long, his brown eyes fierce, and his body spoke of bunched-up tension inside it.

Leofric smiled at the man. It wasn't easy to face so many.

'The archbishops will conduct the ceremony in the next few days, and henceforth, Siward will be a bishop.'

The king didn't allow any time for questions, slowing only to ensure the development was recorded by his cleric before moving on to taxation matters that vexed him. The new bishop sank to his chair again, although it took Eadsige far longer to settle. But Leofric's gaze was arrested by the furious look on Earl Sweyn's face. Apparently, his father hadn't informed him after all. Perhaps all was not well in the House of Godwine.

With half an ear, Leofric listened to the king speaking. And then he focused more intently. He'd thought the discussion was about taxation in general and the need to restrike the coinage once more. But now, it seemed much more involved than that. Leofric shook his head, allowing a spark of frustration to show. The king had spoken to him of the archbishop's infirmity but not his intentions to finance a vast ship army.

'If the attack by King Magnus has done anything, it's shown us not to take England's security for granted. I know many of you may argue that there have been no attacks since King Cnut was king, but I think we can all determine why that has been. King Harthacnut's death has left us with a problem, that of King Magnus and his extended family. His stepmother still lives, and she's the sister of the King of the Svear. The two parties have worked together against King Cnut before. Need I remind you all of the Battle of Helgeå? Cnut may have had the victory, but he could have been overwhelmed. I propose that the ship army be increased. A fleet of thirty-five is adequate during peacetime. But I'll not allow the kingdom to be ravaged again as it was during my father's rule. I suggest we act as though war might come at any moment.'

'King Magnus will eye England again, and now he knows our strength, he'll outfit more and more ships, and we must do the same.'

Leofric couldn't fault the king's logic nor deny that the words sent a tremor of unease through those assembled.

While there were many who'd not been alive when Æthelred was king, there were enough who had been. Equally, plentiful stories had been shared of the almost constant fighting.

'I suggest a geld, raised to fund the ships that must be built. But not this year. I've heeded the warnings of another terrible harvest. The weather has been too warm early on in the year and too damp now when the plants should be growing well. I'll not burden my people further. But, I wish to put the required administration in place and to do that, we need more moneyers. And, if there are to be more moneyers, then it's a good time to reissue the coinage.'

Leofric lowered his head rather than meet the king's eyes. The king's reasoning was sound. It was reassuring to know that Edward has listened to his advisors. Another year of poor harvests and the people of England were already struggling, the livestock as well. Even those who traded fine clothes and exotic spices and herbs were finding little wealth in England.

He listened to the mumble of conversation, most in agreement, even though the king hadn't clarified what the geld would consist of. It perhaps didn't matter. Unlike Harthacnut, if Edward was prepared to accept that the people he wanted to tax were currently unable to provide more, he would likely win acceptance for his plan.

The story of Magnus' attack had caused a shock wave throughout England. Knowledge of the king's success had quickly spread, even to the borders, where the Welsh king had kept his warband inside the agreed boundaries. Earl Siward had mentioned the same happening in the kingdom of the Scots.

Edward was making a reputation for himself, and he meant to grow it further by winning the support of his subjects and menacing his enemies.

'I'll have a new design for the coins. The word 'Peace' will be removed from them. Not because I don't wish peace, but because I'll not have King Magnus or the King of the Svear believe England will capitulate if only to ensure peace reigns. No, I'll have a new design for my coins. A mint will be placed at Sandwich, and the number in London will be increased even further. This is something that can be set in motion immediately.'

'I'll have the Winchester moneyers summoned and set the matter before them. They will aid me in knowing what figures and shapes translate best into the coin dies, and a design can be chosen to be in place and ready for use when we've survived the winter, if not before.' Edward spoke decisively, inviting no argument, and indeed, he didn't receive any, although Leofric was pensive.

Was this the start of Edward ruling with greater authority? He'd cast his mother aside, removed her meddling bishop from East Anglia, led the ship-army against one of England's enemies, and now wished to grow her ship army? And yet, Leofric didn't miss the look that passed between Earl Godwine and his king? It unsettled him, even as his regard for the king grew.

20

AD1044, LEOFRIC

'There are rumours,' the king paused, as though searching for the right words. Leofric suppressed a sigh. So much of the year had been spent listening to rumours. It was sometimes impossible to know where the truth lay. The king looked as drawn as he felt, his sharp eyes downcast. Edward was learning the rigours of being a king when so many worked only for their self-interest.

'That Osgot Clapa was assisting Lady Gunnhild. Do you know of this?'

Leofric considered how to reply. He only knew that Osgot Clapa had attended one of Lady Gunnhild's meetings. He didn't know anything else. Well, he did. He knew that Tovi had fallen out with his father by marriage. He'd not known the details. Perhaps this was the answer he'd been missing.

'I see you do.'

'I had some small suspicion when all this started, but I'd not realised that Osgot Clapa was overly involved.'

'Well, he is, and there's proof, so I must banish him, as I did Lady Gunnhild,' yet the king sounded unhappy with the decision.

'Who brought you the proof?' Just for a moment, King Edward's gaze fixed on Leofric, as though surprised with the question even while expecting it. Did Edward reassess Leofric, then? He wasn't sure.

'Earl Sweyn.'

'Unsurprising,' Leofric mocked. 'He's keen to win back your regard. He's had quite the calamitous beginning in his new position.'

'Are you implying that Earl Sweyn lies about Osgot Clapa?' A thin edge of fury touched the snapped words, showing the pressure the king felt as he was beset from all sides.

'Not at all,' and Leofric held out his hands in a placatory way. 'I'm merely saying that the person who told you has much to gain from winning back your trust. And how did he even come by the information?'

They were seated in a small, private room in Winchester. Edward was rarely resident in Winchester, perhaps because the spectre of his mother hung over the place. Or maybe the king, while reliant on his father's heritage for his kingship, found it easier to remove himself from the heart of it. Æthelred had spent much of his life in Winchester.

'And would you have told me if you'd discovered Osgot Clapa's involvement?'

'It would depend on the seriousness of the matter. I don't yet know what the allegations are. What has he done?'

'He's been in communication with King Magnus, of course, via Baldwin of Bruges. That man also enjoys causing mayhem for England.' A tight knot of disgust formed on Edward's face. Leofric held his tongue. He knew now wouldn't be the correct time to remind the king that Baldwin had sheltered his mother when King Harald had evicted her from England. Perhaps Edward held that against Baldwin as well. Maybe he wished she'd found no friendly port and had been forced to travel to the land of the Rus or even to Rome.

'He's as much to blame as Lady Gunnhild for the attack, then?' Still, the king hadn't told him all the details.

'So it would seem.'

'Then, yes, he should also be banished even though Earl Sweyn alerted you. I assume you've ensured the intelligence you've been given is correct?' Leofric reiterated his concerns, hoping the king would tell him everything.

Although he didn't look happy about it, the king nodded, and then he completely changed the subject.

'Is it always like this?' Edward asked, leaning forward to rest his elbows on the dark wooden desk he sat behind, his head on his upturned hands.

Leofric wanted to laugh, such was his surprise at such a question, but of course, Edward was new to this. He'd not had a lifetime of preparations for the task ahead. He'd not even had more than a year's tuition. It had been a baptism of fire.

'I believe so,' he almost whispered instead and then cleared his throat. 'You're the target, the one that everyone sees. You might be the rightful heir by natural order, as you say, but as you also note, England isn't the place it was when you left her all those years ago.'

'The Danish kings have wrought their changes, some with soft words and others with hard iron, but the transformations are all permanent. You're the embodiment of that revolution. You represent everything the English people want to be restored to them and everything that the Danes hope to continue to hold. And, unfortunately,' here Leofric dared himself to tell the truth. 'There are those who take advantage of you, even now. They do you more harm than good.'

A set line settled on the king's face at the words.

'You caution me about Earl Godwine and his children.'

'I do, my lord, yes.'

'You're jealous of Earl Sweyn's earldom when it should have gone to your son?' Contempt in the tone sought to infuriate Leofric, but he remained calm.

'I'm not jealous of him, but I don't think the appointment was your finest decision to date. He's not, and I think you would admit this yourself, the epitome of your person as he should be.'

'And who should have been placed there? Lady Gunnhild's children, as she requested? Or your son? A man, I would note, who's friendly with Harold Godwinesson, as well as Ralph.'

'I think Harold would have been a better choice if it had to be one of the Godwines. He would not have made the same mistakes. He might be the younger brother, but he's much wiser.'

'But you believe it should have been your son?' Now it was the king who sought to press the point.

'I've never said that,' Leofric retorted. This had started as a discussion about Osgot Clapa but was rapidly becoming an argument he didn't wish to have. 'It could have been almost anyone other than Sweyn Godwinesson. Anyone would have been preferred. Anyone.'

'Earl Siward's son? Lady Gunnhild's son, perhaps even your surviving brother or your sister's husband? Anyone? Really?'

'Yes, my lord king, anyone. Any of those choices would have prevented the upsurge against you, and could have thwarted the request for King Magnus to attack England. Surely, you must see that?' But the king shook his head, standing abruptly.

'I'd ask you to take the huscarls and arrest Osgot Clapa for his treason. Bring him to Winchester for trial. That will be all. Good day,' and the king turned aside, his back facing Leofric. He inclined his head, all the same, as he stood and made his way from the king's presence. Yet, he couldn't stop himself from offering one final comment.

'Not everyone wishes you to fail, my lord king. Remember that.'

21

ÆLFGAR

HE MOVED EASILY THROUGH THE CRUSH OF PEOPLE, EAGER TO MAKE HIS WAY to the shipyard. His father had asked him to check on the king's current endeavour. When he'd spoken, there'd been a far-away expression in his eyes, and Ælfgar detected a memory from long ago.

Now, he only found chaos, and yet there was some order running through it. He was sure of it.

The smell of wood shavings filled the air, a pleasant aroma against the swell of the River Thames at high tide. The river flashed menacingly, far from enticing, and yet Ælfgar felt a thrill of excitement.

The king's fleet, or rather, the enlarged king's fleet, was advancing well. Woodcrafts-people were spending the cold winter ensuring the wood was seasoned and ready to be worked upon as soon as the weather changed. There was an expectation that at least a further twenty ships would be added to the king's fleet before they once more massed at Sandwich the following summer.

Ælfgar feared that might be too ambitious, but he wasn't about to cast doubt on the hopeful faces that peered his way. Men and women worked diligently, all trying to fulfil the king's wishes. They glowed

from the excellent food they'd been provided with; the king determined that those working for him should be well provided for as the
daylight hours slowly shrank between sunrise and sunset. The same
couldn't be said for others he'd encountered on the way to London.

His father was doing his best for those who fell under his control,
Ælfgar and the other Mercian nobility doing the same, and yet there
was simply not enough. The old and the young would perish during
the winter, and the sick and the weak. More than one newborn babe
would fail to thrive because their mother had given away all she
could to feed her other children, leaving herself weak. It was a story
he heard too many times and saddened him every time. He'd even
taken to questioning the benevolence of his God. How could he
punish the weak when the strong, and the ruthless, survived?

'Hail, Lord Ælfgar.' Quickly, he forced the glower of unhappiness
from his face, looking up to catch sight of Earl Sweyn. He'd not
known Sweyn would be in London. He should have been in Hereford,
not here.

'My lord,' he bowed his head, hoping that Sweyn might pass him
by but realising that he wasn't going to be so lucky.

'Such a waste of money,' Sweyn's words were far from gently
spoken, echoing and seeming to grow in intensity for all they were
outside. Ælfgar felt the scrutiny of those who'd heard and was stung
into replying.

'The king doesn't waste his funds. This is done for England's
safety and security.'

'There are more than enough ships already,' Sweyn complained,
lips downcast. No doubt, his experiences made him eager to remain
on dry land. He eyed the proceedings with a furrow on his brow.

'Did your father send you to ensure his investment progressed
well?' Ælfgar was stung by the idea that his father only cared about
his money, but he tried not to show it.

'No, my father asked me to ensure everything was in order with
the entire scheme. The new Mercian ships will be part of the second

set of ships. It's a higher priority to ensure the king's fleet is complete.'

A look of disbelief flashed across Earl Sweyn's face at the statement, and Ælfgar considered what motivated Sweyn. Was it merely the opportunity to enrich himself? He'd made a fool of himself with his antics and the loss of his craft when they'd encountered Magnus' men. Now he seemed determined to undermine the king's intentions. Once more, Ælfgar felt a swell of anger that the king had made Sweyn the earl of Hereford, not him.

'Well, probably better to allow the king to spend his taxes first. The Mercian craft might not be needed.' Ælfgar held his tongue, but only by biting it so hard, he tasted blood. The man had no idea what it meant to rule and keep England safe from the pretensions of those overseas.

'Your father is a wise man. I should have done the same, but unfortunately, I've had to replace the lost ship. The expense has almost beggared me. The earldom is not the most fruitful it could be.'

'Well, there has been a poor harvest,' Ælfgar wondered why he was explaining to the other man.

'Whether there's food or not, taxes must still be paid, if only to keep the king content. Well, that's what I tell those who tithe to me. They know who's at fault, and it isn't me.'

Ælfgar looked away, not wanting Sweyn to see how much his words upset him. Only a few years ago, King Harthacnut had caused outright rebellion with his excessive demands. And Worcester, the scene of the uprising, was close to Hereford. Surely, Sweyn was intelligent enough not to blame the king? After all, Sweyn could have easily forwarded the tithes on behalf of his people. Contrary to what he believed, his earldom was one of the most well-endowed in England. And the king hadn't yet made his demands. They would come in the new year.

'People have until the end of next summer to settle their dues. I hope you've assured those in your earldom of the king's concession. It wouldn't do to cause unease.'

'As I said, they know who demands the additional funds, either by hook or crook. The needless restriking of the coinage won't be enough to satisfy our king.'

Ælfgar had no choice but to clamp his mouth shut once more. It wasn't for him to argue with the king's earl. Yes, he'd inform his father of Sweyn's words, but it was for Edward to handle.

'Well, I must be going. I have business further down the quayside.' Ælfgar nodded, pleased to be released from the man's oppressive presence. It didn't take much to realise that Sweyn had business with the slave traders.

With Earl Sweyn gone, Ælfgar continued his meandering through the hive of activity, even though his thoughts kept returning to the sea battle when they'd sailed away from Sandwich and encountered King Magnus.

Since then, Ælfgar had often replayed the two times he'd clashed with the enemy. He couldn't help wishing that they'd done more to dissuade Magnus from another endeavour, but news from Denmark spoke of him being even more powerful rather than less. Having been declared king by the witan, Lord Svein Estridsson had been overwhelmed by Magnus and his warriors and forced to flee. However, his mother had remained in Roskilde, determined not to relinquish her family's landed possessions.

He knew that the news had upset Lady Gytha, for she too had landed wealth in Denmark, just another way Godwine's loyalty to Edward was tested.

Yet, Magnus wasn't as secure as he might have hoped, for Svein had sought sanctuary with his mother's nephew, the king of the Svear. It was even said that he'd married Anund Jakob's daughter. If that was true, it could only point to unease between two of Magnus' allies, his stepmother and her brother, Anund Jakob.

Once more, the web of alliances in the northern kingdoms had tilted. Ælfgar hoped, as did his father that Magnus would stay focused on Denmark, even if Edward were preparing for another invasion attempt on England. Certainly, Magnus would need to bring more ships than previously.

And the new ships for the king's ship army were definitely needed. The shipmen who'd supported Cnut, Harald and Harthacnut had slowly dissipated until too few remained in England. The king was determined to make good on that oversight.

'My lord,' it was Eowa who called for him, and Ælfgar nodded and made his way to his side.

'Quite a sight, isn't it?' Like Ælfgar, Eowa had come to watch, not take part.

'It is, yes. I take it you know that everything is as it should be?'

'Well, not everything, but certainly, if I were organising such a feat, then I'd be doing it like this. The sails are being constructed away from the quayside, the ship-builders are being kept busy here, and those who will caulk and weather-proof the crafts before they enter the water are downwind, as much as it's possible to be on a day like this, anyway. I approve.'

'And what of the new shipmen?'

'Some have already been chosen; others are yet to be sought. There's no point having shipmen when there are no ships for them. The king's new coins attract men and some women from far and wide. The poor harvests are helping with that. Many are desperate for a means to feed their families. I can't foresee there being any problems in filling the ships. It'll simply be a matter of who'll ultimately have responsibility for them on a day-to-day basis. The king might need more than a reeve for such a task.'

Ælfgar nodded. His father had said the same thing to him.

The king wished to expand his fleet, in fact, double it, and that would make nearly five thousand men and women to be provided with places to sleep, ships to combat the enemy with, weapons, oars, sails, food and of course, wages.

'I'm off to visit the new moneyers. Come with me,' for a moment, Ælfgar thought Eowa might refuse, but then he nodded.

'It's not like I'll miss anything. This will take months,' and he indicated the carcasses behind him, gleaming too brightly, the wood too fresh.

Eowa fell into step beside Ælfgar as they made their way from the quayside. People called to Eowa, some ribald statements, hastily stifled when they realised he walked with Ælfgar. Ælfgar chuckled softly while Eowa looked furious, glowering at all around him.

Once free from the water's edge, Ælfgar struck out to where the blacksmiths and silversmiths could be found, close to, but not too close, to the king's royal house in London. It reassured the king's close oversight, even while ensuring the smell from the furnaces wasn't too much of a blight.

'You're here alone?' Eowa asked when they were finally away from any of his comrades.

'Ælfwine is with me, but he has business elsewhere this morning. I also have my household warriors, but they're assisting Ælfwine with his task.'

Eowa didn't demand to know Ælfwine's business, and that spoke of a man confident that his oath-sworn lord wasn't up to anything he shouldn't have been.

'Explain to me again how the king makes money from this coinage process,' Eowa demanded to know. 'The men tell me you take in a hundred coins and leave with another hundred coins, and they have the same value in the marketplace, they just carry a new image of the king. It makes no sense to me.'

Ælfgar nodded at Eowa's words.

'I know what you mean. It's strange, but it's all to do with the weight of the new coins, not the number of them.'

'The weight?'

'Yes, the melted-down silver is restruck into the same number of coins, just weighing slightly less.'

Eowa looked affronted.

'So the king steals the silver?'

'No, it's a tax, really. And it needs to be done to make the coins legal tender.'

'Let me get this right. The king makes everyone have their coins melted down, lowers their weight, and it has to be done to ensure it's legal tender.'

'That's about it, but it's how the monetary system in England has worked since King Athelstan. Sometimes the king takes weight away from the coins; other times, it might be added. It all depends on what's happening and whether he needs money.'

'And at the moment, he needs money?'

'Yes, to fund the building of the ships and the wages of the crafts-people and then, in time, the new shipmen.'

'I understand now, but it's strange to think that all those ships are being built, and it does not cost the king, or the people of England, any more money than they already have.'

'Exactly.' Ælfgar scented the air, aware the smell of the River Thames had been overlaid with something else now. Not necessarily more pleasant, just different. And then the fug of the furnaces hit him.

But he couldn't enter the work yard yet because a gateway restricted access and two members of the king's huscarls stood there.

'Who are you?' the one directed at Eowa, his eyes bulging in a face that seemed too compact to hold all of the flesh there.

'He's with me, and I'm Lord Ælfgar, son of Earl Leofric. I've been sent on the earl of Mercia's business.' Ælfgar didn't enjoy using his father's name to gain access, but he knew it would be the easiest way.

'My lord, apologies,' the warrior almost bowed but still leered at Eowa.

'This is the captain of my father's ship, and I've invited him to see how the new coinage is struck.'

A knowing nod from the warrior, but a small smile lit his tight face.

'It's fascinating, I tell you. Go and see, but mind, I'll check your pockets before you leave.' Yet the warrior laughed as he spoke, and Ælfgar had the impression this same caution was offered to everyone he allowed inside the silversmith's yard.

'Seek out Brungar, over there,' and he pointed away from the fierce heat of a fire and instead towards a workshop, where three or four men could be seen sitting beside tree stumps that reached just to their knees.

'My thanks,' Ælfgar called, already turning away.

Many men and women were in the smith's workshop, but they knew what they were doing. Ælfgar watched strong lads with bellows pumping the fire to a bright blue flame beneath a cauldron suspended over it while yet more waited to the side, ready to add more charcoal to the molten heat. Not even the bite of the coming bad weather could be felt in the space.

'That's where they melt the old coins down,' Ælfgar informed Eowa. 'See, these are the chests filled with the coins. They count them into the cauldron, and then they know how many to make from the sheet of silver that they produce.'

'And here is where they punch the shapes from the silver,' at yet another worktable, three men were busy beating down with what looked like an iron cutter, the rounds they used ensuring only perfectly formed silver coins were produced.

'As soon as the blanks are ready, they're brought over here to the stampers. Are you Brungar?' Ælfgar asked at an opportune time when the man in question was between the actions of striking or turning the coin.

'Who's asking?' he had a rumbling bass voice, and he didn't look up from what he was doing.

'Lord Ælfgar, son of Earl Leofric.'

'Well, in that case, yes, I'm Brungar. Is this your silver I'm busy with today?'

'Yes, I believe so.' Eowa was peering around Ælfgar, trying to determine what Brungar was doing.

'See,' and Brungar began to offer a commentary without even being asked. 'The die is fixed in place in the hollow in the tree trunk, just there. It's held firm, so it can't move. That, believe it or not, is our king's head.' Eowa looked down and then squinted even closer. The die was, of course, only as big as a silver coin, the detail almost impossible to make out, not helped by the shadows from where the sun was already beginning to move toward the horizon.

Ælfgar knew what Eowa would see, it had been discussed at length before the king had given his agreement, and Leofric had regaled his son with the tediousness of deciding upon the new design. Each coin carried an image of the king's head facing towards the left, a sceptre in front of the king's face, and the king's name and title, so they read Edward and Rex. Well, that's what it was supposed to say. Some of the dies weren't quite as clear as others.

'I get a nice blank coin, still a bit warm from being punched from the sheet of silver over there, and I place it inside the die, in the tree stump, like this,' and true to his word, Brungar did as he said. 'And then, I pick up the other side of the die, see here, it's got the cross on it, and some other stuff, and also my name, so people can bring it back to me if they're not happy with it. I put the die on top of the blank coin, and then,' and Brungar thudded a hammer onto the die with a single, sharp blow. 'I strike it true, and there, a new coin, ready to be returned to its owner.'

Brungar removed the top die and picked up the coin.

'Look,' and he placed it in Eowa's hand, who flinched at the latent heat within the silver.

Eowa held the coin up to the light, ignoring the discomfort, a smile playing on his lips.

'Well, I never,' he almost gushed with delight. 'Just look at that,' but Brungar had placed the next blank into the bottom die and was already striking true again.

'I can do about five hundred in a day,' Brungar stated, as though he were sewing and not using all his upper body strength to ensure the strike was true. 'It gets a bit tiresome after a bit, and you must be careful because if you get too tired, the strike goes awry. The king doesn't like it if half his head is missing or the letters aren't showing. I don't mind if my name looks a bit odd, but others aren't so pleased. Of course, we can melt down anything that's too poor quality and start all over again if it's no good.'

Eowa still held the coin, but he was surveying the workshop.

'How many of you are there?'

'Before the king set us away with the new coin, there were about five or six of us, working all the time, but now there's twenty-eight, well, twenty-nine, we took on a new smith only this morning. We all have our own dies, but they show as being struck in London. It's important, they say, to be able to keep track of these sorts of things.'

Brungar huffed as though it wasn't imperative, but Ælfgar knew the silversmiths took great pride in their work. They didn't appreciate it when people accused them of weighting the coins lightly or striking them poorly. But, as the king had made the decree, there were also many coins to be melted down and restruck. He wasn't surprised to learn how much the workforce had been expanded.

'We have five clerics who ensure the tallies are correct and people get back exactly what they brought in. We don't want anyone levelling accusations at us about it all.'

Brungar hadn't stopped striking, even as he spoke. Ælfgar found the action almost hypnotic as Brungar placed the coin correctly, struck it, and then handed it into a waiting basket. Every so often, one cleric came, took the full basket away, and disappeared into a small building. From inside there, the coins were reissued back to their owners on the production of the required pieces of vellum. Ælfgar understood there was a strong room hidden inside, with a thick door and many locks.

'Keep it,' Brungar said to Eowa as he bent to replace the coin he was still examining. 'We can take one off Earl Leofric's tally. I'm sure he won't mind.' But Eowa looked shocked at the notion and hastily returned it to the basket as though it still burnt him.

'It has that effect on people,' Brungar chuckled darkly. 'No one wants to be accused of being sleight of hand in here, I tell you.'

Ælfgar was sure about that. The king's coinage was a true marvel. He'd heard it said many times that the Norse had come to England because they wanted to own such portable wealth. It was said that in the northern kingdoms, they made copies of Edward's coins. They'd done the same with Harthacnut and Cnut's, but no one had wanted to forge Harald's. The thought of his dead foster brother sobered Ælfgar. A stab of melancholy drove the enjoyment of the mint from his mind.

Eowa noticed his unease, a quizzical look on his face.

'Just thinking of the past,' Ælfgar apologised, turning to thank Brungar for his time.

'You're welcome anytime, my lord. Next time bring more of your coins. I'll have them melted down and restruck in double time.'

'I'll tell my father,' Ælfgar offered, but the other man had turned and was busy haranguing one of the moneyers for some mistake.

'So, it's not thieving at all, then?' Eowa asked, his eyes noticing where the sheets of silver, from which the blank coins had been punched, were being fed back into the cauldron to be once more melted and reformed.

'Not at all,' Ælfgar confirmed, swallowing down his grief. It did no good to rue the past. He needed to look to the future as the king was doing.

22

LEOFRIC

'AH, EARL LEOFRIC. YOU'VE FINALLY DECIDED IT'S TIME TO FACE ME?' LADY Emma's face was twisted with fury, her hands clenched on the two armrests on her chair. They glowed whitely in the gloom.

'My lady.' He'd been prepared for her fury. And she was wrong to think he'd only now dared show his face. There had been far more pressing concerns than rebuilding an always testy relationship with the king's mother. That he'd come at all spoke of his high regard for her, but she wouldn't see it that way.

So far, the winter had been harsh, the snow drifts high enough to block doors and strand the animals in the fields. Even in the towns, it had been hard going. On his journey to Winchester, he'd come across the huddled remains of unwary travellers caught out in the terrible snowstorms. Their deaths would have been cold and lonely, and he pitied every single person who'd suffered.

There'd been no let-up since the poor summer had turned into a violent and unpredictable winter. The only surety had been that many had died. It dismayed him.

'Don't be all 'my lady.' You know what you did when you supported my son when you allowed him to deprive Bishop Stigand of his new position. Look at me. Look how low I've fallen?' Lady Emma indicated her accommodations as she spoke, and he could find nothing wrong with them.

Yes, she was attended by only a handful of men and women, and yes, that wasn't the norm for her, but the hearth was heaped high with good wood, and something that smelled delicious was being prepared for her meal. After what he'd seen that day, he could find no pity for her. She was the king's mother and honoured, as much as she could be, when she did nothing but interfere in the king's affairs.

She had a solid roof above her head, the company of those who esteemed her, and an earl calling to ensure she was well. While Lady Emma might be ignored by her son and ridiculed for attempting to influence another of her children's rule, she'd never be destitute, and the people of Winchester, no matter the king's personal opinion, adored her.

'My lady,' he tried to stop her litany of complaints.

'Don't, my lord, just don't. You forget how long I've known you and your father before that. You pride yourself on always doing the right thing, upholding your oaths, and being the most loyal of servants to the kings you serve, and yet, it's always to your own advantage. Your ability to twist and turn to suit your ends is well-known and reaches far beyond England's shores.'

Leofric nodded. Her words didn't sting, but the fact that she had the audacity to speak them to him was amazing. She'd spent her life being bent and twisted depending on how the wind blew, always ensuring she came out on top, no matter what. Yes, her two husbands had been difficult men, but they were both dead, and she yet thrived.

'I serve my king, always. As an earl in this great country, it's my role to ensure the king's word is heeded and obeyed.'

'As you did with Harthacnut when you stood up for the people of Worcester and Coventry.'

'Would you say King Harthacnut acted as a king should? When he strove to take from the poor because he'd over-exceeded his expenditure and promised his shipmen wealth England didn't possess? On top of that, Harthacnut was a wealthy man. And I've seen the treasury. He was never exactly struggling for coin.'

'He was the king,' her tone was stinging. 'And you say you always do what the king orders, but it seems that only counts when you agree. Therefore, you must have agreed with the king when he cast my bishop aside and pensioned me off to this humble home in Winchester.'

'Your home is hardly humble, and your bishop shouldn't have claimed the abbey as his own. That wealth was not his to have. It seems to me that you, like your Harthacnut, care only about money and not about your responsibilities. You have more than most people, yes, you've lost the ear of the king, but did you truly expect anything else after everything that's happened between the two of you?'

'I am his mother,' Lady Emma almost spat those words, which were more venomous than a snake.

'Then, my lady, you should have always remembered that. You can't suddenly decide you're his mother because he has what you want.'

'I've twice been a queen,' she interjected fiercely, as though that excused everything.

'And twice you've abandoned your son. Are the two things connected?' he angled the complaint at her, one eye raised. Their conversation had gradually increased in volume and was far from private. Yet he didn't much mind. He would do the same to her if she wanted to throw stones at him.

'I'll tell my son of your disgraceful words,' Lady Emma's chest heaved as she spoke, her face black with fury.

'When will you do that? Does he come to you and speak with you and listen to what you have to tell him?'

'Earl Leofric!' It seemed she hardly knew what to say to that. Perhaps, he admitted, it was cruel to show that he knew how much the king ignored her. But, well, he had come to mend fences with her, and she was determined only to argue with him. He knew full well that none of the other members of the witan had spared her even a moment's thought, and this was all the thanks he was going to get. Even his wife had cautioned him against it. While he knew there was a long-standing disagreement between the two women, on this, Lady Godgifu was proving right.

'It is difficult,' and now he spoke more softly. 'To have one's failing so aptly highlighted, isn't it?' He hoped this might end her tirade, but she only lapsed into a furious silence, four fingers drumming on the right arm of her chair.

'You may sit,' she eventually announced, lifting a hand to call for refreshments. Her servant had been stood, waiting, all this time, and now she bustled to attention, offering Leofric a glass of rich wine and a bowl of berries, glistening with the promise of sweetness. He thought to himself, not unlike Lady Emma, even as he nodded his thanks and sipped deeply.

'My son ignores me,' the words cost Lady Emma dear her neck flushed above the expensive brooches that held her dress in position. Her shawl had also slipped, and Leofric caught sight of fine lines in her flesh. They were all getting old, all of them, and she was his elder by several years.

'I know, my lady. Your son is busy managing the affairs of England, finding his place in the country he's been too long absent from.'

'It's not my fault he left England when my second husband Cnut became king. Surely, he should blame his brother, the revered King Edmund, for losing the kingdom.'

'Now, my lady, it does no good to try and rewrite the past either. We must all accept what we once were and what we have become.'

'I'll accept it when my son recalls me to his side. I should be with him. As I was with Harthacnut.'

Leofric allowed the pause to stretch out. Once more, Lady Emma was being economical with the truth. If the tales of fire and brimstone were correct, then surely her tongue should burn for such untruths.

'We tell ourselves stories that help us sleep at night,' he tried again. He was settled in a comfortable chair, the heat of the fire enticing him, the rich wine making him drowsy. Lady Emma still drank from the king's cellars. He considered whether Edward was aware but quickly decided it wasn't for him to inform the king. He hadn't come here to spread greater discord between the mother and son.

'I tell myself the truth,' she hadn't touched her wine, and in fact, her head was held so high, that she didn't even meet his eyes. Leofric allowed himself to huff just slightly.

'What?' she was on to him straight away. 'You think I'm a liar?' Such outrage, such disgust and yet she did lie. He'd seen a copy of her great work written by the monk from St Omer. Throughout it, she'd entirely rewritten the last twenty years of England's history, all the time trying to ensure she appeared benevolent.

For a moment, he considered attacking her with the accusations that Edward often made, that it was her fault Alfred had died, that her older children's absence from England could lie at her feet. But he'd been there. He knew everything. He could see it from both sides of the argument. It didn't help that he esteemed both Lady Emma and King Edward.

They'd both been in impossible situations. Admittedly, Lady Emma had not suffered years of exile and scorn as Edward had.

'Lady Emma, I didn't come here to quarrel with you. I came as a friend. I came as someone who was your ally, and could still be, provided you understand your current, reduced position.'

'You'll help me win back the king's regard? You'll join me in my newest enterprises?' The words were fevered now, and Lady Emma's desperation and delusion were almost unsettling.

'I'll be your friend, provided you do as the king asks of you.'

Now her eyes turned crafty, a sly look in them.

'You should know you're not the only person seeking me out. You aren't alone in thinking that they can win greater regard from the king by reuniting him with his mother.'

'I assume you mean Lord Godwine.'

'I do, yes,' she almost crowed with delight, settling her hand over her crossed knees now, allowing the light to catch the riches on her finger. He noted she wore the ring that Cnut had gifted to her. That alone would have kept her in such a state as she was accustomed to for a good five years, had she found the right person wishing to purchase it.

'He came here, as you did, with talk of the past and the future and how he'll only grow in the king's estimations in good time.'

The news didn't surprise Leofric. The fact that Lady Emma was so desperate for the attention did astound him.

'So you'll win back your son's high opinion, by allying with the other person implicated in the death of Lord Alfred.'

'Lord Alfred was felled at the hands of Lord Ufegat. You know that?'

Leofric didn't deign to reply. He was considering leaving. Nothing good would come from this meeting. His wife had been right. It would have been better to save himself from the king's wrath and just stay away. Yet, his conscience had nagged him. The memory of his father driving him to try and aid the stricken woman. Not, he surmised that she was truly afflicted.

'Earl Godwine tells me his other sons will be made earls, and the king will marry his daughter. He also says that Lord Svein Estridsson has approached him for assistance in combating King Magnus.'

'And does Earl Godwine tell you that the king regrets his haste in making Sweyn an earl, that he says he'll never raise another of his sons so high, and that instead, he'll reward Beorn or Ralph? Does Godwine tell you of the problems with Baldwin of Bruges, the potential for war with Normandy, or the unease in Normandy because of your nephew's death? Or does Earl Godwine merely bring you the tales from the court that might entice you to join forces with him?'

The gloating triumph slid from Lady Emma's face.

'Lady Gytha visits as well.' Her voice was small now.

'And of course, you and Lady Gytha have always been such good friends. Always working for the good of your shared family.' Leofric couldn't keep the disgust from his voice. He'd not appreciated how desperate Lady Emma had become. He should have realised.

'She was my husband's sister by marriage.'

'She was your second husband's sister via a marriage to his sister that saw Lady Estrid's husband being executed for treason.'

None of these facts could be disputed. Yet Lady Emma seemed determined to, even though her hands were now washing one inside the other, her unease evident.

'Do you think it's the best thing for your son to be surrounded by members of the House of Godwine? Surely two earls from one family are enough?'

She chuckled, but the sound was filled with malice.

'Lady Gytha says the king has little choice for a bride. You have no daughter, and neither does Earl Siward. No one will want a bride from another kingdom, not after what happened. Well, what happened to me.' Defiance made her fling those words as though coins on a wooden floor.

'I'm sure the king will decide on a suitable woman to wed, and you've not answered my question.'

'My son needs his family to help him rule.'

'Then, you've already decided that Lord Godwine and his family should over-run England.'

'I didn't say that!'

'I think, my lady, that you did,' Leofric spoke slowly, ensuring she heeded his words.

'What I meant was that he should rule with me beside him.'

'Why? Did you rule beside Cnut or Æthelred? Do you know the procedures and laws that govern all of England? Do you have skills he lacks?'

Again, silence greeted his words. He carefully placed his wine on the table beside him, noting that it wasn't fashioned from wood, but rather marble; cold and icy, as Lady Emma was acting.

'I'm his mother. I'm the Queen Dowager.'

Leofric stood, his eyes never leaving hers.

'If you truly consider yourself his mother, might I humbly suggest that you begin to act like one. A mother's role is to protect her children, to ensure others don't harm them. I don't believe you've yet done that for Edward.'

'I,' her eyes implored him to be kinder, but he had no patience.

'Your son will only allow you back into his life if you begin to place his interests before your own. And, my lady, I can say the same for myself. I thought, between us, we could appreciate what we'd been through, work together, find an understanding, but you, it seems, aren't yet happy to do that. And so, I bid you a good day.'

And without further pause for thought, he swept from the hall, his breath running too fast.

That woman had frustrated him time and time again. He'd offered an olive branch. She'd chosen not to take it.

And yet, the news about Lord Godwine and his daughter was unsettling, not helped by the fact that there was more than a glimmer of truth.

23
LEOFRIC

'MY LORD.'

He turned to face the man who addressed him, still mounted, gleaming with the exertion of a fast ride through the cold day.

'Yes. What is it?'

'I've been bid to bring you this.' The man reached down, offering a letter for him. Leofric nodded, stepping forwards to take it. His gate wardens would have asked all the necessary questions of the man now, all that needed to be determined was whether the missive came from Lady Estrid. Certainly, he didn't recognise the messenger, but she could rarely use the same man.

'I'm to await a reply,' the messenger stated.

'Then you'd best put your horse in the stables and avail yourself of food and drink from my servants. I'll read it and determine if a reply needs to be written.'

A grin split the white-cold face. The roads were thick with mud from heavy rains. Leofric almost wished the temperature would drop low enough to freeze.

'My thanks, my lord.'

Leofric glanced at the letter, a feeling of unease welling in his belly, even though he didn't think to expect unpleasant news. But then he recognised the seal, and he relaxed. Lady Emma. Of course, she would want to have the last word in their argument from a few days ago.

He moved to find a perch to settle on in the busy courtyard. He'd been preparing for a ride out and didn't much want to interrupt his plans.

'My Lord Leofric, Earl of Mercia,' he knew the hand that had scratched the words wouldn't be her own as he opened the letter.

'I must apologise for my harsh words. Your visit was an act of kindness and friendship. I appreciate that now. My son treats me harshly, that is right, but of course, it is not at your instigation. I should have known better than to blame you. And now that my apologies are made, I will inform you of what I know. I made illusions, but it is a fact. Lady Gytha crows that her daughter will wed the king, perhaps not yet, but soon. I don't believe we can do anything to prevent it, but being aware of the development will allow you to plan and plot.'

'I cannot explain my son's actions. Some would perhaps say he has no choice, but, as you and I know, there's always a choice where the House of Godwine is involved. I believe my son acts wilfully, perhaps keen to counter the hopes of Harthacnut, to make a name for himself. He wishes for his independence from me, but all he does is replace me with another malevolent force, not, of course, that I am malevolent.'

'I advise you to do nothing. It must be hoped that the king will quickly tire of his choice of bride, that the marriage will perhaps not take place, and that Earl Godwine won't get his wish. But I doubt it, as I know you will.'

'There is, of course, one option open to us. We could encourage Lord Svein Estridsson to make a move against the king or even King Magnus again. Better to have a king amenable to our wishes than one so greatly in the debt of Earl Godwine. You are right, we have not been unified for some time, and now Godwine seeks to advance while I'm left with nothing.'

'Inform me by return of your plans. I'll add my name and seal to anything you determine to send to Lord Svein or King Magnus.'

'Your friend, Lady Emma, from her humble home in Winchester.'

Leofric was shaking his head by the time he came to the end of the letter. Was Lady Emma unhinged? How could she even make such a suggestion? Lady Gunnhild and Osgot Clapa had already been removed from England, Lady Gunnhild's sons as well, and now Lady Emma planned to do the same! Perhaps Edward knew his mother better than she knew herself. Maybe his plans for the enlarged fleet were based on knowing that others would wish to depose him.

Yet, at the heart of it, he could understand her rage.

What, after all, had Lord Godwine ever done to deserve such reward from the succession of kings he'd served? Leofric couldn't forget Godwine's involvement in the death of Northman, and neither did he want to, and that had merely been the first of many missteps by his adversary. And yet, he still maintained and cultivated the support of Edward.

Even after all this time, was the House of Leofwine nothing more than a tool for the king to use? Did the king have no regard for him, and what such an alliance would do to England? Surely, Earl Sweyn's actions in Shropshire and at Sandwich spoke of a man who had responsibilities above his abilities.

But that was not the matter at heart. Not now, and Leofric determined to think only of Lady Emma's outrageous request that he support an invasion of his kingdom. He wouldn't. Not again. England had suffered more than enough. What the domain needed was peace and good weather, and decent harvests to fill the bellies of the hungry and restore the stability that had disappeared since Cnut's death.

He paced inside his hall, calling for ink and parchment as he went. The startled eyes of the messenger met his, and he nodded. Leofric was sure the man could have no idea of the letter's contents.

Lady Emma wouldn't be so brash as to inform all and sundry that she meant to ferment rebellion against her son.

For a moment, Leofric considered sending a verbal message, but no, he wanted his rejection of her idea to be in writing.

'Lady Emma, Queen Dowager, at Winchester,' the words flowed from him, spiked with anger and frustration.

'I thank you for your apology. I'm keen to be your friend, as we once were. But it will not be brought about by the demand that I support insurrection against the king. He is my oath-sworn lord. He's my anointed king, and Edward is England's natural heir.'

'I insist that you put aside such notions. You must, as I advised you, be the king's mother from now on, and in such a position, it's your responsibility to support him and to accept your punishment as your due. If I hear one more word of such insurrection, I will act to have your current, pleasant confinement changed to something more fitting for the treason you discuss.'

He signed the letter with a flourish, warmed the wax, and imprinted his seal that showed the two-headed eagle onto the rolled parchment. Only when the missive was in the hands of the messenger did his tense shoulders relax. Only then did he stride out of the hall and into the brisk day. He would ride, and he would rage at both Lady Emma and the king's supposed intentions to marry Lord Godwine's daughter, but he knew his place.

Whatever the king decided to do, he would support him. Even if it went against everything he stood for and even if it meant he had to break his oath to Harthacnut. And to himself.

THE HORSE'S GAIT BENEATH HIM WAS SMOOTH, THE MOVEMENT CALMING AS he tried to banish all thoughts of the king and his mother. Ælfgar rode beside him, but he was holding his counsel, which suited Leofric just fine.

They'd not yet discussed what Ælfgar had discovered in London. Leofric appreciated that if there'd been any huge problems, Ælfgar would have told him immediately. His reticence spoke then of all being well, and that pleased Leofric. It was time matters settled down. When Ælfgar did speak, Leofric startled.

'There's to be war in the Welsh kingdoms. I have it on good authority that Gruffydd Ap Llewelyn will move against Hywel Ap Edwin.'

'It's not for me to concern myself with,' Leofric dismissed the notion even though it was unwelcome. 'Earl Sweyn will have to prove himself.'

'And you think he'll do so?' The sting in Ælfgar's voice was easy to hear.

'He'll have no choice. If he fails in such a task, the king might replace him. Edward won't welcome feeble men on his borders.'

'Would the king make war on Gruffydd Ap Llewelyn?'

'I think the king would go to war against anyone who threatened England. He's not afraid to do so; his ship expedition proves that.'

'The new shipbuilding programme progresses well. Even Eowa was impressed with the skill and organisation.'

'There are more than enough ship-builders to do what Edward commands. And many will be desperate to earn a wage and become one of his lithesmen.'

'Yes, when they begin to recruit. Certainly, there'll be coin aplenty to pay them, although, well, I worry the London mint might be making their coins a little light. It seems that more than just Edward will benefit from his new coinage.'

'It's always the way,' but Leofric's lips were sealed in a tight line. 'I inspected the mint at Oxford while you were in London. Beorhtweald assures me that the restrike progresses well and that the weights are good. I believe him. He's never produced shoddy work before. He's doubled the number of moneyers there. There's good money to be made while the king is so keen to fund the ship-building schemes.'

'Eowa thought the king was stealing the silver. I explained the process to him.'

'Good, it wouldn't do for others to believe the king was gaining more than they believed from the process.'

'Tell me,' and Leofric reigned in his mount beside Ælfgar, realising he would have to share the information with his son. 'Did you hear anything of the king's marriage in London?'

'No, I didn't. I had to listen to Earl Sweyn and his belief that Harold will become an earl soon, but nothing about the king's marriage. Why? What have you heard?'

'Lady Emma is adamant the king means to marry Lady Edith.'

'Earl Godwine's daughter? No, that can't be right.'

'I share your thoughts, but equally, who should he choose instead?'

'A bride from the kingdom of the Scots, or perhaps from Normandy. Anywhere but Godwine's daughter.'

'Yes, they would be better matches, but equally, now that I've heard the notion, I can't talk myself from it. I think we should prepare for the king's next act of foolishness.'

'Bloody hell,' Ælfgar exploded. 'It's as though Edward means to undermine himself. Can he truly be making these decisions alone? Or does Earl Godwine know something about him that makes him do as the man commands as though he were a dog at heel?'

'It makes no sense, and yet, it does. I don't know,' and Leofric shook his head, even as he gazed at the ruin of the fields around him. There was no sign of growth. Everything slept beneath the soil. He could only hope that the following year would bring better weather for the crops.

'I don't know why the king would ally with Lord Godwine. He can't be blind to the potential for problems, and if he is, well, how can I talk him from the decision? He's the king. I supported him. I did what Harthacnut asked me to do. Maybe I should have refused the nomination and presented one of King Edmund's sons instead.'

'But, they still haven't been found,' Ælfgar commented, his tone reasonable.

'No, they haven't,' Leofric confirmed. 'Maybe, that should be our priority. Maybe we should send someone to see if they yet live, to encourage them to return to England because although Edward mentioned it, I've heard of no progress being made. I don't know if anyone was ever sent to find them.'

'But is it not treason?'

'Treason would be to proclaim them as king. I have no plans on doing that, but, I should like there to be an alternative. Someone to keep Edward's focus on where it should be.'

'And, of course, the sons of King Edmund would have no love for Earl Godwine. That helps.'

'It would, yes, and no, they wouldn't. Godwine fought for Cnut against his father. It seems that being responsible for killing a brother isn't enough to counter the allure of the House of Godwine. But perhaps, just perhaps, there would be greater loyalty from two men who have no memory of their father or England.'

Ælfgar was silent, and Leofric waited patiently for a response.

'I don't believe it will be enough,' Ælfgar finally admitted. 'If Lady Edith marries the king and gives him a son, it won't matter.'

'Conceivably,' Leofric admitted. 'But I can do nothing. All these years and now Lord Godwine seems ever closer to what he's always wanted. A man with such ambitions, with the morals of an ally cat, shouldn't triumph.'

THE ANGLO-SAXON CHRONICLE ENTRY FOR AD1044

(C - Abingdon)In this year Archbishop Eadsige resigned the bishopric because of his infirmity and consecrated to it Siward, abbot of Abington. He did this by permission and with the advice of the king and of Earl Godwine. Otherwise it was known to few people because the archbishop suspected that somebody else would ask for it, or purchase it whom he less trusted and favoured if more people knew about it. In this year there was a very great famine over all England and corn dearer than anyone ever remembered so that a sester of wheat went up to 60 pence and this same year the king went out to Sandwich with thirty-five ships.

(D - Worcester) In this year Bishop Ælfweard of London died on 25 July. He had first been abbot of Evesham and he greatly promoted the good of that monastery while he was there; then he went to Ramsey, and there he passed away. And Manni, was chosen abbot and consecrated on 10 August. And in the course of the year, Gunnhilde, that noble lady, King Cnut's kinswoman was banished and she then stayed in Bruges for a long time and then she went to Denmark.

(E - Peterborough)This year died Lyfing, bishop of Devonshire, and Leofric, the king's priest, succeeded to it. And in this same year died Ælfstan, abbot of St Augstine's on 5th July, and in this same year Osgot Clapa was expelled.

24

JANUARY, AD1045, WINCHESTER, LEOFRIC

LEOFRIC HARDLY KNEW WHAT TO DO WITH HIMSELF. ANGER COURSED through his body so violently he was sure that others must be aware of the deep unease settled deep within him.

After everything he'd done, Leofric just couldn't understand why the king was repaying him so poorly.

His son had been overlooked for an earldom in favour of bloody Sweyn, an embarrassment to his father, mother, and the king. And now this. Leofric could feel the burn of the king's gaze as he announced to the witan that he'd chosen whom he'd marry and that it was to be Edith, daughter of bloody Lord Godwine.

Leofric had felt his face freeze at the news, hoping with all his heart that his son maintained his calm response, that his oath-sworn men didn't cry out in outrage. And all the time, there had been Lord Godwine, watching him, the smug expression on his face intolerable, for all Leofric could admit, it had been understandable. It spoke of all Lord Godwine had achieved since King Harthacnut's death.

Harthacnut had known what Godwine was. He'd seen right through the man to the simmering ambitions swirling beneath the façade of a courtier. In that, Harthacnut had shown more insight than his father. Cnut had fallen under Lord Godwine's influence, even if he had understood it by the time his reign ended.

Yet, the news that the king would marry had cheered the other members of the witan, almost as though they couldn't see the same ambitions that infected every member of that vast family. Leofric thought of what he could have accomplished if only he'd been able to father more than just one son. He'd always known it was storing problems for the future, and now he felt that even more.

Not only did Lord Godwine have the sons to hold every single earldom within England, but now he'd accomplished the greatest of all feats, marrying his oldest daughter to the king as well.

'You'll have to compose yourself,' Olaf had furiously hissed at him. 'Unless you want bloody Lady Gytha to look down her nose at you even more than she already does.'

Leofric had considered shaking aside Olaf's concern, but he was correct to caution him.

He and his family had survived so much; the brutal assassination of his brother, the loss of his father, the death of his brother, but this? Well. Leofric held to the belief that his father had never been forced to endure all that he had. There were stories that Æthelred had been his own worst enemy, choosing allies who were both liabilities and incompetent to boast, but even Æthelred had never purposefully allowed one single family to gain so much control over him.

Leofric couldn't help wishing that King Harald yet lived. Then, all of this could have been avoided.

'Lord Father,' Ælfgar bowed slightly before him as they converged at the property in Winchester where they were staying, preparing to attend the king's marriage ceremony later that day. His movements were sharp and concise, very unlike him. It showed his suppressed fury as well. Elgiva entered the room behind her husband. She curtsied to her father and mother, but the smile on her face didn't reach her eyes. None of them was pleased about this, yet there was no choice. The king had decided, and the king had resolved to ally himself even more closely with Lord Godwine and Lady

Gytha. Their dynasty, as vast as it already was, would only grow bigger.

And worse, their grandson should, by rights, one day be king of England.

It felt as though everything he'd ever worked for, all his father had sacrificed, including his sight in one eye, had been for nothing. Nothing.

But now Leofric had to pick himself up, and lead his family through what could only be dark days ahead. The promise of the future that he'd dreamed about, when his son would rule with him, had been replaced with the starkness of what could only be a huge power struggle. Yet, they couldn't afford to lose more than they already had.

He found a tight smile on his lips. Here, just the four of them, they could be honest with one another. They might be unable to devise a path back to greatness, but it wasn't all over. It couldn't be. He wouldn't allow it. None of them was dead. None of them was an enemy of the king. There had to be hope in that.

'Today feels like a dark day for our family, I admit it.' Ælfgar's stifled cry of anguish told him all he needed to know about his son's state of mind.

'I know it,' and he nodded at his son. Ælfgar refused to meet his eyes but then met them squarely. This wasn't defiance. This was an acknowledgement that he recognised what the future held for him and his three small sons and daughters.

'We've lived through far, far worse, and our family has always survived. We've prevailed. Danish kings have tried to kill us, English kings have ignored us, and others have struck down men in their prime for doing little more than serving their king. The English queen has used us for her own ends, and Lord Godwine has done all he could to prevail against us. Today feels as though he's won that fight. It felt like it when Sweyn became an earl. In the future, I've no doubt that Harold will follow in his steps, and Edith will birth the king an heir, but we must not give in. No matter what.'

A sift sign escaped Elgiva's lips. Leofric noted that she'd taken particular care with her appearance. Her dress was of the finest linen, family heirlooms of the double-headed eagle were prominent on brooches and in the stitching close to her neckline. She was a member of his family by marriage, yet she'd made the greatest effort to proclaim her fierce loyalty.

He admired her. She wasn't immune to the whims of kings.

'I have three grandsons who will grow to become earls, a grand-daughter who may well marry an earl or even a king. All is not lost. If we can only triumph.'

This time it was his wife who spluttered at his words. Her eyes were flecked with fury.

'In time, the House of Leofwine will prevail once more. I'm sure of it. No man can live forever, and all can change on the last gasp of a dying man.'

He knew it was treason to speak as he did, yet Edward had done nothing to make him regret his desire for the future to be rewritten, and sooner rather than later.

'Today, we'll join the king in celebrating his union with Edith. We'll ignore the supercilious glances from Lord Godwine and his family, the snide remarks from those who attach their star to the House of Godwine. It's been done before, and it can be done once more. We'll do it again.' His voice rang with conviction, and he was pleased with the words.

Leofric took the time to hold the eyes of his son, wife, and daughter by marriage. None of them looked away. They accepted this new, unwelcome task. And he trusted them to do what needed to be done.

They would hold themselves rigid against the criticism, the laughter, the derogatory statements. They would resist being angered when the king seemed to side-line them, preferring the pull of the House of Godwine.

A knock at the door and Leofric winced at the sound.

'My lord?' His servant called to him.

'Yes, what is it?'

'My lord, the king requests your presence immediately.'

The unease in his stomach solidified, and he felt heavier than iron.

'Very well. I'll go to him. Attend upon the festivities at the Old Minster. Be seen, and I'll join you shortly.'

He offered his wife a quick kiss, his son a grip on his forearm. He wouldn't let them see the flash of fear. Was it possible that Lord Godwine had already moved this quickly? Was it likely that all of his words would mean nothing, his intentions would be irrelevant in the face of crushing odds?

Catching the eye of his nephews as he slipped through the exterior door, he raised his chin to them. They'd suffered so much already. He'd never forgive the king if he took yet more from them. To grow to adulthood without a father was already terrible enough. An experience that Edward should have understood.

Outside, the street was a bustling mass of people trying to move towards the Old Minster and away from it. He grimaced, pleased to feel the solidness of Olaf at his side. Even if he wore ceremonial clothes, Leofric believed no man could get the better of Olaf, no matter their weapon skills. Olaf could make use of anything that came to hand.

'Surely he could have sent for you last evening?' Olaf grumbled, even as he forged a path for his earl and brother by marriage. Leofric couldn't deny that this crush only added to his foul mood. Olaf was right. Whatever the king needed to say to him could have been done at any point in the last few months, ever since the king had announced his intention to marry before the witan, giving Leofric no warning. No, for that, he'd had to rely on Lady Emma.

Leofric didn't reply, instead focusing on keeping his clothing clear from others and the quick hands that would attempt to snatch such finery from him, even though he was the king's man.

Along the street they went, the cries of the stall owners rife in his ears, some almost shouting directly into his ear because he was forced so close to the walls. He would have liked to follow one of the side streets that jutted from the main thoroughfare, but even they were crowded. News of the king's marriage had brought men and women from far and wide, hoping to catch a glimpse of the new English king and his pretty wife, despite the terrible cold that froze fingers and toes quickly. There was not a bed to be had in the town. It was chaotic.

'This is intolerable,' he fumed, yanking his cloak free from the press of bodies, ensuring it was held close to his body by wrapping it tightly around him. If the crowd should abruptly melt away, he'd be standing, looking foolish. The thought only added to his black mood.

Finally, up ahead, he caught sight of the towering edifice of the Old Minster, and then, abruptly, the crowd was prevented from surging onwards by a line of the king's huscarls. They allowed Leofric and Olaf easy passage. They were familiar faces to all.

'Thank goodness for that,' Leofric breathed a sigh of relief, taking the time to straighten his tunic and cloak.

Only then did Leofric take notice of his surroundings. There was a steady trickle of royal courtiers inside the church. It was still some time until the ceremony, but some would be content to wait a long time to achieve a better view of what was happening.

Leofric hurried up the few stone steps and into the Old Minster itself. He bowed his head for just a moment toward the altar and then turned to look for the king. He tried not to consider what had happened when he'd last been inside the Old Minster. A reign that had begun with hope was now anything but that.

'Ah, Earl Leofric, my thanks for attending so quickly,' Edward's voice was at his shoulder, and he spun quickly.

'I see the journey has been uncomfortable,' Edward indicated his face and attire, and Leofric winced, even as he bowed.

'There's a crowd out there. Perhaps more huscarls are needed.'

'Yes, I've already instructed that more men line the streets. I'll not have my guests being set upon on their way to the Old Minster.'

Leofric appreciated that Olaf had melted away into the mass of others. Around the king, there seemed to be some sort of honourary circle. No one dared approach him unless he beckoned them closer.

Edward was in his element. His wedding tunic was a bright turquoise, the colour akin to the feathers of a peacock. It suited the king with his greying, light hair and quick eyes. He'd taken a great deal of care when choosing his clothes. Or, someone else had. He was watching everything and everyone. In the future, he would discomfort people with his excellent memory of what they were wearing or whom they were speaking to before his wedding.

'I've been remiss in not speaking to you sooner, but I believe you'll understand my motivations soon enough.'

Leofric was unsure how to respond to the king's comments and decided to hold his tongue instead.

'I know this marriage is not to your liking. I'm not immune to the greed and ambitions of Earl Godwine. He believes he's achieved all he can, and that one day he'll be the father of a king. I wished to assure you that this marriage will not see that happen.' Leofric felt his forehead furrow at the words.

'But surely, my lord king, you'll soon be a father, and Lady Edith will be the mother of those children.'

'That's certainly what Earl Godwine and his daughter believe, but I can assure you, they're both wrong. They're not quite achieving the coup they think they are. Lord Leofric, I wish to guarantee that no children will be born from this union. None at all. Of that, I can assure you. Rather than rewarding Earl Godwine, this wedding is merely a means of punishing him and his deluded son and ruining his ambitions. He could marry his daughter to any king in any kingdom, but no, he has his sights set on me. And what am I to do but give in to his demands.' Edward's lips formed a tight line as he spoke, a tick of amusement on his left cheek.

'I share this with you now because I know you think I'm scolding you for only having fathered a son. But it's not you who's to be admonished, but Earl Godwine. Unfortunately, his daughter must also endure. She's a pleasant enough woman.'

Leofric knew his mouth hung open in shock. He simply didn't know what to make of the king's words.

'Lady Edith won't be the first woman to share my bed, far from it. Landless royal family members hold their appeal for women who think of making their fortune in Normandy, just as anywhere. And yet not a single one of those women has ever produced a child for me. It seems, alas, that I can never be a father, that I lack the ability.'

Only now did Leofric comprehend what the king was telling him.

'Truly, my lord king?'

'Truly, my loyal earl. I erred when I rewarded Earl Sweyn, I'll try not to make more mistakes. And I can guarantee that there'll be no children from this marriage as far as I can know these things. Whoever rules after my death, they'll not be my son, and more, they'll not be Earl Godwine's grandson. And that, I believe, satisfies your oath to King Harthacnut.'

A tight smile played around Edward's face as he spoke.

'But, my lord king, you assign yourself to an unhappy marriage.'

'I do no such thing. I make a political match that will keep my most disruptive earl close to me. It's a shame I don't have unmarried sisters or nieces to marry his sons, but that's something over which I have no control. Know that I take this step willingly. I'll find happiness with Lady Edith, and I hope she'll find peace with me in time. I can also hope for her loyalty, but I think she'll always be torn, her principal ambition to protect her family.'

Leofric nodded, grasping the full implications of Edward's decision. Edward watched him, waiting to weigh his response.

'My lord king, it's a piece of diabolical deception,' Leofric found he couldn't help smiling at King Edward.

'I know it is, Lord Leofric, and Earl Godwine thinks me too thick-headed to devise such a thing, and yet I have, all the same. He'll never even consider that I took such a step with any deceit in mind, which makes it all the sweeter. Now, try and hide your delight while I take my vows, but share the news with your son when you're able. But, for today, please continue as you have before. It only adds to my enjoyment. And please, take this conversation as proof that you've broken no oath to my predecessor. I know it was a heavy obligation to be placed on you and your family. I would hope not to burden you similarly, but of course, I can make no such promise.'

Leofric found himself bowing low unbidden, even as the king turned to attend to his preparations. In a daze, he made his way to the main body of the church, Olaf emerging from the press of bodies to join him.

Yet, Olaf was astute enough to say nothing of what Leofric and the king had spoken about while there were so many ears to hear.

'We'll make our way to our assigned seats,' Leofric muttered. He was keen to be away from those who gossiped and plotted in the clear view of the king. 'Stay with me,' Leofric urged.

At the front of the church, Leofric caught sight of Lord Godwine, Sweyn at his side, and Harold. The two older men looked overly pleased with themselves, although Leofric detected some unease in Harold's bearing. He was an astute young man. Leofric knew that Ælfgar esteemed him, and more than once, he'd wished a different father for the young man.

Lord Godwine caught sight of Leofric's approach, and his broad grin stretched ever wider, almost expanding as much as his inflated waistline. His show of wealth, his fur-trimmed cloak, tunic, arraigned with heavy stitching and gems, spoke of a man who believed his position had just been secured, cemented, before the whole court.

For just a moment, Leofric paused. Had the king truly done what he said? Or was he merely trying to apply a salve to the burn he'd inflicted on the House of Leofwine? If the king could even consider the marriage a trick, was it not equally possible that he could do the same to Leofric? But no, he dismissed the worry. Edward was not his mother to set every one of his loyal earls against the other. In his time as Harthacnut's heir, he'd learned much more than Leofric had realised, and now he was putting it into good effect.

'Earl Leofric,' Godwine's voice thundered, ensuring all heard.

'You're welcome to witness my daughter's union with England's glorious king.'

The words almost caught in Leofric's throat as he tried to congratulate the self-satisfied man. But of course, that was what the king demanded from him.

'I'm pleased to be welcomed and wish your daughter, and the king, much happiness and fruitfulness in their union.' Godwine guffawed at the words, his eyes bright with ambition.

'How can it not be? Her mother and I have eleven children to our name. I'm sure the union will be blessed with the cries of a newborn in no more than nine months.'

Sweyn chuckled maliciously at the words, taking delight in his family's triumph, for once accepting that he was a member of Godwine's family and not Cnut's son. Leofric would have liked nothing more than to wipe the smug expression from his face, but he didn't want to waste his time. There would be a time for revelling in the failure of the House of Godwine's plans, but it wasn't yet.

'Then, I look forward to standing as the child's godfather when the time is right. The House of Wessex can dream of a glittering future.' And so spoken, Leofric walked away and found his place in the congregation, Olaf close behind him.

'Fucking arsehole,' Olaf huffed angrily.

'Always,' Leofric replied, keen to watch all those sycophants who came to make their presence known to Godwine and his sons. Lady Gytha was absent, no doubt assisting her daughter, while the remaining children performed other tasks. But now Leofric watched with detachment. If the king could truly guarantee his wife would never carry his child, then, and Leofric realised he'd only just understood this simple fact, who would rule in the future?

Edward was already older than King Cnut had been when he died, and he'd long outlived Kings Harald and Harthacnut. While he appeared hale and hearty, and certainly his father had lived a good long life, who would be his heir?

But that was not a problem for today, hopefully.

No, as Lady Godgifu made her way to him, he found a tight smile to alleviate the worry around her lined-eyed, admiring her clothing choice afresh.

'Husband,' she curtsied briefly, already turning to pick out the circle of Godwinist adherents.

'The king was well?' she continued as Leofric nodded to his son and daughter by marriage. His nephews followed Lady Elgiva, Wulfstan tugging at his ceremonial tunic with irritation. Leofric suppressed a smirk and found a smile instead for Lady Mildryth. It had been decades since she'd last stepped foot in Winchester, but for such a wedding she'd found the strength to attend. Leofric was overjoyed to see her, especially as she quelled Wulfstan's fussing with a sharp slap on his right hand.

Leofric looked away, not wanting his lighter mood to be seen by any. Yet, his wife had not been his partner for so many years without knowing him well. As the congregation settled, the king standing at the altar, Lady Edith led there by her father, she turned to him and craned her lips to his ear.

'I don't know what the king said to you. But I know it's pleased you, which brings me greater hope than this marriage does.'

Leofric turned to her, noting the assurance in her eyes. He made an arch with his arm, and she slid her arm between it, standing closer together than was perhaps respectable, but he was sure his God would forgive him just this one.

'My lord king is an astute man, a clever man, and one who understands his allies and enemies better than we perhaps give him credit for.'

'Then, I'll enjoy the feast that follows the wedding,' and she lapsed into silence.

Before them, Lady Edith smiled prettily to her father and then turned to her new husband-to-be with only the slightest hesitation. She was a beautiful woman, Leofric would never deny it, and her brightly coloured dress accentuated her beauty and her youth. The ageing Lady Gytha suffered in comparison; her girth expanded beyond even that of her husband. She carried her childbearing years heavily. Leofric appreciated that Lady Edith, or Queen Edith as she would be soon, would never suffer the same fate. She would retain her youthful elegance and svelteness.

And then his gaze was caught by Lady Emma. He'd been unaware that she'd been allowed to attend the king's marriage ceremony, but perhaps the king had deemed her useful for this task. Without her there, his family would have consisted only of his nephew and Beorn.

Lady Emma arched an eyebrow at him, her fury evident in the action. Leofric nodded to her. How he considered, could he convey to her, across the expanse of the magnificent church, just what the king had shared with him? But then, if the king had wanted her to know, he'd have told her? That meant, clearly, that Lady Emma was to remain ignorant. With whom then, had the king decided to share his news?

Leofric couldn't imagine that Earl Siward would have been a recipient of the information. Was it only he?

He kept his eyes on Lady Emma, noticing the care that had been taken with her clothing and hair. It glimmered beneath a covering of the lightest silk, ensuring that the greys were mingled with the fabric's silver, obscuring them, even while leaving them in place.

Lady Emma's dress was of the same shade; her hands clasped demurely before her. To one side stood Ralph, his back to Earl Leofric, although Beorn to the other side of her, half-turned, no doubt curious to see what distracted the king's mother from the union of her son, the only one of her sons to live long enough to marry.

Hard eyes flickered to Leofric, a warning in them, or perhaps, cold indifference. For all his friendship with Lady Estrid, Beorn seemed reticent to allow the same. Leofric inclined his head, a mild greeting, nothing else. Not for the first time, Leofric considered why Beorn hadn't returned to Denmark.

A comment from the bishop and Leofric's gaze was riveted on

events unfolding before him; the king's voice giving the desired responses, Lady Edith's voice lighter, but doing the same. Yet, when he turned, Lady Emma's gaze was still on him. Could she not bring herself to watch what was happening? Perhaps not. It was Lady Edith, who, as soon as the marriage was concluded, would sit in the place she'd thought would belong to her.

While the king had distanced himself from his mother throughout the last eighteen months, this was the moment when all that became irreversible. Leofric didn't believe that Edward would be like his father. He wouldn't allow his mother to raise his children, as Lady Elfrida had done for Æthelred. But no. The king said there would be no children, so it was an irrelevant thought.

But it meant that Lady Emma was being resoundingly replaced. It would be strange to have a new queen. She'd held the position for most of the last forty years. Leofric couldn't help but pity her, and it was evident that Lady Emma followed his thoughts, even though they were so far apart.

She looked defiant. He considered whether she'd genuinely followed through with her desire to approach Lord Svein or King Magnus? Would she rather have anyone as her king, besides her son, provided they were her ally?

Leofric listened to the bishop's intonation, his voice filling the full church as he first joined them together and then offered a Mass in celebration before the anointing of their new queen could take place. It was to be a long and tedious day in the Old Minster

He risked a glance along the row where his family stood to witness the same. His wife's eyes were focused on the king and his new wife, her face betraying no emotion. His son stood beside his mother, his eyes forward, but Leofric wasn't sure whether he watched the ceremony or not. Certainly, it looked as though he did, and his wife, Elgiva, clasped his hand tightly, perhaps in memory of their union.

His sister came next. Ealdgyth met his eyes, a wry smirk lightening her face, reminding him that none of them was young anymore. She rolled her eyes, almost enjoying the moment even though her loyalty had always been with Lady Emma when she'd fallen foul of King Cnut. Olaf kept her close company. Leofric appreciated that of them all, his family had been the first to welcome the Danes into its fold. They'd just done it far more quietly than Lord Godwine. But that was a thought for another day.

His brother also attended, Godwine, unfortunate that he shared the earl's name, but perhaps it only made his desire to stand against him more fervent. And then there was Northman's wife. Lady Mildryth, kept close company by her two sons, both of them strong men, clever men, worthy children of his honourable brother. He knew his father would be proud to see them all. His niece stood with her cousins. The only member of the family to be missing was Brother Leofric, his place at his monastery and not the king's marriage ceremony.

All of them wore the sigil of the House of Leofwine in some way. He had the two-headed eagle's emblem stitched into his tunic and smaller versions cavorted around the hem. His wife wore a golden depiction on the diadem threaded through her hair. His son opted for a similar design to his own, wearing it proudly on his clothing.

Elgiva had a bracelet with a realistic-looking charm on it, the eagles' eyes, particularly drawing the viewer's attention by the tiny dots of ruby in their eyes. His brother stood firm, his stance that of a military man used to facing the borders with the Welsh kings, and yet even he condescended to the small necklace Leofric had gifted to him, showing it proudly. Godwine might not have reached the same level of earl as Leofric had done, but he was an extremely important man in Mercia, as Earl Sweyn was beginning to realise.

His sister hadn't come alone either. Two of her hounds sat attentively, tails silent against the hard floor, and Leofric thought of Hund. He missed the animal's constant attention. It was time he allowed himself to replace the animal.

Leofric's pride at his family and their honourable ways threatened to spill over. He couldn't deny that they'd all managed to smooth away the fury of the king's marriage, just as he'd commanded, and that filled Leofric with renewed resolve.

His family were united, always united. His father had ensured they all understood their position and roles in life, and his brother and sister had ensured their children knew it as well, just as Ælfgar did. And that was something that Lord Godwine could never claim while his eldest son was unruly in his position of an earl, his daughter wed to the childless and almost friendless king, and the other children, jealous of those that had achieved more than them.

With such unity within his own family, perhaps the uncertain future was to be welcomed, after all. His family was equal to that of Lord Godwine's even though he'd succeeded in the matter of the king's bride. Leofric almost relished seeing how much his oldest adversary enjoyed that when the truth became undeniable.

No, he'd not managed to do as Harthacnut had demanded him to do, how could he? Not when Lord Godwine was as invidious as he was, but King Edward had heeded his half-brother's words. He was both rewarding Lord Godwine and admonishing him, all at the same time.

But that was for him to know and not to share.

He smiled, the first genuine grin in some months.

Everything was all still in play. He and his family were far from the spent force Godwine believed them to be.

THE ANGLO-SAXON CHRONICLE ENTRY FOR AD1045

(C - Abingdon) *included in 1044.* And in the same year, King Edward married Edith, daughter of Earl Godwine, ten nights before Candlemas.

THANK YOU

Thank you for reading The English King.

If you've enjoyed the book, please do consider leaving a review on Amazon or Goodreads. Thank you in advance.

If you would like to keep up to date with my writing projects and special offers then please sign up for my newsletter. I send out monthly emails, and subscribers then have the option to sign up for a weekly reminder email containing special offers. https://mailchi.mp/d0f05800d212/mjportersubscriber

The King's Brother will be released in June 2023.

HISTORICAL NOTES

THE IDEA OF NATIONALITY AS WE KNOW IT TODAY was not evident during this time period. As Katherine Cross has noted in her book '*Heirs of the Vikings*' the inhabitants of England, Normandy, Denmark, Norway and Sweden were all 'northmen/women'. This is an important factor to consider when trying to make sense of the events that led up to the Norman Conquest. That isn't to say that people didn't make decisions based on what they considered their home country to be. Earl Leofric appears to have been very anti-involvement in anything that wasn't directly related to England, Earl Godwine, perhaps not so much, but then, Godwine had a pan-European family. He had nephews and nieces as far away as the Holy Roman Empire and as close as bordering his own landed interests. It would be intriguing to know how close the family was and whether or not they did advance one another's interests.

What is probably more important is the idea of an 'extended family.' As such, we find King Edward bolstering his small power-base by bringing family members to his court. We might find it strange to discover his nephew Ralph, and his 'cousin' (through a complex set of indirect marriages) as King Edward's greatest 'friends'. It's possible that he also considered Earl Godwine and his sons as his relatives if we follow through with the idea that Beorn Estridsson was his cousin, but potentially not, as otherwise, he married his cousin. Perhaps, as so often the case, it was dependent on what people at the time thought.

We're rapidly coming into a period of events that many people will believe they 'know' and 'understand' but I'll continue to challenge the accepted timeline because that is the joy of writing historical fiction and not non-fiction. And, equally, it's important to understand that what we learned at school or through accepted books might no longer be the current thinking. History is not quite as staid and settled as many will believe it to be.

For those interested in what was happening in Denmark during this period, please consider reading Lady Estrid, which covers the period to 1050, and is a standalone novel, but can be read as a companion to the Earls of Mercia books.

It's not known why Lady Gunnhild was banished from England, alongside her sons. I've made some suppositions and put together a few pieces of known 'fact' to determine that she was the one encouraging King Magnus of Norway to invade England (not that he needed any great encouragement), alongside Osgot Clapa, who was also banished. King Magnus based his claim to England on the alliance he had forged with Harthacnut, in which they had both named each other as their heirs.

Some might have thought this only applied to Denmark, but King Magnus, even as young as he was, had high ambitions and was the stepson of Lady Astrid, the sister of the King of the Svear (Sweden). It doesn't take too much of a stretch to think this was an attempt to knock the family of Cnut off every throne they claimed and to repay them for the years of war and subjugation that they'd endured, especially in Norway.

There is a gap in understanding when I turn to King Magnus of Norway. His invasion of England in AD1043 is my invention to explain why Lady Gunnhild was banished and why he might have felt welcome in England in the first place. Yet, it is right to point out that under Edward, England had her first king since 1016 who wasn't either Danish, or related to King Cnut directly through blood and marriage – Harald was his son with Lady Ælfgifu, Harthacnut his son with Lady Emma – on the other hand, Edward was Lady Emma's son, and perhaps more damningly, the son of King Æthelred II. By now, Æthelred II was deemed a failure in his attempts to combat the invasions of King Swein of Denmark and his son, according to the chronicles, which I think might just have been subjected to a little bit of rewriting after the events.

The events of 1043 and 1044 might be seen as a precursor to AD1066.

Gunnhild took herself off to Flanders, as Lady Emma had done when she was banished by King Harald, and eventually returned to Denmark, where I've not yet been able to track her down.

Her identification as King Cnut's niece, as mentioned in the Anglo-Saxon Chronicle, is perplexing, and I'm wondering if it comes not from the fact she was his biological niece but because of her marriage to Earl Hakon, who was Cnut's nephew, the son of one of his older sisters, Lady Gytha and Earl Eirikr. That said, I've struggled to find Cnut's other sisters. He had five in total – Lady Estrid and Lady Gytha are the most well-known. So, it is possible that Gunnhild was his niece, and I'm looking for problems where none exist. Her second husband, Lord Harold, is identified as the son of Earl Thorkell the Tall, the famous Jomsviking, and Cnut's foster father (although this is disputed). She was undoubtedly, therefore, a high-status woman, married to an earl and then the son of an earl, and her sons could have had an expectation of being rewarded.

Since introducing Ralph, Edward's nephew, as a character in this series, I've read that there is no evidence he was in England before the 1050s, but I've already brought him to England, so he'll have to stay!

It's impossible not to think that Edward struggled to find his feet as England's new king, and some of his decisions appear strange in hindsight. Certainly, it seems that those he should have been able to rely on, his mother most of all, either weren't able to put aside their rampant ambitions or entirely misunderstood Edward's intentions.

Many will feel that the reign of Edward the Confessor is more like 'real' history than earlier periods. There is certainly far more information about him, and the events feel more like we would expect from 1066 onwards. However, I've stuck to my intentions to offer an accounting based first and foremost on information recorded in the Anglo-Saxon Chronicle and only consulted secondary sources where necessary to fill in unexplained gaps.

There is no suggestion that King Edward knew he was unable to father children before his marriage to Lady Edith. I've made the leap because I find it difficult to reconcile his actions in marrying Lady Edith and making Sweyn an earl. Yes, the House of Godwine was powerful, and the argument could be made that Edward had no allies in England, but there were more earls – Leofric was a staunch Englishman, who had shown himself to be loyal to English kings in the past – I'm thinking of King Harald when I say that – and I believe that Edward would have had other options if he'd wanted them. It's impossible to forget that Earl Godwine was responsible, in a large way, for the murder of his brother, Lord Alfred. If Edward couldn't forgive his mother, why would he have forgiven a man who was a stranger to him? And not only that but advanced his son and his daughter?

I have never considered that Edward was a military man, but it's an idea suggested by Tom Licence in his new monograph on Edward the Confessor. It's a beguiling idea. After all, he had attempted to 'invade' England at his mother's request when Harald was claiming the kingdom and the ASC is adamant that he took 35 ships from Sandwich in 1043 or 1044. There is some confusion with the date. Edward's father, the man he could claim the right to rule through, was a weak military commander, only leading one expedition into Cumbria and then deputising others to stand in his place. Edward would have wanted to make a name for himself.

The names I have used for Edward's moneyers are men who really existed. I'm grateful to the following article for the information. THE *PACX* TYPE OF EDWARD THE CONFESSOR by Hugh Pagan, freely available to download via the internet, with pages of photographs of the coins being discussed. I find the whole system absolutely fascinating, so I apologise if you didn't enjoy that particular scene. England's monetary system was a sophisticated and complex operation, and it's believed that the coinage was re-struck every two years.

The locations I've used for the properties belonging to the House of Leofwine are taken from Appendix 1 in 'The Earls of Mercia: Lordship and Power in Late Anglo-Saxon England' by Stephen Baxter and refer to properties assigned to the family members when the Domesday Survey was compiled. Ælfgar is assigned the third penny from Oxford and twenty dwellings there which had to keep the wall repaired.

For information on Winchester, I've consulted Winchester: A City of Two Planned Towns by Martin Biddle.

And to the *Encomium Emmae Reginae*, which I've mentioned but only in passing– to quote Pauline Stafford in her book 'Queen Emma and Queen Edith', 'The Encomium was meant to influence that future, through a version of the past which met the questions of the present. It was aimed at her sons, and more widely at the great men of the English. It was a political work, from a political woman in the thick of politics.' (p. 29). I don't believe it was appreciated by Edward and certainly did Lady Emma no good.

With more and more information available for this time period, it's now possible to make more mistakes, and so, I apologise for any I've made and hope they don't detract from the story.

NOTES ON THE ANGLO-
SAXON CHRONICLE

THE ANGLO-SAXON CHRONICLE SURVIVES IN SEVEN 'recensions' – the simplest way to explain this is to say that there is a 'base' document (now lost), and these seven versions all share common elements of the base document, but that they were then kept in regional centres and reflect the bias there. There was no attempt to ensure the same information was recorded in these regional copies.

The Winchester Manuscript (known as version A) is the oldest surviving manuscript of the Chronicle. A copy of it was made and sadly lost in a fire at the Cotton Library in 1731, although it had been copied in 1641, and this edition does survive.

There are two versions of the Abingdon Manuscripts. The first was written by a single person in the second half of the tenth century, and ended in AD977 (version B). This edition was used to make a compilation for the second of the two manuscripts, although details were added at this stage, in the middle of the eleventh century (version C). It is this version that contains what is known as the 'Mercian Register' containing details of AD902-924.

The Worcester Manuscript (version D) was written in the middle of the eleventh century, probably at Worcester, as it contains some local entries for AD1033 onwards. This seems to have been based on a lost Northern Recension as the diocese of Worcester and York were closely connected as they shared the same incumbent between AD972-1016.

The Peterborough Manuscript (version E) was written from AD1121 onwards, and is in one hand until that date, and probably copied from a Kentish Chronicle.

The Canterbury Manuscript (version F) was written at about AD1100.

I have made use of the entries for versions C, D and E when writing The English King. E is assumed to take the stance of the House of Godwine, C, that of the House of Leofwine. E, as noted above, was written in one hand, from AD1121 onwards. Version C is more contemporary to the events I'm writing about, and, for those who've read the Tenth Century books, provides invaluable information from that time period not found elsewhere. D is seen as more neutral.

To complicate matters, D and E versions normally begin the new year at Christmas and before 1st January. C usually began the year at 25th March, hence why the king's marriage is noted in AD1044 in version C although it took place in AD1045.

My preferred edition of the ASC is that edited by Michael Swanton but I've also made use of the version in English Historical Documents Volume II in writing this novel, and free versions are available on the internet.

CAST OF CHARACTERS

THE HOUSE OF LEOFWINE

Leofric, born AD998

m. **Lady Godgifu** in AD1018

Ælfgar, son, born in AD1018

m.**Lady Elgiva**, the daughter of Morcar (a thegn murdered by Eadric Streona) and Ealdgyth, the niece of Ealdorman Ælfhelm, (murdered on Æthelred II's orders early in his reign).

Burgheard – b. AD1038

Eadwine – b. AD1039

Ealdgyth – b. AD1041

Morcar – b. AD1042

Ealdgyth, Leofric's sister born AD1000

m. **Olaf** son of **Horic** (fictional, but neither is Ealdorman Leofwine's daughter – just the vague understanding that he had five children, one of whom is unnamed.) Two children

Brother Leofric of Peterborough (historically accurate, although perhaps not at this time)

Æthelflæd (fictional)

Godwine, his younger brother born AD1002,

Eadwine, his younger brother born AD1006, Sheriff of Shropshire, dies in AD1039

Leofwine, father of Leofric and his brothers and sister, Ealdorman of the Hwicce/Earl of Mercia under Cnut although difficult to pinpoint where his power was based (dies AD1023). Son of **Ælfwine** who dies at the Battle of Maldon in AD991.

    m. **Æthelflæd**

Northman, Leofwine's oldest son born AD996, executed AD1017 on the orders of Cnut.

    m. **Mildryth** in AD1011(fictional)

    Wulfstan born 1012 (fictional)

    Ælfwine born 1014(fictional)

LEOFRIC'S HOUSEHOLD

Orkning (son of Horic, one of Leofwine's household troop)

    Otryggr – his son

    Olaf (son of Horic) married Ealdgyth, Leofric's sister (not historically attested)

    Godwulf member of Leofric's household troop

    Winhus member of Leofric's household troop

    Scirwold member of Leofric's household troop

    Eadsige door warden in Oxford

    Cena member of Leofric's household troop

    Æthelheard member of Leofric's household troop

    Magnus the illegitimate son of King Olaf Haraldson of Norway, becomes King of Norway in AD1035, following Swein Cnutsson's exile, and with the support of two regents, and his father's wife, Astrid, who was not his mother, but was the sister of the king of the Svear (Sweden) Anund Jakob.

    Æthelred II of England (dies April AD1016),

m. 1) **Ælfgifu of York**

Has nine children – six sons and three daughters, of which the below are mentioned.

Edmund Ironside (d.AD1016) marries the widow of Sigeforth before his death. Two sons;

Edward the Exile

Edmund Ætheling

Eadwig

m. 2) **Emma of Normandy**

Lord Edward

Lord Alfred (dies AD1037)

Countess Godgifu, Dowager Countess of Vexin

m.1 Drogo, Count of Vexin (dies AD1035)

Walter

Ralph

Fulk

m.2. Eustace of Bolougne

Swein Forkbeard of Denmark (dies AD1014)

Cnut (son) of England (from AD1016 with Edmund/AD1017 sole ruler of England) and Denmark (from AD1018, after the death of his brother, Harald).

m.1.**Lady Ælfgifu**

Swein, King of Norway (AD1030-35)

Harald, Regent/King of England (AD1035-1040)

Secretly marries **Alfifa,** one son, **Ælfwine** (he is mentioned in the historical record)

m.2.**Lady Emma**

Harthacnut, King of Denmark AD1035-1042, King of England AD1040-1042

Gunnhilda, married to **Henry**, son of **Conrad II**, Holy Roman Emperor, she dies in AD1038, but has a daughter, **Beatrix**, before her death.

Harald of Denmark (from AD1014 when his father, Swein, dies in England until AD1018 when he dies).

Lady Estrid, daughter of Swein Forkbeard, wife of Earl Ulfr, with whom she has two children
Svein Estridsson (take their mother's name, not their father's.)
Beorn Estridsson

Olaf Tryggvason, King of Norway, dies AD1000 at the Battle of Svølder (ties with the House of Leofwine)

Mac Bethad Mac Findlaich, King of Scotland (Macbeth in Macbeth) from AD1040

Duke Robert of Normandy, Emma's nephew. He left one illegitimate son, who would become **William the Conqueror.** Died in AD1035 returning from a visit to the Holy Land, along with Lady Godgifu's first husband.
William of Normandy, still very young at this stage

Gruffydd Ap Llewelyn – King of Powys and later Gwynedd

Gruffydd Ap Rhydderch – King of Gwent

Hywel Ap Edwin – King of Deheubarth

CNUT'S WIVES

Lady Emma, Queen Dowager (King Æthelred's second wife – mother of Edward, Alfred and Godgifu) (King Cnut's wife from Summer 1017 – mother of Harthacnut (son) and Gunnhilda (daughter))
Lady Ælfgifu (King Cnut's first wife, even though also married to Emma – sons Harald and Swein.)
Her brothers are **Ufegat** and **Wulfhead** who were blinded by **Æthelred II** when their father was murdered, the Ealdorman of

Northumbria, **Ælfhelm**, by **Eadric** in the early 1000's. Now both dead.

EARLS, NOBLEMEN/WOMEN AND OTHER COURT NOTABLES

Earl Hrani (Herefordshire), dies AD1042
    Earl Godwine (of Kent and later Wessex)
        Married to **Lady Gytha**, sister of Earls Ulfr and Eilifr
        Their children,
        Sweyn, Earl of Hereford from AD1043
        Harold
        Tostig
        Edith
    Gyth
    Leofwine
    Wulfnoth
    Elgiva
    Gunnhilda
    Earl Siward of Northumbria married to Ealdred of Bamburgh's daughter, Eadwulf of Bamburgh's niece.
        Osbjorn – his son, with first wife, not the Earl of Bamburgh's daughter/niece
    Earl Leofric of Mercia (see above)
    Earl Sweyn of Hereford – takes over Earl Hrani vacant earldom
    Osgot Clapa, not an earl but a prominent thegn
    Tovi the Proud, one of Harthacnut's allies
    Gunnhild, niece of King Cnut, m.**1) Earl Hakon**
    m. **2) Lord Harald** (son of Thorkell the Tall).
    Hemming
    Thurkill
Holy Men
    Archbishop Eadsige – Archbishop of Canterbury, resigns in

AD1044 due to infirmity, Siward replaces him as Bishop of Canterbury. Eadsige remains as the figurehead.

Brother Leofric (Leofric's nephew – historical, although perhaps not at this time.)

Bishop Ælfweard – Bishop of London

Bishop Brihtwold – Bishop of Ramsbury

Bishop Siward – of East Anglia, during AD1043, previously a royal priest with ties to Lady Emma. He is removed from post by the king.

Bishop Ælfwine – bishop of Winchester

Bishop Wulfsige – bishop of Lichfield

Bishop Eadnoth – bishop of Dorchester

Abbot Ufi of Bury St Edmund's

MISC (MOSTLY FICTIONAL)

Lord Otto – ally of Harthacnut's from Denmark

Karl – named as one of the huscarls

Urk – named as one of the huscarls

Thored – names as one of the huscarls

Ælfstan, Lyfing, Odda, Dodda, Wulfnoth, Kinewerd, Toking, Ulfcytel – all historically attested members of the witan,

Brythnoth – in Shropshire

Eadwig – Sweyn's reeve

Oswald – Leofric's horse

Dunston – fisherman in London

Commander Eowa – Leofric's ships commander

Brihtric – sailor

Brungar – silversmith in London (historically attested)

Beorhtweald – silversmith in Oxford (historically attested)

PLACES MENTIONED

St Peter's Church, London – would become Westminster Abbey

Deerhurst – ancestral home of House of Leofwine (this is my assertion)

Oxford –House of Leofwine holds land there (according to Domesday Book).

Shropshire – on the border with the Welsh kingdoms

The Land of the Scots – not yet Scotland, but getting there!

The Foss, Ermine Street, Icknield Way, Watling Street – the oldest roads in England

Sandwich – busy harbour, where Harthacnut claimed the English crown

Coventry – part of Mercia. According to Domesday Book, Leofric held land there.

Ditton Priors, Wellington, Ford, Ellesmere, Emstry, High Ercall, Crudington, Doddington – all places named as belonging to the family of the House of Leofwine in Shropshire in Domesday Book

ABOUT THE AUTHOR

I'm an author of fantasy (Viking-age/dragon-themed) and historical fiction (Early English, Vikings and the British Isles as a whole before the Norman Conquest), born in the old Mercian kingdom at some point since the end of Saxon England. I like to write.

You've been warned!

facebook.com/mjporterauthor

twitter.com/coloursofunison

instagram.com/m_j_porterauthor

tiktok.com/@mjporterauthor

amazon.com/mj-porter

bookbub.com/authors/mj-porter

BOOKS BY M J PORTER (IN SERIES READING ORDER)

Kingmaker

The King's Daughters

Viking King

The English King

The King's Brother

Lady Estrid: A novel of Eleventh-Century Denmark (related to the Earls of Mercia series)

Fantasy

The Dragon of Unison (fantasy based on Viking Age Iceland)

Hidden Dragon

Dragon Gone

Dragon Alone

Dragon Ally

Dragon Lost

Dragon Bond

As JE Porter

The Innkeeper

20th Century murder-mystery

Cragside – a 1930s mystery

The Erdington Mysteries

The Custard Corpses

The Automobile Assassination

Made in United States
North Haven, CT
08 September 2023

41311813R00153